One Last Thing Before I Go

Michele Brouder

This is a work of fiction. Names, characters, places and incidents are either a product of the author's imagination or are used fictitiously, and any resemblance to actual persons, living or dead, events, or locales is entirely coincidental.

Editing by Jessica Peirce

Book Cover Design by Rebecca Ruger

One Last Thing Before I Go

Copyright © 2023 Michele Brouder

All Rights Reserved. No part of this book may be reproduced or transmitted in any form or by any means, electronic or mechanical, including photocopying, recording, or by any information storage and retrieval system, without permission in writing from the author.

Chapter One

Carol

CAROL RIMMER SAT IN a booth in the Chat and Nibble Café on Main Street in Hideaway Bay, fidgeting with her paper napkin before crumpling it up in a ball. Despite the time—late morning—the sky was dark, gunmetal gray. Outside, the rain slammed down, bouncing off the pavement. Cars rolled along Main Street, their rear lights red bars in the darkness as their tires splashed water up onto the sidewalks. Supposedly, spring was on its way, but so far March had been a washout.

"Aren't you hungry?" her friend Lottie asked from across the booth.

Carol had been friends with Lottie Gallagher Prescott for most of her eighty years. She couldn't have been closer to a sister if she'd had one. Lottie had driven Carol to her medical appointment earlier, and afterward, the two of them had stopped for a late breakfast.

She had always liked this restaurant. Booths lined the perimeter of the rectangular room, and tables that sat two or four occupied the rest of the interior space. Currently it was decorated for St. Patrick's Day: shiny green shamrocks, leprechaun hats, and rainbows covered the walls. Last month it had been hearts and Cupids, and next month it would be cheery pastel-colored Easter eggs and rabbits. The place was simple, nothing fancy, but the food was good. Except for today, and that was no fault of the chef's, it was that she had no appetite.

Carol looked down at her plate, the eggs gone cold and the toast rubbery. She speared a piece of home-fried potato and put it into her mouth, chewed a bit, and then scrunched up her nose in distaste. She managed to get it down but pushed her plate away, frowning.

"I guess I'm not hungry," she said.

She looked across at Lottie's meal. Lottie had ordered eggs Benedict and there was nothing left on her plate. Carol was glad someone had an appetite.

"Look, this doesn't have to be the end," Lottie said, leaning slightly forward over the Formica-topped table. She tapped a pearly pink polished nail on its surface. "Let's get a second opinion. We could go to Sloan Kettering and see what they say. I'll go with you."

until she got sick. Having been the town's librarian for so long, it seemed the natural thing to do. She wasn't even sure if the book club met anymore.

Lottie shrugged, leaned against the back of the vinyl booth, and folded her hands on the table in front of her. She had rings on every finger. The spoon ring on her index finger had been there since the '70s when she'd hosted a Sarah Coventry party. Carol still had the jewelry she'd bought from that party, in her jewelry box in the top drawer of her dresser.

"Thelma's club is mainly for widows and widowers, and they play a lot of cards. Della said hers was going to be more like a club for getting together and doing different events. She said something about watching movies on the beach and parasailing," Lottie said. "Can you imagine?"

Carol could, and she thought it was a good idea. "Is it a singles club?" She'd joined her fair share of those over the years with no luck. But she'd never been the 'woe is me' type when it came to life's disappointments.

"No, she said it was open to everyone of all ages."

"Oh, it sounds nice. I'd love to watch a movie on the beach," Carol said. "It would kind of remind me of the drive-in."

"Now that's something I miss," Lottie said with a soft smile. "I used to love the drive-in."

"I know." Carol laughed. "You cried for days when they closed it down."

"I still miss it." Lottie appeared thoughtful for a moment and said, "Maybe we could go together?"

Then she froze when she realized her faux pas. "Oh, Carol, I'm so sorry, I didn't think—"

"Come on, Lottie, we've been friends long enough, don't apologize," Carol said, trying to reassure her friend. "And who knows, maybe I'll still be here when that happens. And we could go together."

"All right," Lottie said, but she remained unconvinced.

Suddenly, Lottie put her head in her hand, her eyes covered. Her chin quivered.

"It's not fair, Carol," she said, her voice breaking.

Carol reached across the table and took her friend's other hand in hers and gave it a squeeze. "That's life. We know it isn't fair. I've no complaints. I've had a *good* life."

Lottie lowered her hand and turned away to look out the window, but not before Carol saw that her eyes were wet with tears. "I don't know what I'm going to do . . ."

"It'll be all right, you'll see," Carol said.

Lottie snapped her head back in Carol's direction and laughed. "Here you are, comforting me. It should be the other way around."

Carol's heart burst with love for her friend. "It's been pretty even throughout our lives."

The unshed tears in Lottie's eyes made them appear bluer. She nodded. "I suppose."

"Come on, let's get the bill and go," Carol said, inching her way out of the booth, the vinyl squeaking beneath her.

"I'll pay for it," Lottie offered.

"Nope, I pay. That's the deal. You drive me to my doctor's appointments and chemo and radiation appointments, and I treat us to a meal."

"For which I'm grateful. You know how I hate cooking," Lottie said.

"I do know."

Carol set her purse on her lap and dug out her wallet and left a tip on the table. Slowly, she made her way to the counter and paid the bill.

They walked out together, both of them lifting their hoods up onto their heads against the splattering rain. By the time they walked around to the parking lot in the back, the hem of Carol's pants was wet. Anxious to get home, she walked a little faster but still had trouble keeping up with Lottie.

Inside the car, Lottie opened her purse to pull her phone out to check it. Carol spied chocolate candy wrappers and laughed. Lottie looked at her.

"I see you're still hiding candy," Carol said, amused.

"I keep it in my purse. Those grandchildren are rascals. They're always rooting around, looking for things."

Although she sounded annoyed, Carol knew Lottie was anything but. She adored her grandchildren.

"What are you doing for the rest of the day?" Lottie asked as she turned on the engine. It was a brand-new vehicle; Lottie had only driven it off the lot the other day. Carol closed her eyes and breathed in the new-car smell.

"The usual I suppose," Carol said. Her routine consisted of reading, lots of it since she retired, and of course there was Melvin, her gray-striped cat, to consider.

But the bigger question was: what was she going to do with what was left of her life?

Chapter Two

Jackie

Jackie Arnold pulled the plastic tote off the front porch of her house on Starview Drive in the little town of Hideaway Bay.

After a rain-soaked March, April had heralded the arrival of spring sunshine, a soft breeze, and dry days. The cool air smelled like wet earth: damp and mossy. It was time to bring out the Easter decorations.

"Mommy, I can carry that," Anna said from the porch. At four, she already had ideas about how things should be done. Like her mother, her hair was blond, but whereas Jackie's was golden and honey-colored, Anna's was still pale, almost white, like Jackie's had been at that age. The two of them were clothed in jeans and fleecy jackets, and Anna had also added a pair of pink sunglasses with kittens all over them, an item she was so fond of she wore them in the house and sometimes to bed.

Jackie set down the tote on the path that led from the porch steps.

Immediately, Anna put her small hands on either side of it and tried to lift it, but it wouldn't budge. The little girl groaned, her face scrunched up in effort.

"Why don't you let me help you and I'll open it," Jackie said.

"All right, Mommy, but I want to do the decorating," Anna said.

"Right," Jackie said with a laugh. She pulled the lid off the tote, revealing a multitude of decorations.

"Oh, he's cute," Anna said, digging through the pile and pulling out a wooden stake in the form of a white bunny with big buck teeth, holding a vibrant orange carrot in his hands. She turned it around in her hands. "Can I put this in my room?"

"No," Jackie said firmly.

"Aw."

"Let's put that over there," Jackie said, pointing to the small, round flower bed with two shrubs and a boulder that her husband had managed to transport from the beach with the help of friends.

She had a hard time looking at that sand-colored boulder between the shrubs. It always took her back to that day when Jason had spotted it at the far end of the beach and said it would be a perfect addition to their front garden. And she'd been doubtful, immediately voicing her concern about how he would move the sizeable boulder from the beach to their front lawn. By the weekend, he'd gathered a group of his buddies and using his engineering expertise, managed to get the boulder off the beach. That had been a great day. Afterwards, they'd had a barbecue with their friends in the backyard, and Jason had manned the grill while Jackie walked around with the baby on her hip. Yes, those had been happy days.

The familiar sting of tears pricked her eyes, and she distracted herself by showing Anna how to stick the stake in the ground.

"I want to do it," Anna announced.

"All right."

The ground was soft, so Anna was able to place the stake into the flower bed. Satisfied, she stepped back, smiled until all her teeth were showing, and clapped her hands. She returned to the tote and pulled out the next decoration, a small plastic rabbit.

"Can I put this one in my room?" she called out, standing next to the tote.

"No."

"Where can I put him?"

"How about over there." Jackie pointed to the bed that ran along the front porch.

"Why do you cut back your bushes so short like that?" a voice said behind her.

Jackie was startled and gasped.

Her elderly neighbor from a few doors down, Thelma Schumacher, laughed and said, "I'm sorry, Jackie, I didn't mean to scare you."

"No, that's all right," Jackie said, laughing as well. "I didn't see you there. Which bushes do you mean?"

"Over there," Thelma said, pointing to the rosebushes that ran along the front of the house.

Currently, they were short and stubby as Jackie had pruned them back at the end of winter. That used to be Jason's job, but now she was doing his jobs as well as her own. She didn't mind as it kept her busy and kept her mind off things.

"I think it improves them." She knew this sounded lame, and she was embarrassed at being caught out. She wasn't really sure why they needed cutting back; it was one of those things Jason had done with no explanation. And as they'd always had beautiful roses during the summer, she figured she'd keep doing it. A thought occurred to her, which she verbalized so she didn't appear like a complete idiot. "By the end of the summer, they're too high and they get a bit straggly."

"That makes sense," Thelma said with a nod.

Both women stared at the rosebushes for a moment.

"I don't know how you find the time to keep up with your landscaping all year round," Thelma noted with admiration. She swept her hand over the vista that was the front yard of the Arnold household.

"It helps to be organized," Jackie said.

"You would have to be," Thelma said. "It can't be easy. You're raising a child by yourself, working and running a household. I've been there." The older woman sounded sympathetic. She said again, her voice dropping, "It's not easy."

Jackie could not allow this conversation to segue into how she was coping after Jason's unexpected death. He'd been gone two years now. And even though Anna had no memory of him, everywhere Jackie looked she was reminded of him. Every time she sat on the front porch in the summer and the scent of roses reached her on the breezes blowing in off the lake, she thought of Jason at the nursery, choosing only those rosebushes that had a fragrance. Before she went further down that rabbit hole, she crossed her arms across her chest and changed the subject.

"Do you have plans for Easter, Thelma?"

"Yes. I've been invited by Lily Monroe. The girls are having a big dinner and at my age, I never turn down an invitation for a meal."

Jackie laughed. Out of the corner of her eye, she kept watch over Anna, who was digging through the plastic tote. She currently held two small plastic eggs in her hand, studying them. One was lilac colored, the other pink. Jackie would soon string those from the maple tree in the center of the yard.

As Jackie stood on the sidewalk chatting with Thelma, Anna soon abandoned the plastic eggs and pulled out another decoration. This time a cardboard cutout of a gnome with a multi-colored Easter egg.

"Can I keep this in my room?" Anna yelled.

"Still no," Jackie replied.

Thelma laughed. "She keeps you on your toes."

Jackie grinned and gazed at her child, her heart warm. "She sure does."

Chapter Three

Carol

She didn't *feel* like she was dying. Oh, she was tired, and sometimes she lacked the "oomph" to complete tasks, but that could also easily be chalked up to her age. Living eight decades took its toll.

And yet there was so much she needed to do with the time she had left. As she sat at her kitchen table with Melvin circling her legs and meowing, she pulled a small box toward her. Inside were numerous notepads and all sorts of pens, pencils, and fine-tipped markers. She'd never met a notebook or pen she didn't like. Thumbing through the small stack of notepads, she pulled one out and a pen, ready to make her to-do list.

She wanted to sort out her house and her personal possessions to pass on. She'd heard too many horror stories of problems with wills or the deceased's wishes not being carried out. Her plan was to gather everything that was of personal value to her and decide who to pass it on to. To make sure things she valued and treasured were passed on *before* she died.

She'd made prearrangements with the cemetery. There was room in the family plot, but she had her own reasons for not wanting to be buried there. It wasn't due to any drama, it was that she'd been a separate entity for so long that she'd be alone in the cemetery as well. It didn't bother her.

Not one to sit around and wait for things to happen, she'd keep busy with organizing her life and what was left of it. She'd also need to make plans for her end-of-life care. She would have loved to stay home, but as there was no one to take care of her—and who knew how long she'd linger—she would probably have to go into the hospice. That was fine too. What she didn't want was to become a burden to those she loved. It was best to be practical about these things, she reminded herself.

In the short term, she would continue living as she had: reading lots of books, taking care of Melvin, seeing family and friends. And as her strength would permit, she'd get out and about in Hideaway Bay.

Her most pressing concern at that moment was a visit to Ben, who'd just had a knee replacement. The hospital, a rectangular, utilitarian three-story building of blond brick with steel-gray windows, wasn't that far from the highway, an easy drive from Carol's house on Sand Hill Street.

"I'm here to see my brother, Ben Anderson," she said to the receptionist when she arrived. The receptionist gave her Ben's room number and a visitor's badge and pointed her to the bank of elevators on the other side of the lobby, which hadn't been necessary, as Carol knew the layout of the hospital like the back of her hand.

The other half of the lobby was closed off with yellow plastic signs as a maintenance employee used a commercial buffer on the floor. The machine made a constant low humming noise, which Carol found pleasant.

She'd brought a box of chocolates and the newest Michael Connelly book, knowing the author to be a favorite of Ben's, and also knowing Ben to have an interminable sweet tooth.

Ben had inherited the family farm and currently ran it with one of his sons, Tom. Their family-owned business, Anderson farms, sold all sorts of fresh, in-season produce and canned goods throughout the year in their little stand on the edge of their land at the corner of the highway and Erie Street. Despite coming from a farming background, Carol had never had any interest in working the land, always preferring books and the written word. Luckily, like her father and grandfather, Ben and Tom lived and breathed farming. Carol had inherited a two-acre plot behind the fruit-and-veg stand with the hope that she might build a house there someday, but it had never happened. She had been happy living in town, within walking distance of the library.

There were sixteen years between them, but despite the age difference, she and Ben had always been close. And as they got older, the age difference seemed to matter less and less. It would have been very hard not to be close to Ben. With his sunny disposition, she doubted anyone who'd met him would dislike him.

His room was the first one when she stepped off the elevator. Ben was in the bed by the window, and his face lit up when he spied her walking through the door.

Carol nodded acknowledgment to Ben's roommate in the bed nearest to the door.

She set the book and the box of chocolates on the over-the-bed table and bent over and kissed his forehead. She glanced at his leg, which had an intermittent pneumatic compression sleeve wrapped around it.

"How's it going?" she asked, wincing.

"Good. The knee was more painful to replace than the hip," he said. Despite this, he smiled. "Sit down, Carol." With a nod he indicated an armchair near the window.

Carol dragged the chair closer to the bed and glanced out the window. He had a good view. Beyond the highway and over the copse of bare trees, you could make out

Lake Erie, whose color, a churlish gray, indicated that spring hadn't arrived fully.

"Did Lottie drive you?" he asked.

Carol shook her head. He went to protest but she held up her hand. "I'm fine. When the time comes that I can't drive, I will call you or Lottie. Okay?"

He grumbled his assent, clearly not happy about it.

Carol looked out the window again and changed the subject. "You've got a nice view."

"So I've been told," he said with a laugh.

"When will they let you go home?" she asked, settling into the chair. She tucked her purse between the armrest and her thigh.

"In a couple of days."

"Crutches?"

"Yeah, for six weeks," he said.

Carol frowned. "What about the farm?"

"Tom is going to do what he can but he's pretty busy with the vineyard," he said.

Tom Anderson had started a vineyard with Ben's blessing, and like any business start-up, it required a lot of time and attention. Carol worried that Tom would be pulled in too many directions.

"I hired two kids to man the stand," Ben continued. "A nice part-time job for both of them."

"Anyone I know?" she asked.

"I bet you do. Kyle Koch and Mimi Duchene, Martha Cotter's granddaughter."

Carol nodded. "I heard Martha's granddaughter was living with her now."

She knew who Kyle was: his father taught at the elementary school and used to bring his class into the library when she worked there. But that had been years ago.

"More importantly, how are you feeling?" he asked, shifting in the hospital bed and grimacing with pain.

"Fine, nothing new," she said truthfully.

He nodded and looked as if he wanted to say something, but didn't. The only wobble in her steely determination to live out the remainder of her life as she wished was when she'd told Ben about her terminal diagnosis. He'd broken down and cried in front of her.

"How's Dawn?" she asked of his wife, anxious to change the subject.

"She's good but I sent her home before dinner. She was here all day."

Carol laughed. She liked Ben's wife. She was diminutive but a force to be reckoned with. She wondered whether the other woman ever slept.

"You know how she likes to run things," he said with a wink.

Carol laughed again. "I do. That's a good thing. It's how things get done."

Ben narrowed his eyes and said, "But she's up to something, I can tell."

Carol shrugged. "I'm sure she is. Grass doesn't grow under her feet."

Ben rolled his eyes. "You know how she is. She loves surprises. So many secrets."

"Well, we all have our secrets," Carol said evasively.

Ben pulled up the blanket and sheet on the hospital bed. "Except for you, Carol. You are an open book."

She smiled wanly and thought, *If you only knew.*

CHAPTER FOUR

Jackie

THE FINE WEATHER BROKE at the end of April and Jackie stared out her front window, watching the rain pour down on all their Easter decorations. She cradled a cup of coffee in her hands and brought it to her lips, sipping it.

Behind her, Anna sat at the kitchen table, her head pressed in the palm of one hand and the other hand lifting spoonfuls of cereal into her mouth. Milk dripped everywhere.

Jackie smiled to herself. The only way Anna resembled her was the color of her hair. Her face was the image of her father's and every time Jackie looked at her, she was reminded of Jason.

"Can we go to the beach today?" Anna asked.

Jackie turned around and smiled at her. Anna was half hidden behind a vase of tulips in colors of red, yellow, pink, and orange. Jackie's mom was always bringing flowers over, to cheer the place up, she said.

"I have to work today. You're going to Grammy and Papa's for the day," Jackie said. With a glance back out the window, she added, "Besides, it's raining out."

"I don't care about that," Anna said.

Jackie grinned at her. "Spoken like a true beach lover."

"Can we walk to Grammy's house?" Anna asked, her mouth full of Cheerios.

Jackie shook her head, walked over to the sink, emptied her coffee cup, and placed it in the top rack of the dishwasher. "Too wet. Come on, finish up and drink your orange juice. We need to leave soon."

"When are we going to Disneyworld?" Anna asked for the umpteenth time.

"I don't know yet," Jackie replied. And that was the truth.

Anna had been on a Disneyworld kick for a few months now with no sign of letting up. There would be nothing Jackie would love more than to take her, but a trip like that was not in the budget. Between the small life insurance settlement and her part-time job, Jackie was scarcely able to keep their heads above water.

But someday, she hoped to make it happen.

Jackie placed Anna's backpack by the door. Inside were various toys and books she liked to bring with her wherever she went.

After breakfast, Anna had a mini meltdown over the clothes laid out on her bed.

"I don't like that shirt," she said, her arms crossed and her lower lip jutting out.

"But it has flowers on it," Jackie said.

"I don't like *those* flowers," Anna shot back.

Impatient, Jackie said, "Pick another shirt, then."

"I want to wear the shirt with the daisies on it."

Jackie had been afraid she'd say that. She looked up to the ceiling, rolled her eyes, and sighed. The white cotton shirt with the daisies on it was Anna's favorite. But yesterday, she'd spilled spaghetti sauce on it at dinner despite wearing a bib, and currently it was in a small plastic tub on top of the washing machine, soaking.

"It's in the wash."

"But I want to wear that one," Anna insisted.

"Look, you can't, it's in the wash. End of. Pick something else out of the drawer or I will. Now let's go, I'm going to be late for work," Jackie said firmly. Rather than engage further, she warned, "You've got two minutes, Anna Catherine, or there'll be consequences."

Before the child could respond, Jackie headed to the hall closet to retrieve their rain jackets. As she waited by the door, she heard the dresser drawer slam shut and some muttering from Anna's bedroom. *Her teenage years will probably be so joyful.*

Anna came stomping out of the bedroom, and Jackie handed her her jacket and let her put it on. When she was in this kind of mood, she'd want no help. Once Jackie got her into the car, relief finally set in. A quick glance at the dashboard told her she had just enough time to drop Anna off and head back home, where she worked remotely for a health insurance company. The job was perfect. She could work from home, and they allowed part-time hours, so Jackie worked three days a week while her parents babysat Anna. If it weren't for them, she didn't know what she would do.

Her parents, Helen and George, lived three streets over, on Moonbeam Drive in the house where Jackie grew up. The sight of the house, a Dutch colonial similar to others on the street with its magnolia-colored siding, forest green shutters and redbrick chimney, always brought a familiar comfort.

As she pulled in the driveway, her father came outside with an umbrella over his head.

She rolled down her window. "Dad, I would have brought her in."

"No, you'll be late for work," he said, opening the back door to get Anna. "Hello there, young lady."

Anna giggled. "Why do you always call me young lady?"

"Well, you're not a young man."

This resulted in another round of giggles.

George unbuckled the seatbelt of Anna's car seat and she sprang out of it.

"Kiss your mother goodbye," he instructed.

From behind her, Anna wrapped her little arms around Jackie's neck, and Jackie moved her head slightly so she could plant a kiss on her daughter's forehead.

"Be good for Grammy and Papa," she said.

"Aw, what do you mean? She's always good for us," her father said, putting on a gruff voice.

"Watching more John Wayne movies, Dad?" Jackie asked.

"What else can you do when it's raining? Let's go, Anna," he said.

As they walked up the driveway, he said to Anna, "Do you like westerns, young lady?"

Anna shook her head and they disappeared into the house.

Chuckling, Jackie reversed out of the driveway and headed back home to work.

The mistake she'd made was stopping into the olive oil shop for some balsamic vinegar during her lunch break. She was drawn to the barrel that read "Popcorn toppers, 3 for 2" and she was debating on a third flavor—she couldn't decide between Buffalo Wing or Dill Pickle—when she was cornered by the owner, Della Rossi, and her assistant, Sue Ann Marchek. Both women enthused about Della's new social club and were currently trying to recruit Jackie into coming to the preview night at the parish hall.

"We've got so much planned," Della said. Her chestnut-colored hair glimmered in the lighting of the small shop, and her dark, mascara-fringed eyes were wide with enthusiasm.

"There's going to be something for everyone," Sue Ann chimed in.

"Oh, I don't know," Jackie said vaguely, not really wanting to commit.

She had her back to the shelves with the two women in front of her. There was no escape. On the outside, Della and Sue Ann gave the appearance of what they were: two lovely, personable ladies. But when they ran with an idea—like their current one—they would put the most persistent telemarketer to shame.

"Come on the opening night," Della said. "I think you'll find something that might interest you."

"No obligation," Sue Ann said.

"It's not a singles' club, is it?" Jackie asked, wary. She'd been roped into one of those by a well-intentioned friend and she'd been horrified. In her mind, she was still married to Jason.

Della looked at her assistant and said, "No, of course not. It's for all age groups, men, women, married, single, whatever."

"But no obligation," Sue Ann said again gently, noting Jackie's reluctance.

Della repeated, "No obligation, of course. Sue Ann, why do we sound like we're selling time shares?"

Both women got a fit of the giggles and pretty soon, Jackie found herself smiling with them. Slowly, she began to inch away from the shelves so the women were no longer directly in front of her.

"Where's it at?" Jackie asked politely as Sue Ann checked out her purchases. Next to her, Della put Jackie's items into a brown paper bag with handles.

"The parish hall on Thursday night. It was the only night available," Della said.

"I'll have to check my schedule," Jackie said.

Her breathing relaxed when she was able to slip away. As she headed toward the register, she called out, "I'll certainly keep it in mind."

Before she departed from the shop, she heard Sue Ann say to Della, "Gee, do you think we're coming on too strong?"

Chapter Five

Carol

"Hi, I'm Gail Hartling, I'll be your primary hospice nurse while you're in the program," said the tall, thin, angular woman as she stepped across the threshold of Carol's house.

Carol shook the woman's proffered hand. With her translucent skin, Gail was one of those women who could get away with minimal makeup. Her eyes were large, and her eyebrows were dark.

"Carol Rimmer," Carol said softly, indicating that the nurse should follow her into the house. The place smelled of lemon-scented furniture polish. Lottie had been by earlier in the day and had dusted and vacuumed for her.

Unlike most people who lived in Hideaway Bay and preferred to be as close as possible to the lake, Carol had chosen a house off a side street off Erie. She and her former husband had purchased it because it was within walking distance of the library, and she'd lived there ever since, even after the divorce. It had always suited her needs down through the years.

There was a small den off the kitchen, and Carol sank down on the middle cushion of the sofa as the hospice nurse took the wing chair directly across from her. Gail set her black nursing bag down at her feet next to the chair.

The den was Carol's favorite room in the house. The walls were lined with shelves crammed full of books. The small television in the corner of the room was rarely turned on and when it was, it was more for background noise than anything else. The dark carpeting was plush, and she'd treated herself to a recliner that had all the bells and whistles. It basically did everything except wash the dishes. As she grew older, she found herself spending more and more time in this room with Melvin. It was her happy place.

Carol's physician in town, Dr. Morrison, had referred her to hospice after Carol's most recent office visit. A nurse from the admissions department had been out two days earlier to admit Carol to the program and go over the paperwork. Even when you were dying, there was still a ton of paperwork to go through.

Gail spoke about how she would visit Carol every week to gauge her progress with her life-limiting disease. She reached over and set a magnet on the coffee table and instructed Carol about the emergency number that was available twenty-four hours a day, seven days a week, should the need arise.

"I hope I never have to use it," Carol said, fingering the magnet.

"We hope not too, but if you get any uncomfortable symptoms like pain or shortness of breath, call us right away," Gail told her.

"What happens when I can no longer be alone?" Carol asked. This thought kept her up at night. "There's really no one to take care of me." She couldn't impose on Ben and Dawn; that wouldn't be right. Or even Lottie. Her friend had her own family and lots of grandchildren.

"We have an inpatient unit for end-of-life care," Gail informed her.

"And I'd be able to go there?" Carol asked.

Gail nodded. "Yes, if you were unable to continue at home, then when the time came, that would be an option."

That was a relief. It was one more thing she could check off her list.

"I would like to stay at home as long as possible," Carol said.

That was the truth. She didn't want to spend her last days in an institution; she still had some living to do.

"Have you thought about a DNR order?"

The admissions nurse had discussed with her the idea of a Do Not Resuscitate order and at the time, Carol had said she'd like to think about it. Even if CPR were successful, what would she be brought back to? She'd still have cancer. Over the last two days, she'd mulled it over and had made her decision.

"Yes, I'd like to sign one, please," she said. She folded her hands in her lap and sat up straight.

Gail removed a folder from her bag, opened it up, and pulled out a sheet of paper. She stood and handed it to Carol, showing her where to sign. She took another sheet and said, "Here's a copy stating that you have a DNR order. Keep it on the front of your fridge."

Carol nodded, looking at it.

"You'll also have access to a social worker, a chaplain, an aide for personal care, and a music therapist if you like. What I suggest to all my patients is to let all the disciplines come out for an initial visit to meet you, and you can decide from there if you'd like to continue."

Carol nodded again. There was a sense of relief that there would be comprehensive support.

"It's funny, but I don't feel like I'm dying," Carol admitted. "I mean other than the fatigue."

"That's good," Gail said. "But as your disease progresses, you might begin to have symptoms other than fatigue."

"Like what?"

"Increased weakness, for example." Gail dug through the bag at her feet and pulled out a five-by-seven booklet that was done up in soft pastel colors of pink and peach. She slid it across the coffee table toward Carol.

"You can read that when you want, but it's basically for patients and their caregivers about what to expect during the process."

Carol glanced at it and set it down, thinking she'd look at it later.

They spoke for a few more minutes and then Gail pulled out her stethoscope and blood pressure cuff and began a physical assessment of Carol.

"Are you going to remain with Dr. Morrison or will you be followed by one of our hospice doctors while you're in program?" Gail asked, putting the earpieces of her stethoscope into her ears.

"I'll stay with Dr. Morrison, he knows me well," Carol said.

He was relatively new in town, but he was a great doctor and had been overseeing her care since her initial diagnosis. He had an innate ability to put a patient at ease no matter what the problem.

"Perfect," Gail said, removing the blood pressure cuff from Carol's upper arm. The nurse's perfume was light and reminded Carol of honeysuckle.

Gail finished her visit with a promise to call Carol on Monday mornings to set up a day and time for the weekly visit.

As Carol walked her to the door, Gail said, "But if any symptom should show up, call any time, day or night."

"I will," Carol promised. She hoped she would never have to use the on-call telephone number, but it was reassuring to know that help was only a phone call away.

After the hospice nurse departed, Carol made her way back to the kitchen, where she sat at the table with notepad and pen in front of her, continuing where she'd left off previously.

The first thing she wrote on her list was "will." She'd made a will years ago, but she should review and update it with her attorney, Art Stodges.

Something out the kitchen window caught her eye, and she was momentarily distracted by the birds gathering outside on the back lawn near the feeder she'd filled just the previous day. Warmer weather must be on the way. Every year, she recorded the date she first heard birdsong again. To her, that day signaled the end of the winter and the heralding of spring. She wondered what would happen to her house when she was gone, and would the new owners feed the birds? She hoped the presence of the bird feeder would nudge them in the right direction.

Her worries about the birds were interrupted by the doorbell.

Slowly, Carol rose from her chair.

She heard the front door open and a voice call out, "Carol?"

Tilting her head, she recognized the voice as belonging to Baddie Moore.

"Come in. I'm in the kitchen," she replied. With relief, she sat back down.

She twisted carefully in her chair as Baddie appeared in the doorway. He was bundled up in a yellow and blue North Face jacket. Despite it being April, there was still a bit of a nip in the air. The big jacket did nothing to hide his physical appearance: tall, broad-shouldered with thin legs. She often wondered how his legs supported all that top-heavy weight. Even in the winter, he sported a buzz cut. She was older than him by at least ten years.

"Hey, Carol," he said.

In his hand, he held a bouquet of sunflowers tied with bright orange twine and wrapped in clear yellow cellophane.

"Hi, Baddie, how are you?"

"I'm fine. Are you up for a visit?" Looking at her, he added quickly, "A short one."

Despite feeling drained, she was in the mood for company. "Sure, Baddie, come on in."

She waved him to the chair and told him to sit down.

He held out the flowers for her. "I brought you these."

"Thank you, I love sunflowers. They're so cheerful."

"Yes, they are." He looked around. "Do you have a vase I can put them in?"

"That would be great," she said. She was tired and didn't have the energy to get up. "There should be a vase beneath the sink."

"Okay," he said, lumbering over to the sink with the bouquet in his hand. He soon returned with the sunflowers in a cranberry-colored Fenton vase filled with water and set them in the middle of the kitchen table.

She'd become good friends with Baddie after his wife, Leslie, had died and he'd wandered into the library, a little lost. She'd recommended a book to him, and he'd admitted he hadn't read a book since college. She handpicked a series about a former athlete who was now a private eye in Florida, and Baddie was hooked. Became a voracious reader because of that first book.

He sat down at the kitchen table across from Carol. When she offered him a beverage, he declined.

"I heard your news. I wanted to stop by and see how you're doing."

"I'm doing as well as can be expected," Carol said. "I've got a hospice nurse coming out to the house once a week to check on me."

"Good. They're a great organization," Baddie said.

"Yes, they are. My nurse is a lovely woman."

"That's great, I'm glad to hear it," he said.

"How's Ben doing?" she asked.

His stepson, Ben Enright, was a partner in a law firm with Alice Monroe. He had a history of alcoholism, but he'd been in rehab recently. Baddie had always looked out for Ben, especially since Leslie's death.

"He's doing great. Been sober for . . ." He cocked his head up toward the ceiling and closed one eye and appeared to think for a moment. "For almost six, seven months."

"I'm glad to hear that," Carol said, and she meant it. Alcoholism was a serious problem and ruined lots of lives. The whole town was rooting for Ben.

Baddie nodded. "Me too. His mother would be so proud."

"Yes, she would," Carol said, remembering Ben's mother, who loved reading cozy mysteries and must have read all the books in that genre in their small library before moving on to audiobooks.

"Carol, is there anything I can do for you?" he asked quietly.

She shook her head. "No, not really. There isn't anything to be done."

"Do you need a ride to anywhere? Doctors' appointments or hospital visits?"

"Not necessary. There are no more appointments, and Ben or Lottie are usually around to give me a lift when I need one."

"You have my number if you need anything."

"I do, and I appreciate that, Baddie," she said. She appeared thoughtful for a moment and asked, "Do you mind if I ask you a question?"

"Shoot."

"How did you end up with the name Baddie? And what is your real name?" Not wanting to appear too nosy, she said, "Feel free to tell me to mind my own business if you'd prefer not to say."

Baddie grinned, and the laugh that burst forth was deep and rich. "Nah, Carol, I don't mind. My real name is Robin Moore."

Carol arched an eyebrow and Baddie laughed, sliding his arms forward onto the kitchen table and folding his hands. "I know, right? I don't look like a Robin. Not a real tough name for a linebacker. When I was in college, the guys on the offensive line kept ribbing me about my name and finally, after one game and a good performance on my part, one of them said I was bad, real bad out on the field. And it kind of stuck."

"Thank you for enlightening me," Carol said. *That's one mystery solved.*

"Not a problem."

Carol yawned, and the sudden urge to doze off overwhelmed her.

Baddie took the cue and stood. "I won't keep you, but if you think of anything, anything at all, you'll call me, right?"

Carol smiled. "I will, thank you, Baddie."

"Even if you need me to pick up some groceries, I can do that, too," he said. "Or I can pick up a meal from the Chat and Nibble if you'd like."

She smiled again. "Thanks." She couldn't help but be touched by his thoughtfulness and willingness to help.

"I'll show myself out, don't get up."

"Thanks again, Baddie," she said. "And thanks for the beautiful sunflowers. They're my favorite flower."

"Lucky guess on my part," he said.

After Baddie was gone, Carol made her way to the den, carrying the vase of sunflowers with her and setting it on a table where she could look at them. She spent a long time staring at the flowers in the vase, enjoying the sight of them, thinking of how they were a cheerful flower. As she stared, she started to drift, until she dozed off, sitting in her chair, dreaming of golden fields of sunflowers.

Chapter Six

Jackie

Jackie thought no more of Della's invitation until her parents showed up Thursday night after dinner. Immediately, Anna lunged for them, and both grandparents enveloped the little girl in a hug.

"What are you doing here?" Jackie asked, wondering if she'd forgotten a get-together or something. She racked her brain for a previously arranged meeting but came up blank.

"We ran into Della earlier today," Helen said.

"Ran out of cherry-flavored balsamic vinegar," George said with an expression that implied that that situation was unacceptable.

"And she mentioned that she told you about the social club meeting tonight up at the parish hall."

"And you said you might go," George said.

Both her parents smiled. She knew they were worried about her, but she was quick to reassure them.

"Oh! Wait a minute, I appeared interested to be polite, but I never had any intention of actually going," Jackie said. *No, no, no.* She wasn't going out tonight. Or any night.

"Anna, how would you like Grammy and Papa to babysit you tonight?" Helen asked excitedly.

Anna jumped up and down, her hair flying around her, shouting, "Yay!"

"Mom, that's not fair," Jackie hissed.

Her mother adopted a stern tone. "It's time to rejoin the land of the living."

"And you think a new social club is the answer?" Jackie asked in disbelief.

"It doesn't have to be," her dad chimed in. "But it's a start, honey."

"You have to have a life," Helen said, her tone still firm. "You can't continue hiding in your house."

"I'm not hiding in my house," Jackie said, her voice rising. "I'm raising my daughter."

"You're using your daughter as an excuse to hide in your house," Helen said.

Jackie was about to bite back; the words were right there on the tip of her tongue.

But her father spoke. His voice was soft. "As a parent you can understand how worried your mother and I are about you. You never leave the house. You work from home, you don't see friends anymore . . ." he said, waving a hand around and letting his voice trail off.

She got the idea and sighed.

Helen put a hand on her daughter's arm. "Try it. Go out for a bit. An hour. It'll do you good. And it'll do Anna some good."

An hour seemed like a long time to Jackie.

Her mother mistook her silence for acquiescence. "Good. Now go fix your hair and do something with your . . ." Helen circled her finger around Jackie's face.

George attempted a softer approach. "Just for an hour, Jackie. It won't hurt. We'll be fine. And so will Anna."

But will I? Jackie thought.

Anna pulled her grandparents by their hands into the living room, where she wanted to show them what she'd been working on in her coloring book, leaving Jackie standing in the middle of the kitchen, unsure.

"Fine!" she said tightly, heading off in the direction of her bedroom.

She plugged in the curling iron, telling herself she wasn't going to fuss. She was clipping her hair up and she was only using the curling iron to fix her bangs. Roughly, she pushed hangers back along the closet rack, trying to decide what to wear. Finally, she threw an ivory-colored turtleneck on the bed and pulled out a clean pair of jeans. After fixing her bangs, she applied a bit of mascara and some lip gloss.

"You look nice," her mother crowed. "It's nice to see you wearing some cosmetics for a change."

"Now don't rush back," George said as Jackie shrugged on her coat, grumbling under her breath about how she'd be back shortly. Hopefully, within fifteen minutes.

So much for a quiet night at home with Anna. But then every night was at home with Anna and not necessarily quiet. Her friends had rallied around her after Jason's death and in the beginning, obligingly, she met them for lunch or dinner, but she found that after a while she couldn't enjoy herself. She'd spent the time half listening to the conversation and checking the time on her phone and worrying that Anna was all right. When it became uncomfortable, she stopped meeting friends out. She'd have them over to her house, but they were all married, and she felt as if she no longer had anything in common with them. And then after a while, the stream of phone calls and invites thinned out. Probably for the best, she'd told herself.

Although it would have been a brisk fifteen-minute walk, she opted to drive as the night was dark, damp, and misty. Plus, Jackie was anxious to return home. Although she hated to admit it, Anna had barely lifted her head when she'd called out goodbye as she headed out the door.

The parking lot of the parish hall was packed. After circling around the building twice in search of a parking spot, she spotted an irregular one at the end of a row, kind of narrow but Jackie was going to make it work. She pulled in, parked, and slid out sideways as her car was right up against the neighboring vehicle.

As soon as she opened the door to the parish hall, she was blasted with heat and noise. The building, constructed back in the forties, was terrible for acoustics, and voices echoed and boomeranged around the hall. The block walls were painted a maize color, and brown industrial tile covered the floor. The hall felt damp, and Jackie chose to keep her coat on. The smells of brewed coffee and lemon-scented disinfectant comingled in the air. The place was in disarray. Everyone was mingling, and she couldn't see either Della or Sue Ann. She hoped the meeting would start on time.

"I'm glad to see you here," said a voice behind her.

Startled, Jackie turned and came face to face with Thelma Schumacher.

"Thought I'd check it out," Jackie lied. No sense in telling anyone her parents had strong-armed her into coming.

"Good."

"I didn't know you'd be here."

Thelma ran her own group for the widows and widowers of Hideaway Bay. From Jackie's understanding, they played a lot of cards. Thelma had invited her several times to join the group, but Jackie had been horrified. She didn't want to sit with much older people who'd lost their spouses to be reminded that Jason's premature death was not the natural order of things.

"I had to come and check out the competition," Thelma said with a wink. "I must admit, she has a good turnout."

"She does," Jackie agreed, wondering if she slipped out if anyone would notice her absence. Probably not.

She was just thinking of turning around and exiting the building when Thelma said, "Come on, we can sit together."

They took a seat toward the middle. Jackie scanned the crowd and saw lots of people she knew. The Monroe sisters were there with their significant others: Simon Bishop, Jack Stirling, and Joe Koch. Mr. Lime from Lime's Five-and-Dime sat in the front row, his hearing aids visible on both ears. Baddie Moore and his stepson, Ben Enright, sat behind him. Tom Anderson was there. Jackie knew him by sight. He belonged to the farm family up at the corner of the highway and was the new owner of Hideaway Bay's first vineyard.

Della stood at the front of the room, getting her PowerPoint presentation ready. Sue Ann and her boyfriend,

Dylan Sattler, assisted her. Both Della and Sue Ann had recently returned to Hideaway Bay after being away for many years. Although Jackie wasn't familiar with Della's story, she knew that Sue Ann had lived in Florida for years and had come back home after a bitter divorce.

Next to her, Thelma removed her coat, saying, "Might as well get comfortable."

Jackie did not want to get that comfortable.

Della stood in front of the microphone and began to speak, but no sound came out. Dylan leaned forward and adjusted something on the side of the mic.

Della tried again and this time, her voice boomed throughout the hall. It brought everyone to attention, but some people covered their ears and grimaced.

Dylan stood next to Della and made another adjustment to the mic and when Della spoke into it, this time her voice was perfect: neither too loud nor too low.

"Sorry about that," she said with a warm smile. Her eyes scanned the crowd, sweeping left to right, and she broke into a big smile. "This is a fantastic turnout. I'm pleased to welcome you to Hideaway Bay's newest social club. Open to everyone ages eighteen and older. Although you may not be interested in everything, there will be something for everyone!"

There was some clapping and when it died down, Della started the presentation. She went through the various offerings, and even Jackie had to admit that there were some things that interested her.

Lily Monroe was slated for a three-hour workshop on the history of beach glass in Hideaway Bay (where it was bountiful) as well as other beaches in the United States. She was also going to demonstrate making crafts using beach glass. It was well known that she and her boyfriend, the writer, Simon Bishop, went on frequent trips to other beaches in the continental US in search of glass.

Tom Anderson of Anderson Farms was going to give a talk on pairing wines with various kinds of cheeses. If she'd been inclined, she would have chosen that one. She loved wine and cheese and thought they married well.

Jack Stirling was hosting a volunteer cleanup on the beach followed by a barbecue to kick off the summer season. There was also mention of how Della and Sue Ann were going to set up movies on the beach once a month. There was a survey to fill out with what movies people might want to see. Mr. Lime piped in from the front row with "*Jaws, Titanic, The Poseidon Adventure.*" Everyone clapped and cheered him on. His wispy voice added, "A nice disaster on water." People around him laughed.

"I see a navigational theme with all of those movies," Thelma quipped, leaning into Jackie.

"Also we're going to have a book fair," Della announced. "So bring all those old paperbacks and hardcovers you want to get rid of but aren't sure what to do with."

There was a murmur through the crowd.

Jackie wasn't much of a reader, but she thought she'd bring Anna, who was fond of books. And it would be good value.

"For the more adventurous of you out there," Della started. "We have looked into a company up in Buffalo to come down and rent out Jetskis for a day as well as parasailing."

"I'll give that one a miss," Thelma whispered. "Don't need a broken bone at my age."

Jackie had to agree with her. She preferred her feet firmly on the ground.

"The Pink Parlor has graciously agreed to host an ice cream social one summer night where there will be old-fashioned prices of one dollar."

The murmuring picked up and Della said, "And of course, the social club will be renting a bus to go up to Buffalo for various outings. There will be trips to the casino, and to watch the Bills and Sabres play."

"This has been well thought-out. Good for them," Thelma said.

"And finally, on the fifteenth of every month, we'll celebrate all the birthdays of those members in the club, of which we hope there will be many. There'll be cake, ice cream, and beverages."

"Now for the bill," Della joked. "All these activities will cost money. There will be a flat annual fee—"

"Like a country club!" someone yelled from the back.

Della laughed. "Not quite. As I was saying, there will be a flat annual fee and we will be doing fundraisers to offset costs, so we'll try and keep it down. For those activities that might be more expensive, people who sign up may have to contribute for the difference."

Jackie thought this was fair. She was glad for the citizens of Hideaway Bay. The community had a lot to offer. If she were in a different position, she might try some things out. But she had more important things going on right now in her life: namely raising Anna.

"I hope you'll join some of these events," Thelma said. "It might be good to get out for a change."

Jackie didn't respond directly to the other woman's comment. "They certainly have a lot planned."

At the end of the presentation, Sue Ann stepped up to the mic and announced, "There are refreshments at the back of the hall."

Everyone turned their heads, looking to where Sue Ann had pointed. A table had been set up with carafes of coffee and tea and plates of pastries. Stacks of paper plates and napkins stood ready at the end of the table.

The crowd stood and mingled or began to disperse.

Jackie felt her coat pockets for her phone and car keys. "It was good seeing you, Thelma."

"Aren't you staying? Have a cup of coffee or something?" Thelma asked.

Jackie shook her head. "Can't." And offered no more explanation.

She excused herself out of the row as some people had remained seated. The exit was within her sights, but she was intercepted by Alice Monroe, the youngest of the Monroe sisters. Alice had been two years behind Jackie at high school. And Jason had gone to school with Alice's sister Lily.

"Jackie! It's great to see you," Alice gushed. The harsh lighting made her abundant curly hair appear even redder than usual. "Gosh, I haven't seen you in ages."

That was one of the problems with working from home. You hardly got out, but Jackie wasn't complaining. At home, she had everything she needed.

"It's been a while," Jackie said. "Everything is going well, is it?" she asked with a nod to Alice's engagement ring, a sparkly solitaire.

Alice's smile was broad and beautiful. "It is. We'll be planning our wedding soon."

"That's wonderful. I'm happy for you," Jackie said truthfully. The day she got married had been one of the happiest of her life.

"Thank you."

They were joined by Alice's older sister Lily. They exchanged greetings and Jackie said, "You've really created a niche business with the beach glass." She'd seen some of Lily's crafts in the shops on Main Street: from Christmas ornaments to picture frames with beach glass adorning them. She seemed to be doing well, and Jackie was glad for her.

Lily nodded, her fine blond hair bobbing up and down. "I have. I'm so lucky."

Alice reached over and squeezed her sister's arm and smiled.

"That's great. And are you still working for Simon Bishop?" Jackie asked, realizing her news was old and she was out of the loop.

"I am, but only part time now. The beach glass keeps me pretty busy," Lily said. "I hope you'll come to the workshop."

"It sounds interesting," Jackie said. And it did, and maybe in another life she would have signed up for it. She trotted out her usual, convenient excuse. "But I'll have to see what's going on with Anna that day."

"Hopefully, you'll be able to do other things with the group," Alice chirped in. "It looks like it's going to be a lot of fun."

Not wanting to find herself in a position where she overextended herself or committed to something she'd regret later, Jackie started making noises about needing to leave.

As they parted, Lily said, "Stop over any time. Bring Anna with you. We'd love to see her."

"I will, thank you," Jackie said with a wave, heading out.

As soon as she was clear of the exit, she hoofed it to her car, anxious to get home.

Chapter Seven

Carol

Carol sat in the cab of Ben's truck. She'd asked him to take her for a drive around the farm as she wanted to see it and she had something on her mind.

Over the past few nights, she'd lain awake thinking about her legacy. She was certain people would remember her for her role as the town's librarian, but was that enough? Was finding the perfect book for someone or helping a child with their school project memorable? There must be something more she could do for the town. She was driven by the need to do something for the residents of Hideaway Bay. Except for a six-month stint living with her aunt in Pennsylvania, Carol had spent all of her life in the lakeside town.

Although the fields were pale yellow and brown, leeched of the bright colors she loved so much during the summer months, she still loved looking at the expanse of it, thinking of how many times as a child she'd coursed through these fields that brought her out by the parish hall on Erie Street.

The farmhouse she grew up in was still there, now lived in by Ben's oldest son, Tom, who would one day inherit the farm. He'd renovated parts of the house and when she was last in it, she was pleased with the changes and told him so. It was nice to see property passed on, and it was also nice to see it upgraded and modernized. Ben and Dawn had moved into the long, low ranch bungalow on the other side of the property, which had once belonged to Carol's grandparents.

Though her grandparents and parents were long gone, there was some contentment knowing that the farm carried on in the Anderson family. Carol had been very happy that it had been left to Ben. He had loved everything about the farm from the time he could walk, unlike Carol, who had never wanted anything to do with it. She had been more than satisfied with the two-acre plot she'd inherited. And although nothing was ever done with that plot, she had an idea for it now.

The day was dull and overcast. As they drove around, they were enshrouded in a fine mist that never seemed to settle but remained suspended in the damp April air.

Ben headed away from Erie Street to the opposite end of the farm, which ran north along the highway. Traffic was light and Ben stayed in the right lane.

Acres and acres of fledgling grapevines stood row after row. They'd survived their first winter. Ben had been encouraging when Tom said he wanted to turn a portion of the farm into a vineyard. Ben felt it was important to diversify to keep the farm going. Carol had driven past it numerous times on the highway but it was nice to see it from the back end, too.

Ben pulled his truck over near a small, steel-framed building that served as Tom's office and storage for supplies for the farm and vineyard. There were plans to build a winery, and ground had been broken on that up near the highway.

Carol waited for Ben to come around to her side of the truck to help her out. He walked slowly, testing out his new knee. The ground was uneven, and she took her time, leaning on his arm.

"We're quite the pair," Ben joked.

"That we are," she agreed with a laugh.

"Come on, Carol, let's get you inside," he said, walking her to the front of the building. The color matched the sky: gray.

He opened the door and guided Carol through.

"Tom?" Ben called out.

"Right here, Dad," was the answer.

Carol looked around. With its concrete floor and corrugated metal walls, the space was cavernous and cold, and the interior was dark with only one overhead light for illumination. Most of the space was in shadows. Black steel shelves ran from the floor to the rafters. To her right was an office with a Perspex window.

Tom Anderson emerged from the office and broke into a wide grin when he spotted Carol.

"Aunt Carol!"

Carol's heart lurched every time she saw Tom as he bore such a strong resemblance to her late father. Named after him, he possessed the same dark hair, intelligent eyes, and the familiar square jaw. Like her father, he sported the perpetual farmer's tan.

Tom embraced her in a gentle hug and kissed her cheek. "Why didn't you tell me you were coming over?" With a laugh, he added, "I would have put the heat on."

Carol had to laugh despite the damp seeping into her bones. Her body ached. She wouldn't be able to stay long.

Tom waved them into the office, offering Carol his arm. He closed the office door behind them. Inside, a space heater blasted heat that enveloped Carol like a warm hug. Tom pulled his desk chair over nearer the space heater for Carol and invited her to sit down.

Carol immediately sank into the chair, grateful. A whiteboard ran across the back wall of the office, opposite the window that looked out over the vineyard. On the narrow side of the wall stood two four-drawer file cabinets with a metal tray on top of each one.

On the other narrow wall hung an artist's watercolor renderings of the building that would house the wine for sale and have a small gift shop.

Tom pulled out a black binder, opened it, and placed it in Carol's lap.

"I'm glad you're here, Aunt Carol. I want to show you what the future will look like for the Hideaway Bay wine label."

Slowly she leafed through the pages, each showing another watercolor rendering. On the first page was the label and the logo. It bore the image of an orange sun setting over a lake. The lake was represented by three stripes in alternating colors of blue. Carol smiled. The new family business. She was so pleased.

The following pages depicted the fields with the vines and the exterior and interior of the shop. The shop was to be built at the north corner of the farm near the highway. She delighted in the detail of the drawings of the interior, showing all the shelves and the displays of wine and other goods to be sold, and there were even customers in the drawings. Everyone was smiling.

When she finished leafing through the binder, she looked up at Tom and smiled proudly. "These are beautiful, Tom!" Her happiness was tinged with sadness knowing she wouldn't live long enough to see it come to fruition. But she brushed those thoughts away as one swats a pesky fly.

"It's finally taking shape," he said excitedly. "I've already got two businesses who will display their wares in the shop when it's finished. They'll be on consignment, of course."

"Who?"

"Della Rossi from Hideaway Bay Olive Oil Company is going to have a large amount of space here for her goods, and Lily Monroe will have a small table showcasing her beach glass art."

"That's wonderful," Carol cried. This was the future of the farm. How far it had come from when she was a child, hiding under a porch to read books while corn grew in the fields around her.

"I'm so excited for you, Tom."

Tom stood a little taller, arms folded over his chest, grinning. "Thanks, Aunt Carol. I wouldn't have been able to do any of this without your help."

Carol waved his thanks away. When she first found out she was sick, she had gifted money to him and his brother. As it turned out, you certainly couldn't take it with you. Both boys had used the money for good things. Tom's brother, David, had put a deposit down on a house. Carol had been pleased. They were such good boys.

She was going to miss them. She sighed. That was the problem with dying. Leaving all those people you loved and journeying on by yourself.

When Carol expressed interest in the finer points of the business, Tom launched into a detailed list. He was up early, before five, and stayed late at night trying to get his baby off the ground. You'd think he'd be exhausted but he was so enthusiastic about it that he didn't even appear tired.

After an hour during which Tom gave her an impromptu tour of the site while Carol leaned on Ben's arm, Carol had to refuse his offer for lunch. All she desired was to go home to her warm house and take a nap in her chair with Melvin on her lap. Besides, she was expecting Gail, the hospice nurse, later that afternoon for her weekly visit.

On the way out, Carol asked Ben to pull over at the produce stand so she could take a look at her piece of the farm.

The white-painted stand at the corner of the highway and Erie Street was surrounded by loose gravel that kicked up a lot of dust in the summer. There were no formal parking spots, and Ben pulled around the stand and parked in the back.

At this time of year, there wasn't a lot of produce to sell, but Ben's wife, Dawn, carried on the tradition of selling canned goods and jams and preserves throughout the winter months. Currently, eighteen-year-old Mimi Duchene manned the stand. Carol had wondered about the girl being there on a school day, but Ben had informed her that she had the day off. Ben and Dawn were beginning to pull back from some of their work and had hired part-time help to run the fruit-and-veg stand. Carol could remember back when her grandparents had operated it more than seventy years ago.

The young girl stood there dressed in a winter hat, turtleneck, heavy hoodie, and a pair of jeans. Her winter hat had a furry pom-pom. She was a pretty girl, Carol thought, with her nut-brown hair and peaches-and-cream complexion.

"Hi, Mr. Anderson," Mimi called out with a smile.

"Hey, Mimi, how are things going today?"

"Great. I'm almost sold out of the strawberry jam and the peach preserves."

"Good, you're a natural-born saleswoman," Ben said. Gesturing to Carol, he said to Mimi, "Have you met my sister, Carol Rimmer?"

"Hi," Mimi said, lifting up a hand wearing purple fingerless gloves.

Carol said hello, and she and Ben walked behind the stand and looked out at the two-acre plot owned by Carol. It was long and narrow in depth, but it would suit her purposes perfectly.

They stood there for a few minutes and stared at the fallow, barren field. Carol had dreams for this field in the time she had left and because time was important, she needed to share her idea with Ben and get it off the ground.

"I've got an idea about what I want done with this field," Carol said.

Ben turned to her, his expression serious. "Carol, you can count on me to carry out your wishes."

She patted his arm and said with a smile, "I know that, Ben, and I appreciate it. But my plan is grand, and you won't be able to do this by yourself."

There was a slight lift to his mouth as he arched an eyebrow and said, "I'm all ears."

Carol turned her attention back to the field and squinted, unsure if it was the solitary breeze or feelings that had made her eyes sting.

"I've been thinking a lot lately of what I'd like to leave behind."

"Leave behind? You mean like your legacy?"

Although that's how she'd been referring to it in her mind, when he said it, it sounded pretentious. Carol scrunched up her nose. "That's kind of a stuffy word."

"Maybe so, but your legacy as Hideaway Bay's longest-serving librarian is well in hand. Think of all the students you've helped with school projects and all the kids and young mothers who came to your story-time circles, and all the charity book drives you've organized."

She shrugged. She didn't want to say she'd just been doing her job, because it had been more than that: reading had been her vocation and she'd wanted to share the joy of it with everyone that walked through the doors of the Hideaway Bay library. She hoped she had.

"I know that," Carol reluctantly admitted, "but I'd like to honor my connection to this place. Our family has been farming this land since well before the town was built, and it's only now that I'm starting to appreciate the significance of that."

Ben returned the smile. "I know exactly what you mean."

The two of them surveyed the two-acre plot.

"Now, what is your idea?" Ben asked.

"I want to leave something behind, something for everyone, not only my family but for everyone in town," she said

Ben waited patiently.

"I'd like to turn my plot into a field of sunflowers," she said.

The thought of it, a field full of sunflowers, growing tall and leaning toward the sun, filled her with immense joy. She verbalized this thought to Ben. "Think of how lovely it would look to people driving off the highway, all those rows of sunflowers with the lake in the backdrop."

"That's a great idea," he said. "I'll make sure it happens."

Carol shook her head. "No, I want to start now, before I go. I'd like to see some of it."

"Okay," he said slowly.

She was quick to reassure him. "Ben, I don't expect you to do this all by yourself. I know you and Dawn have stepped back and I would not ask any more of you."

"We wouldn't mind," he said eagerly.

She laughed. "No. You can oversee it if you want, but I'll find someone who can do the actual planting and growing and tending."

"Tom—"

She closed her eyes and said gently, "No. Tom is busy enough. He's got the winery to get off the ground. Leave him out of it. I couldn't possibly ask him. It wouldn't be fair." Ben and Tom were the sorts to volunteer to help regardless of their own commitments and obligations.

"I don't think Tom would mind doing this," he said. "I know he wouldn't."

Carol knew that too but still, she shook her head. "Nope. If you want to advise and Tom wants to manage it, fine, but I'm going to hire someone to plant and tend the field."

"Do you foresee this being an ongoing thing?" Ben asked.

She nodded. She'd given it quite a bit of thought over the past few days. "I do. You can sell bouquets of sunflowers at the stand." It would provide more income for the farm.

Ben's brow furrowed and he appeared deep in thought. "Carol, do you know anything about growing sunflowers?"

She laughed. "No, not a thing. But come on, we're from a farming family, how difficult could it be? I'm going to read up on it."

He started laughing.

"What's so funny?" she asked, smiling at him.

"I guess there's a book for everything."

"Of course there is!"

"What gave you this idea?" he asked.

"Baddie Moore stopped over the other day and brought a bouquet of sunflowers with him. They cheered me up to no end and I started thinking and one thing led to another—"

"Proving that thinking can be a dangerous pastime," Ben teased.

"Maybe."

He looked around the lot. As he did, a truck pulled in and a couple got out and approached the stand.

Carol regarded them. "It's great that there's still some business even this early in the year."

"We're blessed," Ben said. "And it's a good thing the growing season is coming because we're almost out of everything: canned goods, jams, and preserves."

"It's a good problem to have." She rubbed her forehead, closing her eyes briefly.

"You look tired, Carol. Do you want me to take you home?" he asked.

"I think so. I'm ready for a nap. I've got Gail coming over later."

"All right, let's get you home and we can discuss your sunflower field on the way."

By the time they arrived at Carol's house, she was bone tired and would have loved a nap. But this desire to do something for the town gnawed at her and she knew as soon as she put her feet up, there'd be no resting because this idea had taken hold of her mind. It occurred to her that as your life wound down, there were always going to be things to do and that quite possibly, you never got everything done. She'd have to make peace with that.

But she loved this idea so much and she could visualize it so clearly that she wanted to get started on it right away and bring it to fruition. Granted, it wasn't something that would happen overnight, but she hoped and prayed she'd live long enough to see it. As she watched the rain splatter the windows, she knew she had to wait until there was no more frost at night before seeds could be planted. Impatience hounded her.

Ben insisted on making her a cup of tea, and she humored him and took a sip when he handed her the cup.

"As you can imagine," she started as soon as he sat down on the sofa, "I'm anxious to get someone to plant the field and get started."

"I think between Tom, Dawn, and me, we could get it going," Ben said again. That was the problem with Ben and it was a good problem: he was always eager to lend a hand.

Carol shook her head. "No, Ben, we've already had this discussion. No need to go over it again." She hadn't wanted to hurt his feelings. Not Ben, the least of all people. "But I would like you to be there in an advisory capacity."

He nodded.

"Especially if I'm not here when it's finished—"

"Don't say that, Carol," Ben said, his voice laced with panic. "Of course you'll be here."

He knew as well as she did that her days were numbered. She had the scans to back it up. Why did people do that, she wondered, protest the inevitable by disputing the cold, hard evidence. She was guilty of it herself. She supposed there might be two reasons: first to cheer the dying person up and give them hope. And second, maybe it was to forestall their own feelings of grief about the loss of a loved one. Human beings were such wonderfully complicated creatures!

"All right, but in the event of . . ." And her voice wandered off. Before he could protest, she said, "Now all we have to do is find someone to work it."

"A volunteer, you mean?"

Carol shook her head. She'd given this a lot of thought as well. This was going to be an involved, labor-intensive, time-consuming project for the next few months. She'd worked out that she could pay a wage, and a decent one by Hideaway Bay's standards.

"I'm going to make it a job and give someone a wage for it," she said firmly.

Ben protested. "You don't have to pay anyone, Carol. There'll be plenty of people who would gladly volunteer."

"I know that, but I need more than a volunteer, I want someone who can commit one hundred percent to my project. I can't have someone who can only do it for an hour on the weekends. Besides, it won't be that long, probably not for more than six months, tops."

"Well, no rush," Ben said softly.

Carol laughed; she couldn't help it. "Well actually, there is a rush."

Ben looked horrified but as soon as he saw the mirth in Carol's expression, he relaxed.

"Ben? Can I be honest here? I don't want to tiptoe around the fact that I'm dying," Carol said plainly. "And it's okay to make a joke about it."

Ben lowered his head and his voice became gruff. "I don't think it's funny, Carol."

She realized he was trying to get control of his emotions. She was overcome with feeling for him because despite their age difference, she couldn't love him any more if she tried. "From where I'm sitting, there has to be humor or I won't be able to get through it."

Quickly he lifted his eyes and met hers. "All right, Carol. I'm just not used to joking about death."

The subject was beginning to skate around the edge of the pond of maudlin and Carol reigned it back in, bringing it to safer ground. "Do you know anyone in need of a job who'd like to take on a project like this?"

Hideaway Bay wasn't that big and between the two of them, with her being the town librarian and Ben running the produce stand all their lives, they'd met practically everyone in their small town on Lake Erie.

Ben leaned forward, folding his hands. After a moment, he shook his head. "Not off the top of my head. But I'll ask around."

"Okay. Because I'd like to get started sooner rather than later."

He paused, regarding her. "There is one person who knows everyone in town and would probably be in a better position than either you or I to find someone . . ."

Carol held up her hand. "Don't say it, Ben."

She knew he was referring to Thelma Schumacher. Thelma had been a transplant from Buffalo to Hideaway Bay, a divorced mother of one when she arrived in the beachside town. She ended up marrying Stanley Schumacher, the owner of the Big Red Top restaurant. Carol had dated Stanley briefly and she had been hopeful about him; he came at a time in her life when she could have used some kindness, and it was a trait he had in spades. But it wasn't meant to be. He'd always loved Thelma, or at least that's what she'd heard.

Thelma Schumacher was loud and gruff, and Carol had told herself on more than one occasion that this was the real reason they'd never get close, but deep down she knew it was because of the lost opportunity with Stanley.

Ben shrugged. "I know you're not a big fan of hers, but once you get to know her, she kind of grows on you."

"I don't want her growing on me in the time I have left." She couldn't imagine that. Didn't want to.

Ben went to say something else, but Carol cut him off. "Hopefully, it won't come to that. We should be able to find someone ourselves." She was confident of this even if Ben wasn't.

But after two weeks, when it felt as if Ben had talked to everyone in the farming community and beyond, it was deemed necessary to contact Thelma. Carol practically winced at the thought of it.

She didn't know if she was up for Thelma, not because she wasn't a big fan of the other woman, but she'd been having more pain, so much so that she'd had to call her hospice nurse. Gail popped out to see her and reviewed in detail Carol's level of pain, then made a call to Dr. Morrison, who ordered a painkiller. Gail reviewed with her the dosage and the possible side effects of the new medication, but at that point, Carol didn't really care about side effects, she only wanted relief.

By the time Thelma arrived, Carol had already taken one dose of the pain medication and although it hadn't totally relieved it, it had taken the edge off it to the point that it was tolerable. Gail had warned her to stay on top of her pain management.

Thelma Schumacher had never been inside Carol's house before. As she walked through, led by Ben, she took in the shelves crammed with books.

"Gee, you'd never know you were a librarian by the inside of your house," Thelma cracked with a grin.

Ben laughed and even Carol had to smile.

Thelma took a seat on the sofa, next to Ben.

"How are you feeling?" Thelma asked, removing the strap of her purse from her shoulder and setting it on the floor next to her feet. She slid out of her spring jacket, one arm at a time.

"I'm as well as can be expected," Carol said. She didn't want to relate her whole issue with pain, not that she didn't want to share this detail with Thelma, but she didn't want to worry Ben.

"Ben said you needed help with something," Thelma said.

"I do, and we've wracked our brains trying to figure out who might be well suited for the job, but we've come up blank."

"Well, if I can help, I will," Thelma promised.

Years ago, Thelma's hair had been red and wild and curly. Now, the curls remained, but they were steel gray. The years had gone by so fast. Carol could still see Thelma standing up on one of the vinyl booths in Stanley's restaurant decades before, taping Christmas decorations above the windows.

"Carol?"

"Huh?"

"Thelma asked what kind of help you needed."

"I'm sorry, right!" she said, coming back to the present.

Carol explained her idea and what was needed and for how long. At the end, she reiterated that it wasn't a volunteer position, that it would be paid a wage in line with the cost of living. Hopefully, there was someone out there in the community who was looking to earn an extra bit of money for the summer.

Thelma smiled. "I think a sunflower field is a wonderful idea. And although I can't think of anyone off the top of my head, let me sleep on it and I'll find someone to plant those sunflowers for you, Carol."

Carol hated to admit that she felt a little lighter knowing Thelma was going to help in her search. Although she had never formed a close friendship with Thelma, the other woman's ability to get things done in Hideaway Bay was legendary. Now she was sorry she hadn't asked her sooner.

Ben seemed to share Carol's relief. "That's great. Because we're almost in the window where the frost is behind us, and we need to get things planted."

Thelma stood.

"Wait, would you like some tea? I've got a lemon meringue pie," Carol said. She'd forgotten her manners. Lottie had dropped off the pie earlier in the day.

Thelma shook her head. "No, thanks. As much as I love lemon meringue pie, I've got to get going."

As Ben walked her out, she said goodbye to Carol.

"Let us know if you find someone," Carol said, clinging to hope.

"Oh, I'll find someone, I'm not worried about that at all," Thelma said before she left.

Chapter Eight

Jackie

On Saturday morning, Jackie took Anna and met her parents for breakfast at the Chat and Nibble on Main Street.

Laid out on the table in front of them was a veritable feast: a Belgian waffle with strawberries and whipped cream for Jackie, chocolate chip pancakes for Anna, a western omelet for George and a feta-and-spinach omelet for Helen. The table was crowded with plates, half-drunk mugs of coffee so strong it could put hair on your chest, placemats that doubled as a coloring book, and the odd broken crayon here and there.

Anna tried to speak to her Grammy, but her mouth was full of pancake and syrup.

"Anna, don't talk with your mouth full," Jackie said.

Papa winked at her and Anna giggled, syrup dripping from her mouth and down her chin.

"Really, Dad?" Jackie said. "You're not helping."

"Sorry, Jackie," he said, but he sounded far from remorseful.

"What are your plans for the week?" Helen asked, spreading strawberry jam on her rye toast.

Jackie shrugged, forked a piece of waffle, and wiped it around on her plate, picking up a bit of strawberry and some whipped cream. Her fork paused midair as she answered her mother. "The usual. Working three days. That's it."

"You need to get out more," her mother said. "It's not healthy being stuck in the house all the time."

"I'm not 'stuck' in the house, Mom," Jackie said. "I'm working, and I have Anna there."

"You need a social life."

"Why?" Jackie asked, waving her empty fork around. She wanted someone to answer that for her. Why did she need to get out of the house? Especially if she didn't want to.

"You need to have a life of your own, *separate* from Anna," her mother said, dropping her voice to a whisper.

Jackie looked to her father for help. "Dad?"

"Would it hurt to go out once in a while?" he asked delicately.

Jackie pressed her lips together and pushed her plate away, her appetite gone. She was about to say something when they were interrupted by the arrival of Thelma Schumacher.

"Hey Helen, George, Jackie, Anna, I see the gang's all here," she said, standing at the edge of their table. She was dressed in jeans, a long-sleeved turtleneck, and a quilted purple vest.

"What's new, Thelma?" Helen asked.

"Actually, I'm putting the word out," Thelma said.

"About what?" George asked.

Thelma explained to them about Carol Rimmer's project as well as her failing health.

Jackie thought a sunflower field sounded hopeful, but where would they get a volunteer for a part-time job like that? She glanced at her mother, who sipped her coffee, and Jackie could have sworn she saw the wheels turning in her head.

"It sounds like a great idea," George said. "If I were younger, I'd volunteer."

"We'd all do it if we were younger," Thelma agreed. She looked at Jackie, narrowed her eyes and said, "Gee, Jackie, a thought just occurred to me. You'd be perfect for a project like this."

Jackie put her hand to her chest and said, "Me?"

Thelma nodded enthusiastically. "Yes, you!"

Jackie shook her head quickly. "Oh, I couldn't commit to something like that. I've got enough on my plate as it is."

"I think Thelma is right. You would be perfect for this project," George piped in enthusiastically.

"Not helpful, Dad," Jackie said under her breath.

"It would be mean not to want to help a dying woman," Helen said pointedly, looking at Jackie.

Jackie tilted her head to the side and raised her eyebrows as if to say "Really, Mom?"

Thelma's gaze followed Helen's, and she placed Jackie under her own thoughtful scrutiny.

But before either woman could say anything, they were interrupted by Baddie Moore.

He stood next to Thelma and thumped on the table with his forefinger.

"Hello, everyone."

"Hi, Baddie," they all said, not quite in unison.

Everyone knew Baddie. Like Thelma, he was involved in just about everything in town, even at seventy.

"Hey, Baddie, what's new?" Thelma asked.

"Not much," he said, rubbing the back of his neck.

"We missed you last Tuesday at the social club," Thelma said.

"I went up to Buffalo to give my sister a hand. She's downsizing."

"That's a big change."

"I'll say. Boy, the amount of stuff you can accumulate in a lifetime," Baddie said, shaking his head.

Thelma snorted. "Tell me about it."

Helen picked up the thread of the previous conversation. "We were just talking about Carol Rimmer and her sunflower project."

Baddie's expression brightened. "I think it's a wonderful idea. Has she found anyone yet?"

"No, but the search is active," Thelma said.

Helen cleared her throat and then cleared it again, until Thelma and Baddie looked at her, their expressions expectant.

Jackie's eyes widened in alarm, and she mouthed across the table, "Mom."

"I think Jackie here would be perfect for the job," Helen said.

Oh no.

Both Thelma and Baddie stared at Helen, then swung their gazes to Jackie and back to Helen.

"You're right, Helen. Jackie, you would be perfect for this," Thelma said, running with the idea.

"I really can't," Jackie started.

"It's only a part-time thing for the summer," Thelma said. "And you'd be paid for it."

Helen chimed in. "You'd be able to put that money toward a trip to Disneyworld—"

Without looking up from her coloring, Anna threw her fisted hand, which held a broken red crayon, into the air and yelled, "Yay, Disneyworld!"

"And you could probably bring Anna with you to the field," Helen continued. "What a wonderful experience for a child."

"That is not helpful, Mom," Jackie said through gritted teeth.

Jackie's parents, Thelma, and Baddie focused their stares on her. Even Anna, who'd been immersed in her coloring, paused, chewing on a mouthful of pancake as she looked from one adult to another before finally landing on Jackie.

Anna leaned forward and stage-whispered, "Are you in trouble?"

I think I am, Jackie thought, but she laughed nervously and said, "Not yet."

Anna pulled her bottom lip down to the left and raised her eyebrows. "That's not good."

"No, it isn't," Jackie agreed with a sigh.

When Jackie arrived at her parents' house with Anna the following day for Sunday lunch, she couldn't believe Carol Rimmer's sunflower field was still a topic of conversation that included her. She thought for sure after a good night's sleep, her mother would have come to her senses and crossed Jackie off her mental list.

The roast beef dinner with mashed potatoes and gravy and green beans, which originally Jackie had been looking forward to, had now lost its appeal. She leaned over and began to cut the meat on Anna's plate.

"What do you mean you're not interested?" Helen asked. Her mouth slackened and she appeared to be at a loss for words, which was highly unusual for Jackie's mother.

Jackie looked beseechingly at her dad, who threw his hands up in surrender.

"I think it might be a nice little project for you," he finally admitted.

She skinnied her eyes at him and thought, *Not you too.*

"You spend a lot of time outside. And look how well you've kept up all the work Jason has done," her mother pointed out.

"That's beside the point," she shot back.

"It *is* the point," Helen said.

Jackie couldn't believe this conversation was actually taking place. How had going out for breakfast on a Saturday morning devolved so quickly into people thinking she could plant a sunflower field? The fact that there were four adults in Hideaway Bay who thought she could do it scared her. One person would have been bad enough, but four?

"If things were different, it might be something I'd be interested in," she conceded.

But things weren't different. They had changed dramatically. One moment her life had been one way and in the next instant, it had gone sideways.

"What conditions have to be met for you to take on this project?" her father asked.

Jackie ignored the question. "Why is it so important to you both that I do this? Plant these seeds and grow sunflowers?" She realized there was a plaintive tone to her voice, but she didn't care, she felt desperate. Why couldn't people leave her alone?

She pinched her eyes shut and rubbed her finger between her eyebrows. She couldn't understand why her mother was so excited about this. And then they arrived at the part of the conversation where Helen mentioned that she'd rung Carol and told her Jackie would do it.

The world seemed to lurch on its axis. Jackie's eyes widened and she stared at her mother, gape-jawed, as what she was telling her began to sink in.

"What?" Jackie asked. She couldn't have heard her right.

"I told Carol that you could do this, grow her sunflower field," Helen said, looking around to make sure all the dishes were on the table. She picked up a white ceramic pitcher and poured thick, rich gravy over her mashed potatoes.

ONE LAST THING BEFORE I GO 81

Jackie blinked several times, a jumble of thoughts crowding her mind, unsure of what to say next or what question to ask as all her thoughts piled up on one another. Finally, she came out with, "Why would you do that?" Her voice was laced with anger.

"Because it's perfect for you," Helen said.

Her certainty that Jackie was the right person for the job was both humbling and scary. "You need a little extra money," Helen continued. "This is a temporary, paid position, and Carol needs help right away. She doesn't know how much time she has left."

Although Jackie felt sorry for this woman she barely knew, she was also practical. And the pragmatic side of her was throwing up red flags and sounding all sorts of alarm bells in her head.

"Mom, I appreciate your concern, but I'm the last person to be running this project." Jackie started with this, hoping to be the voice of reason. She was barely keeping her head above water; she certainly couldn't be a flower grower.

"You're the perfect person," Helen said.

"Stop saying that," Jackie cried.

"It'll be good for you," Helen said with a tone that indicated the subject was closed.

To Jackie, the subject was anything but closed.

Her father remained quiet, slicing the roast with his electric carving knife before passing the plate of meat around.

"Can I point out one thing? Well, maybe two or three?" Jackie said, brushing her hair off her forehead.

Her parents looked at her with smiles indicating all was right with the world. At least their world.

"I know absolutely nothing about growing flowers, sunflowers or otherwise," Jackie said.

"Pffft," Helen said, still smiling but giving Jackie a dismissive wave of her hand.

"Mom, I don't even garden!" Jackie hissed.

"Of course you do," her father said brightly. "Look at your gardens at home."

"I simply maintain what Jason put in place," she cried out. Her eyes filled at the mention of his name.

Her parents looked at each other and then down at their plates.

"We're worried about you, Jackie," her father said quietly. "We know you miss Jason, and we understand you're still grieving."

Jackie looked at her father, trying to control the tears that were swimming in her eyes, not wanting them to spill over. "You don't understand what it's like."

"No, we don't," her mother said. "But you're our daughter—we love you and we want to help you."

"How can growing sunflowers help me?" Jackie asked.

"We will support you in any capacity," George said. "We'll help you plant the seeds. We'll watch Anna every day. We'll do whatever it takes to help."

Was she that bad? Yes, she was sad, but she was functioning. Wasn't that enough? She picked up her napkin and dabbed her eyes.

"Can I make a suggestion?" Helen said.

Jackie eyed her mother, wary.

"I told Carol we'd stop over tonight. You and me. Dad can watch Anna."

Jackie looked at her mother in disbelief. "That soon? Tonight?" A million excuses flooded her mind as to why she couldn't go. But none of them were valid.

Seeing her daughter's distress, Helen sighed. "Well, we can't back out now. Besides, time is of the essence. Let's go and see what she has to say and if at any point it feels too much or you're not interested, I'll tell her it's not for you. That way the onus is on me and not you."

"Okay," Jackie said, weary. She only had a few hours to come up with a solid reason not to take on this project and to let a dying woman down gently.

"Let's eat now," her father said. "This beautiful dinner is starting to get cold."

Jackie hadn't counted on liking Carol Rimmer. That had blindsided her.

She had marched into the woman's house, following her mother, going over in her head the list she'd compiled that afternoon of all the reasons she *wasn't* the person for the job. Her plan had been to articulate these reasons when they sat down with Carol, and hopefully, she'd be back home in time to watch television and read a story to Anna before she went to bed.

But she'd been distracted as soon as she stepped into Carol's house.

The house was warm—almost tropical—and there were books everywhere: jammed on shelves, piled on tables and chairs. A hutch against the wall in the kitchen was filled with pieces of Blue Willow patterned service ware. The walls in the den were covered in dark paneling and shelves with more books. The addition of houseplants of various sizes in ceramic pots gave the place a cozy feel.

Carol was not alone. Her brother, Ben Anderson, who had answered the door, was also there. Jackie recognized him from the fruit-and-vegetable stand up at the corner of the highway and Erie Street. His son, Tom Anderson, sat next to Carol with a sober expression. His face had the rugged look of someone who spent a lot of time outdoors. He regarded her with a nod of acknowledgement.

But the retired librarian had beguiled her. Although Jackie knew her by sight, she was surprised at the change in her appearance. She'd gone from appearing robust to frail. Jackie tried to remember the last time she'd seen her. Before Christmas? Her skin was pale, almost translucent. Deep purple circles sat beneath her eyes. She wore a colorful headscarf wrapped around her head with the tail of the scarf hanging over a bony shoulder. And although she moved slowly, she moved with purpose.

There was evidence of sickness Jackie couldn't ignore: The walker parked next to Carol's chair. The various bottles of medication littering an adjoining table. And then there was the DNR paper in stark black and white, held by a magnet to the refrigerator, that Jackie had glimpsed on the way in.

Things were dire for this woman, and that was the instant Jackie began to cave.

Both men stood when Jackie and her mother entered the room, and Carol attempted to stand but Helen frowned and said, "Carol, no need to get up."

With relief, she sat back down.

"This is my daughter, Jackie Arnold," Helen said.

"I'm Ben Anderson and this is my son, Tom," Ben said with a nod.

Jackie gave a quick smile and stepped forward to shake their offered hands. Both men's hands were large and calloused. When she shook the thin, frail hand of the retired librarian, she did so gently.

Carol swept an arm toward the sofa and invited Jackie and Helen to sit down. Once they were seated, the men resumed their positions on what looked like kitchen chairs brought in for the meeting.

Carol didn't waste any time. "Your mother has said you might be interested in running my project for the next few months."

This was the opening Jackie needed, had hoped for. But she could not find her voice to express her protests. Instead, she found herself saying, "Well, I'm interested in hearing more information."

Her mother stared at her and blinked.

Carol launched into her plan and her vision for the field. When she mentioned the remuneration starting immediately and continuing until the end of the season in October, Jackie did some quick math in her head and realized with that money alone, she'd be able to take Anna to Disneyworld in the spring.

Carol had to stop when she burst into a fit of ragged coughing and leaned forward, trying to get her breath.

Ben and Tom jumped up and were at Carol's side in a flash. Tom ran to the kitchen and got a glass of water. By the time he returned, the coughing had subsided. Carol thanked him for the water and took a few sips before setting it down on the crowded table next to her.

"I'm all right," she said, reassuring them.

Slowly, they backed up and sat in their chairs, not taking their eyes off Carol.

Carol leaned back, wiping her eyes. It was evident the coughing had cost her for suddenly, she appeared wrecked.

"Aunt Carol, why don't you let me explain it, so you can catch your breath?" Tom suggested.

Carol nodded, brought a tissue to her mouth, and let out a few more coughs. "I'd appreciate that, Tom."

Tom, dressed in a checked shirt and jeans, leaned forward, resting his elbows on his knees, and clasped his hands together.

If she'd been interested, Jackie would have thought him ruggedly handsome with his dark wavy hair and his deep-set eyes the color of espresso. He had a cleft in his chin that she found very interesting.

"Aunt Carol's field is two acres in size—"

Immediately, Jackie held up her hand. "Can you tell me roughly how big two acres is?"

He looked up to the ceiling, thinking. "It's about the size of two football fields."

"Oh," she said, deflating. That sounded pretty big.

Sensing her uncertainty, he said, "It's manageable for one person. The biggest job will be getting the field ready and planting the seeds."

His voice was rich like molasses and she found herself being lulled, almost to the point where she was ready to tackle this project.

"Once the seeds are planted, it's simply maintenance and dealing with problems as they pop up," he said.

"And Tom and I will be there to advise and help," Ben interjected.

Jackie's mother nodded next to her. Why did everyone make it sound so easy? So simple. She was sure it was not.

"I don't mean to sound rude," Carol started, slowly, "But I asked Ben to show me where you live. I wanted to get a feel for you as a person."

Jackie hoped who she was wasn't based strictly on the curb appeal of her house.

"We were impressed by your gardens," Ben said. "It looks like they receive a lot of tender loving care."

"My husband designed the gardens and planted all the shrubs and rosebushes," Jackie said. There was no sense in having them labor under false delusions. "I maintain it."

"A very important job," Carol said.

"You're doing a great job," Ben said.

It was nice to be complimented by people she hardly knew. However, she hoped their kudos wasn't born of desperation.

"Do you currently work?" Tom asked.

Jackie nodded. "I'm a remote worker, three days a week, for a health insurance company."

"So you would have the time to do this?" Carol asked, her voice tinged with hope.

There was a wave of optimism about the grand ideas and plans sweeping through the room, and Jackie could feel herself getting caught up in it.

"I should also tell you that I have a four-year-old daughter, and she would have to come with me sometimes."

"That's fine," Ben said. "You'd want to keep an eye on her as it's right near the highway."

"Of course."

"When can you start?" Ben asked.

"I was hoping to have a chance to think about it," Jackie said.

"I'm sure they're going to need a decision soon," Helen interrupted. "It's May and those seeds need to be planted."

Jackie shot her mother a look.

"The last of the frost is behind us. Your mother is right, we'll want to get those seeds into the ground"—Tom glanced at his failing aunt—"the sooner, the better."

"Can I ask a question?" Jackie said.

"Sure, you can ask anything you'd like," Carol said, taking a sip of her water.

"Why do you want to do this?"

Sometimes the why of something, the impetus behind a goal, was just as important as everything else, the driver of both the motivation and the subsequent execution.

"As you might know, my diagnosis is terminal and I'm currently under hospice care," Carol said.

Ben paled, and Tom lowered his head.

"I'm sorry to hear that," Jackie said softly.

Carol shrugged and gave a reassuring smile. "I can't complain, I've had a good life."

Even though Carol appeared to be at peace with her fate, the looks on the faces of Ben and Tom indicated they felt otherwise. But then that was the problem with death, wasn't it? The impact on the people who were left behind, who didn't stop loving you just because you were no longer there. Death did not end a relationship.

"Anyway," Carol continued, "I love this town. Always have. I never had any desire to leave as some people do. Everything I ever wanted or needed was always right here in Hideaway Bay. I had my dream job at the library and well, I consider myself blessed. And I wanted to do something nice. I chose sunflowers because I love their height and they *are* such a cheerful flower."

Jackie agreed with her there. She was partial to sunflowers herself.

Carol continued. "And you know, I thought it might be kind of nice as you drove down the highway and made that turn onto Erie Street to see a vast field of sunflowers right there, spread out before you." Her dreamy gaze indicated she was looking at it herself.

Jackie squinted a bit, letting Carol's vision come into focus and agreeing with her that it would be nice.

"Is this going to be an annual thing?" she asked.

Carol glanced at Ben and Tom. "I hope so, but I'll let Ben make that decision. Going forward, they could host events connected with the field and of course sell sunflowers at the stand."

"We'll make it work, Aunt Carol," Tom said.

Jackie thought Carol was lucky to have such support from her family.

She liked Carol, and she believed in Carol's vision. How could you not?

"Aunt Carol, would you mind if I asked Jackie some questions?" Tom said.

Carol hesitated but then said, "No, of course not."

Tom directed his warm brown eyes toward Jackie.

"Have you ever worked on a farm before?"

"No."

"How about a florist shop?"

She shook her head. She shifted a bit in her seat. Was he trying to make her uncomfortable?

As if reading her mind, he said, "I'm sorry for all these questions but I'm trying to gauge your knowledge, so we know how we can help you."

That was fair enough. "I don't know what I don't know," she admitted.

His grin was wide and his eyes twinkling. "Noted."

"And I'll be around to offer any advice," Ben said.

"Sunflowers are some of the easiest flowers to grow, Jackie," Tom said. "You really can't mess it up."

Just watch me, she thought, but she smiled politely.

"Good. Now, any more questions?" Carol asked.

"What about equipment and supplies?" Jackie said. Had they expected her to front all of this?

"There's a storage shed behind the fruit-and-veg stand. Everything you'll need will be in there," Ben said. "I'll make sure of it."

"And seeds?" Jackie asked. "How many packets will I need?" She wondered what kind they wanted planted.

"I'll order a couple of bags of seeds, some different varieties, from our supplier," Tom said.

Bags?

"Thanks." One less thing for her to worry about.

Helen looked over at her. "All set? We should get going."

Somehow Jackie found herself setting up a meeting with Carol and Ben at the field during the week and exchanging phone numbers with all three of them.

As they left the house, she couldn't help but wonder what had just happened in there, and what she had committed herself to.

Chapter Nine

Carol

*T*HAT'S SETTLED THEN.

It was a big load off her mind. Prior to meeting Jackie, Thelma had called her and told her she had the perfect person for the project. Carol hoped she was right.

After Jackie and Helen left, Tom put on a pot of coffee. Carol liked how familiar they were in her house: they came over, they got comfortable, made themselves something to eat or got themselves something to drink. This was exactly what she'd wanted with Ben and his family. She was grateful for it, grateful for her close family.

It was almost nine, and she didn't know how Tom drank coffee this late in the evening. How it didn't keep him up all night. Ben had declined his offer for a cup and had put the kettle on for tea instead.

"Carol, do you want a cup of chamomile tea?" he asked from the kitchen.

"That would be nice," she said. She liked to drink a cup before bedtime.

As much as she loved their company, she hoped they wouldn't stay too late. The later it got, the weaker and more fatigued she became.

The previous night, she'd stayed up too late reading and had to rest on her way to her bedroom. That morning, when Lottie came over and Carol told her what had happened, Lottie moved some chairs along the pathway to the bedroom so in future Carol could sit down as needed on her route to bed or to the bathroom. But going forward, she was going to get in her bed by eight or nine and read there instead of in the den.

Even if she lived to be one hundred, she'd never read all the books she wanted to read. She let out a soft chuckle, amused at all the things that would be left undone. But she would be satisfied if she could get that sunflower field up and growing. She prayed she'd live long enough to see it. Her first impression of Jackie was that she liked her; she had faith in her.

Of course she knew Jackie's sad story. Everyone in Hideaway Bay did. Their little daughter had only started walking and talking when Jason Arnold had been the victim of a hit-and-run while out jogging. He was found dead on the side of the highway, the driver never caught. It had been a great shock and the community had rallied behind his widow. It couldn't have been easy to be left alone so young with a small child. Carol's heart went out to her.

Both men reappeared in the living room. Ben placed her cup of tea to her right and sat down next to her.

Tom was quiet as he sipped his coffee. He leaned back in his chair, one leg crossed over the other, looking thoughtful.

Carol picked up her teacup, loving the look of the golden chamomile tea, and took a tentative sip, gauging the heat.

"I think Jackie's going to work out fine," Ben said, sipping from his own teacup.

"I think she will too," Carol said.

"We'll keep a close eye on her," Tom said. "I didn't know she had a young daughter."

Carol nodded. "Her husband was killed by that hit-and-run driver about three years ago."

Shock registered on Tom's face. "That's *her*? I didn't put two and two together." As he continued to sip his coffee, he appeared to contemplate this.

"Put the grapes down from time to time and try to pay attention," his father teased.

Tom laughed good-naturedly. "Hardy har har, Dad."

Ben slapped his thigh and guffawed.

Carol always enjoyed witnessing their easy relationship.

They spoke of general things about the farm, the stand, the vineyard, and news they'd heard about the community.

Tom finished his coffee, stood, and announced, "I better get going. I'll order those seeds first thing in the morning."

"Thank you," Carol said. She was so grateful for their help.

"Aunt Carol, do you need any help with anything before we leave?"

She shook her head. It wasn't too late. She'd take her time and make it to bed.

But Ben hung around, made sure she got to her bed all right, and then turned off the lights and locked the doors. He was so thoughtful; she felt herself lucky. She read one chapter in her book but couldn't keep her eyes open. She bookmarked the page and set the book down on the bedside table.

An audible sigh escaped when her head hit the pillow and she closed her eyes. There was something to be said for a comfortable bed and pillow. In the dark, drifting off, she found herself wandering back to the past as she'd been doing these past few weeks, going over things again in her mind, wondering if things could have turned out different, but always coming up with the same answer: no.

PART 2

1950

Chapter Ten

1950

Carol

Alva Anderson stepped out onto the front porch of the old farmhouse that faced the highway but whose best views were at the back of the house, which looked over fields of corn and offered sparkly, sun-dappled glimpses of Lake Erie through the copse of trees beyond.

The wooden screen door creaked behind her as it closed. With a sigh, she muttered, "Where has she gone now?"

Squinting, she surveyed the rows of corn to either side of the house and then swung her gaze to the right in the southwest direction toward the fruit-and-veg stand that her husband's family operated at the corner of the highway and Erie Street. The gravel lot in front of the stand was full as people clamored for fresh tomatoes and ears of corn.

Finally, she scanned Erie Street for any glimpse of the reddish-brown hair and lanky legs of her only child. She'd be hard to miss, but there was no sign of her.

She stepped forward, leaned over the porch railing, and called, "Carol! Carol!"

After waiting a few minutes, she gave up with an exasperated sigh and headed back into the house. A quick glance at the clock above the fireplace mantel reminded her to remove the loaf pans of banana bread from the oven.

It was eleven in the morning and Carol's chores weren't done. Alva shook her head. Her daughter knew the rule, so there was no excuse. Do the work first and then you could do what you wanted. Granted, it seemed the work was never-ending, but that was how it was on a farm. It annoyed her because now she'd have to dole out a punishment to her daughter, and she hated doing that.

Without a doubt, she knew Carol had slipped off somewhere to read her book. No one understood better than Alva the desire to read one more chapter. She herself had always been a big reader. Until she'd married Tom and learned that being married to a farmer didn't allow as many opportunities to read as one would like. On a farm, the work had to be done first.

It had been a rude awakening for Alva when she'd married Tom. She'd come from the town proper of Hideaway Bay. Her father had worked in the bank and her mother had been a seamstress, and that lifestyle had afforded her not only books but a lot of time to read them.

Now, she was up at the crack of dawn with her husband, making him a hot breakfast and then getting on with her own chores, which never seemed to end. But there were stolen moments of the day when Carol was busy and Tom was out in the field and she was caught up on her tasks, and she could sit and read one more chapter from one of the books her sister had given her.

Carol's absence was forgotten as Alva pulled multiple loaves of banana bread from the old stove and set them on the counter to cool down before she wrapped them up in blue-checked gingham cloth to sell up at the stand. That had been Alva's idea, to sell baked goods at the stand, because after reading, baking was what Alva loved doing most. Her father-in-law, who'd been skeptical, had agreed to a trial basis of thirty days. It had taken off, and Alva squirreled away the extra money, allowing herself the occasional purchase of a book for herself or something nice for Carol.

As she removed her oven mitts and laid them on the table, she thought if she could do it all over again, she would have liked to own a bookshop in town.

Beneath the front porch, ten-year-old Carol leaned against the cool stone of the basement wall and peered out of the latticed siding. She flicked off her flashlight, set her book down, and held her breath. There was a list of chores as long as her arm, but she couldn't put down the book she'd been given by Lottie's older sister. *The Lion, the Witch, and the Wardrobe* by C. S. Lewis. Carol much preferred to read this than do chores.

She waited until she heard the slam of the screen door and the receding sound of her mother's footsteps into the house.

She bit her lip, wanting to stay and read more but knowing the longer her mother waited for her return, the direr the consequences that awaited her and the less time she'd have to read later.

With a sigh, she opened the empty metal box next to her, slipped the book inside, and laid the flashlight on top of it. She closed the box and pushed it up against the stone wall before clambering out from beneath the porch. She stood and peered around, hoping no one saw her crawl out from her secret hiding spot. One of the barn cats, a regal black cat Carol had named Katharine, eyed her with curious ambivalence.

After she brushed off the seat of her dungarees, she ran around to the back of the house and accessed the kitchen from there.

The kitchen smelled of baking, and Carol saw the source of the sweet aroma: loaves of banana bread lined the counter.

As she opened the door, their dog Scruff ran past her, tail wagging, being shooed out by her mother.

"That's your last warning, Scruff! Go on now, or you'll get no more from my kitchen."

That was an empty threat. Her mother wasn't too keen on the rest of the farm animals, seemed to detest the barn cats, but Scruff was her dog. His bed—made by her mother and stuffed with old, clean rags—had the spot closest to the hearth. His dinner was the scraps from every meal. Carol's father had once suggested that the dog should sleep outside with the rest of the animals, but Alva had simply shaken her head and said, "No. He stays in the house with me."

Carol stepped closer to the banana bread, the scent becoming stronger. Her mouth watered. What she wouldn't give to sneak one warm slice, slather it with butter, and settle down behind her favorite tree out back with her book. She had lots of secret spots on the farm for reading.

Her mother stood there, her floral apron covering a floral shirtdress, her hands on her hips. She had the same reddish-brown hair as her daughter and was tall for a woman and spare. The fine lines around her mouth and eyes were more pronounced than usual as she stared at Carol. "I have been looking all over for you, Carol Prudence Anderson. Didn't you hear me calling you?"

Carol was smart enough to appear contrite. "I'm sorry. I was out back."

"Did you do your chores?"

Carol was about to nod but her mother tilted her head to one side and widened her eyes, challenging Carol's answer.

"Your father's going to be here for lunch soon and none of your chores are done? How are you going to explain that to him?"

Carol gave a shrug. Her father wouldn't be happy with that. "Where is Dad?"

"He's next door helping your grandfather with the tractor. It broke down this morning," Alva explained.

Carol stood there, motionless.

"Well, what are you waiting for? Go on, now! Collect the eggs first as I used the last ones in the banana bread. Then clean out the henhouse—don't give me that look, Carol, I know it's unpleasant, but it has to be done."

Carol nodded and bounced out the back door, glad to be out of the house again. She looked left toward her grandparents' house. It was in the distance, with a large portion of the farm between the two houses.

When her parents had gotten married, her father's parents had given them the farmhouse to live in, and her grandparents had built a modest ranch house as Grandma Anderson could no longer go up and down the stairs.

As she made her way to the henhouse out back, she wondered if she could walk to town later and see if Lottie was around.

Only last year, her parents gave her permission to cut across the fields, where she'd end up on Erie Street by the parish hall and head into the town of Hideaway Bay. She'd done it a few times, feeling emboldened and a little bit more confident each time. She liked the town with all the little shops and colorful awnings. There was a gazebo in the town's green space next to the granite war memorial. Plus, her best friend, Lottie, lived in town and Carol loved going to Lottie's house. She had lots of brothers and sisters, and her house was pure bedlam, but Carol had always found it entertaining.

Once her chores were done, she called out to her mother that she was going into town to see Lottie. But she soon discovered that Lottie wasn't home. She'd gone to her cousin's house. Carol wandered around town, not anxious to return home, in case her mother had more chores for her to do.

She soon found herself at the local library. Located on one of the side streets off Erie Street, it was near the rest of the municipal buildings of the lakeside town. The unrelenting heat forced her inside.

Large fans turned lazily, creating a constant clicking noise. The lights were dim in the library, and it smelled like nothing else she'd ever smelled before. Namely, it didn't smell like farm animals and manure. It was a combination of scents: of paper, old things well preserved, with a woody hint. For the rest of her life, she would love that smell.

Behind the desk sat a young woman with bright red lipstick who wore her dark hair short and curled and tucked behind her ears. Her gray print dress had a red belt, and Carol glimpsed a pair of small feet tucked into a pair of stylish red shoes beneath the desk. She was in awe of the fact that the woman's shoes matched her belt.

In front of the smartly attired woman, on the desk, was a nameplate reading "Miss Woodbridge."

As Carol tentatively approached the desk, unsure of what to do, the librarian smiled, revealing small white teeth.

"Can I help you?"

Carol, unsure, shrugged.

"Would you like to check out a book?" the woman asked.

When Carol didn't say anything, Miss Woodbridge stood from her desk, the skirt of her dress swirling around her. She looked over her shoulder and beckoned Carol with a wave. "Come with me, young lady."

Intrigued, Carol followed her until they stood in between two bookshelves.

"Do you like to read?" the librarian asked.

"I like to read in school," Carol said.

"So you do have a voice!" Miss Woodbridge said with a grin.

Carol smiled and looked down at her shoes.

"Let's find something for you to read." Miss Woodbridge ran her finger along the spines of the books crammed on the shelves. "Ah, here we are." She pulled a book out and handed it to Carol.

Carol held the book in both her hands. *The Secret of the Old Clock* by Carolyn Keene. She could not take her eyes from the cover.

"Have you read this one before?" Miss Woodbridge asked. "It's the first book in the Nancy Drew Mysteries series."

Carol shook her head.

Miss Woodbridge lowered her voice. "When you step into a book, you can be all sorts of things, go all sorts of places. Every book is a wonderful adventure."

Carol followed her back to the front desk, fascinated by the swish of the librarian's skirt.

"Now, you can sit here and read a few pages and see if it's to your liking," Miss Woodbridge said, pointing to a small round wooden table with a smooth surface and four wooden chairs.

Immediately, Carol pulled out a chair and opened the book to the first page.

"I'll leave you to it," Miss Woodbridge said, and she returned to her seat behind the desk.

Carol became oblivious to the passing shadows on the wall. She opened the book and by the end of the first chapter, she'd fallen into the story. She kept reading, the only sounds the turning of the page, the tick of the clock on the wall, and those ceiling fans. Later, when she paused and looked at the large clock on the wall with its black hands against a white face, she became alarmed. She'd been gone much longer than she was allowed. Trouble waited for her at home. She closed the book and carried it to the librarian.

"Did you enjoy it?" Miss Woodbridge asked. There was a slight smudge of red lipstick on her front tooth. But Carol still thought she was pretty.

"Yes, but I'm not finished. Can I take it home?"

"Do you have a library card?"

Carol frowned and shook her head.

"You'll need a library card to check the book out."

"How do I get a library card?" Carol asked. "And how much does it cost?"

"Bring your mother or father in to sign the form. And they're free, they don't cost anything."

She couldn't see her mother driving her into town to get a library card. How many times had Carol asked her to take her to the Pink Parlor for an ice cream cone? Or for some saltwater taffy at Mr. Lime's Five-and-Dime? The answer had always been no. But the perk was that this was free. Maybe she could try it from that angle.

"Okay," Carol said, not feeling particularly hopeful.

She left the book with the librarian and headed back out into the harsh sunshine.

It had been a wonderful day.

She ran all the way up Erie Street until she reached the parish hall and cut through the field behind it. She didn't know why she was running as there was only going to be trouble when she arrived home. What was the hurry? Out of breath and her face red and sweaty, Carol slowed to a leisurely pace, cutting through the rows of strawberry runners. There was no worry that her mother would spot her in the open field as there was a giant oak tree blocking the windows on that side of the house.

Strawberry season had come and gone. It only lasted about three weeks in June and then it was over. She had stood out there in the warm afternoon sun with her mother, the dirt dusty, picking strawberries and tossing them into a basket. Smooshed strawberries had stained the pale wooden strips of the bushel basket a pinkish red. Her mother had then sorted through them, tossing the bruised or damaged ones to the side for the birds. They hauled pint-sized wooden baskets brimming with ripe strawberries on a flatbed up to the whitewashed fruit-and-veg stand at the corner. Carol didn't mind strawberry season, at least you could eat them. Her fingertips would be stained red with strawberry juice by the time she was done picking.

As she arrived at the back door of their farmhouse, Carol stood at the bottom of the steps feeling slightly queasy. Before she could start her climb, the screen door burst open and her mother appeared, a tight set to her jaw. She held open the door and said tightly, "Get in here right now."

Carol bolted up the stairs and breezed past her mother, trying to stay out of reach of her mother's hand. She'd been a recipient on a few occasions, and it was an experience she didn't care to repeat.

Her wariness was forgotten when she spotted her father standing in the middle of the kitchen. His denim overalls were dusty and there were dark, damp circles beneath the arms of his shirt. He was in dire need of a shave, and there was a mark along the top of his brown hair from the hat he wore to protect himself from the blazing sun. His hair was damp and plastered to his head.

Carol knew she was in a pile of trouble, more so than if it were only her mother. She swallowed hard as her mouth went dry. Her father was always gone before she got up. He showed up at one sharp for his midday dinner and then did not return until it was almost dark. The fact that he was here now in the house in the middle of the afternoon did not bode well for Carol. There was a grim set to his mouth.

Carol's heart sank and her shoulders slumped as her heart rate picked up in anticipation of the corporal punishment that awaited her.

"Where have you been? We've been looking all over for you," her mother said.

Carol dragged her gaze from her father and looked at her mother, whose eyes sparkled with fury.

"I-I-I went to town to see Lottie—" Carol said, each word diminishing in volume.

"You did not. I called over there and Mrs. Gallagher said you weren't there," Alva said. "She said Lottie was over at her cousin's house."

"I know, she wasn't home."

"Where were you, Carol?" her father asked quietly.

"I went to the library," Carol said hurriedly. "I started reading a book and I guess I forgot about the time."

"Are you telling us the truth?" he asked.

Carol's eyebrows became two dark slants on her face, drawing downward and knitting together in a scowl. "I was at the library. I even met the librarian, Miss Woodbridge. She said I could get a library card and take books out."

Her mother studied her but remained silent.

"A library card?" her father repeated.

This was something he did, repeating a phrase as he turned an idea around in his mind, considering it. Thinking of arguments against it. It amazed her that there were never arguments for things. Like, it's a hot day, we should go get an ice cream cone.

Carol couldn't help gushing out, "I was reading a book about Nancy Drew and I didn't get a chance to finish it and there are more books in the series and if I had a library card, I could take them out."

"I'll think about it," he said.

Carol hung her head and mumbled, "I'm sorry. I lost track of time."

"I've got to get back to work," her father grumbled. "I've lost enough time today."

He brushed past Carol without a word and went out the back door, grabbing his hat off the peg by the door and settling it on his head.

"Go on, Carol, you can weed the back garden," her mother said.

She turned around, her back to Carol, and busied herself at the sink.

ONE LAST THING BEFORE I GO

The following Saturday morning, Carol brought in the eggs from the henhouse in the wicker basket as Alva was putting the breakfast down on the table. Since the incident at the library, Carol had tried to be good. She did all her chores without her mother having to ask her a second time, and she was up in the morning before her mother called her. As a result, there was peace in the valley as her father was apt to say.

That wasn't to say she didn't think about that book. She'd thought of it nonstop. She wondered what happened next, but she supposed she'd never know. She thought of ways she could get a library card. She wondered if her grandparents or her teacher would help her. But as it was still summer, there was no way she could see her teacher to ask. Besides, she'd be going into the fifth grade and that meant a new teacher, a teacher she didn't know all that well. She could hardly approach her on the first day of school and ask her to get her a library card.

Carol took the basket of eggs out to the sink in the back hall, rinsed them quickly, and set them on the folded towel to dry. She put the basket on the floor near the back door and took her seat at the table. Before her was a white-enameled plate with fried eggs, bacon, sausage, and one piece of toast. She picked up the glass of orange juice and sipped from it before digging in to her breakfast.

Her father came in, washed his hands up to his elbows at the sink in the back hall, and took his seat at the head of the table.

"Carol, after breakfast, you can go into town with me," her mother said, eyeing the table to make sure everything was on it.

Carol looked at her mother.

Every Saturday, her mother went into town to do the shopping, and Carol was always left behind with a list of chores to complete before her mother returned. Her father also went to town for parts for the tractor if needed, or to the grain-and-feed store for the livestock. She'd gone with him from time to time if only to escape the monotony of farm life and the interminable list of chores.

She shrugged, stuffed half a piece of bacon into her mouth and said, "Okay."

"Doesn't she have chores to do?" her father said, breaking the yolk on his fried egg and mopping it up with a piece of buttery toast.

"She can do them when she gets home," her mother said, not making eye contact with her husband. She gave Carol a quick smile across the table.

Carol didn't care if she accompanied her mother to town or not. Her plan was to finish her chores and then disappear, staying out of her parents' way lest they get any ideas for more chores.

When she was finished, she scraped the bits off her plate into the dog's bowl, and Scruff's nails clattered on the kitchen floor at the promise of food. She set her plate and silverware in the soapy water in the big, white porcelain sink.

Out back, behind the house, her mother's 1943 DeSoto, whose color was a dark burgundy, was parked in front of her father's black 1938 Ford pickup truck.

Her father jumped into the pickup, started the engine several times before it kicked to life, reversed, then drove around her mother's car, heading to another part of the farm, the frame of the truck bouncing up and down as he drove along the rutted trail.

Carol climbed into the front seat of the DeSoto and waited for her mother. When she slid behind the steering wheel, Carol noticed she had changed her clothes and fixed her hair. Alva had a few dresses she wore to town; Carol knew her mother would never be caught dead in town wearing the clothes and aprons she wore around the farm.

They drove to town with the windows rolled down, and Carol hung her arm out the window, letting the slight breeze tickle the fine hairs on her arm. She loved looking at all the colorful awnings of the shops in town. When they passed the library, she looked at it with longing.

Alva didn't say much on the ride over to the grocery store.

Carol lagged behind her mother as she pushed a shopping cart around Milchmann's grocery store on Main Street. Alva picked items up off the shelf, put them in the cart, and ticked off the things on her list. Carol read everything she passed, from advertisements to labels. At the back of the grocery store, Alva rattled off her list to Mr. Milchmann, who ran the butcher counter. When he handed her a stack of meat wrapped in individual brown wrappers, she thanked him and placed it in the cart.

At the front of the store, once the bill was paid at the cash register, the cashier handed over a strip of green S & H savings stamps, which her mother tucked into her purse.

As they walked out of the store, Carol looked over at the Pink Parlor, thinking an ice cream cone would be just the thing, but her mother either didn't see it or ignored it.

With a sigh, Carol got into the front seat of the car and looked out over the town again, wishing she didn't have to go home. She wondered what Lottie was up to. There was no way she could ask her parents to go and visit Lottie, not after the other day. It would be a long time before she'd be allowed to walk back into town by herself. She'd probably be a grown woman with kids. Feeling logy, she stared out the window, unblinking.

But her mother didn't head in the direction of home, and Carol wondered if she had another stop to make. She remained mute.

She perked up when her mother pulled the car in front of the library and threw it into park.

"Now how about that library card?" Alva asked with a smile.

With a broad grin on her face, Carol popped open the door and jumped out, already on the steps to the library by the time her mother had closed the driver's-side door.

With her mother behind her, Carol pulled open the heavy door of the library using both hands and stepped into the cool air of the front room. Miss Woodbridge was right where Carol had last seen her: behind her desk.

Carol smiled to herself; all was right with the world. She looked up at her mother and hesitated. But her mother strode confidently toward the desk, her purse slung over her arm, hanging from the crook of her elbow.

Carol followed her mother wordlessly and with a beating heart stood next to her at the desk.

"Hello, Elizabeth," Alva greeted the librarian.

"Alva, it's good to see you again," Miss Woodbridge said. Her dress today was sky blue, and at her ears were big white clip-on earrings. A wide white belt cinched her narrow waist. Her hands were small and delicate with bright red painted nails. "It's been a while."

Alva sighed. "You know how it is. The farm is so busy during the summer there's hardly any time to wind your watch much less read." She thought for a moment and added, "Can't wait for winter."

"I bet." Miss Woodbridge glanced at her and smiled. "I didn't realize this young lady was Carol."

Carol frowned. Her mother had mentioned her by name to the librarian? Her mother *knew* Miss Woodbridge. They chatted away like old friends.

"What can I do for you today?" Miss Woodbridge asked.

"I don't have a lot of time, but Carol needs a library card." Alva glanced around the library and added, "And if you could recommend a book for me. I won't have time to browse through the shelves." Her voice was wistful.

"Certainly." Miss Woodbridge pulled open a side drawer in the oak desk and pulled out a piece of paper. "If you would fill this out, I'll type out Carol's library card as quick as I can."

"Thank you," Alva said. She took the offered pencil and paper and quickly filled out the form as the librarian stepped away from the desk, browsed through the return cart, and pulled off two hardbacks.

They exchanged items; Alva handed Miss Woodbridge the filled-out form, and the librarian gave her the two books. "I thought you might be interested in these. Look through them and I'll type out Carol's card." To Carol, she said, "Why don't you go pick two books off the shelf to check out."

"Don't be long, Carol," her mother instructed, glancing at her watch.

Her mother needn't worry, Carol knew exactly which two books she was taking out. The first books in the Nancy Drew series.

Aware that she was in a library, she had to temper her excitement, and she walked quickly to the shelves where Miss Woodbridge had showed her the books by Carolyn Keene. Her hands were damp, but she sighed with relief when she spotted the book she'd started reading the other day. Next to it was the second book in the series, *The Hidden Staircase*. With great satisfaction and anticipation, Carol pulled that one out as well. She didn't want to keep her mother waiting. When she walked around the corner of the shelves, she spotted her mother chatting and laughing with Miss Woodbridge.

She set her books on the desk and said, "I'll take these two out."

"Good choice," Miss Woodbridge said with a smile. She stamped the cards at the back of the books and handed them over to Carol. "Remember, they need to be back in two weeks or there'll be a fine."

Carol nodded and held the books carefully to her chest with both hands.

"Come on, Carol, say thank you," her mother prompted behind her, tucking her own library book close to her.

"Thank you!" Carol said loudly.

The librarian put her finger to her lips in a *sh* gesture, but her smile reached her eyes.

Carol planned to do all her chores quickly when she arrived home and then find a quiet spot to read her books. She couldn't wait.

As they walked out, Carol studied the covers of her books.

"Now there's a great job, working as a librarian," her mother said.

Carol looked back at Miss Woodbridge seated behind the desk with a nameplate on it, wearing pretty clothes and surrounded by all those books.

She had to agree with her mother. Miss Woodbridge had the ideal job.

Chapter Eleven

1952

"Carol, you have a phone call!" her mother called up the stairs.

Carol looked up from her book. Her chores were done, and currently, she leaned back on a pillow she'd propped up against the headboard of her bed. Her book rested on her upraised thighs. Frowning, she asked, "I do?"

She rarely received phone calls. She couldn't imagine who it could be. Carefully, she placed her bookmark—one she'd made herself of construction paper and gold stars—inside the book, closed it, and set it aside. She jumped off the bed and dashed down the stairs.

She picked up the heavy receiver of the black Western Electric rotary phone that stood on the small table just outside the kitchen. Tentatively, she said, "Hello?"

"Hi, Carol, it's Lottie!"

"Oh hi, Lottie," Carol said, slightly disappointed. She had expected someone a bit more exotic. But still, she was happy to hear from her friend.

"Can you sleep over tonight?" Lottie asked.

"Let me ask my mother," Carol said.

Before Lottie could respond, she set the receiver down on the table and went into the kitchen in search of her mother.

She found her at the kitchen sink. On the drainboard lay the carrots Carol had pulled from the back garden earlier that morning. She still had the dirt beneath her fingernails to show for it. Her mother was brushing the dirt and dried mud from the carrots one by one and running them under the cold water tap.

"Can I sleep over at Lottie's tonight?"

Her mother turned her head slightly, glancing over her shoulder, the water still running from the tap.

"Oh, I don't know . . . I wanted to take you up to the stand to help your grandfather out," she said.

"Awwww," Carol whined.

"Carol, you know your grandmother can't help out anymore since her stroke." She turned off the faucet, picked up a towel, and wiped her hands. "Can you go later this afternoon?"

Carol nodded quickly before her mother could change her mind and ran back to the telephone to give Lottie a resounding "yes."

Lottie and her mother, Mrs. Gallagher, pulled into the produce stand late in the afternoon. Mrs. Gallagher drove her 1940 Buick Estate Wagon over the loose gravel, the panel-sided car bumping along over the ruts and dips of the parking lot. As soon as she parked, next to an older Ford pickup truck, Lottie bounced out of the car and greeted Carol with a broad, sweeping wave.

Carol was glad to see her. It had been a long afternoon.

Under her mother's direction and with her grandfather's encouragement, Carol had been kept busy at the stand since late morning. Her mother showed her how to line up the baked goods and the jars of jam on one side of the sloping whitewashed shelves out front. Then she carried the heavy sandwich board touting "Fresh Corn" and "Fresh Tomatoes" out to the edge of the highway. With her grandfather's permission, she painted over the sign to read "Sweet Corn" and "Juicy Tomatoes."

Business had been brisk but began to fall away midafternoon. Her grandfather left to check on her grandmother, and her mother went home to pack a bag for Carol's overnight stay at Lottie's. There were a few stragglers and with diminished supplies, Carol wished she'd brought her book with her. She'd know for next time.

"Mother, can I go now?"

Alva nodded. "Have fun."

Mrs. Gallagher approached the stand. Whereas Carol's mother was tall, spare, and lean, Mrs. Gallagher was petite and curvy with pale skin, and hair as dark as midnight. "Oh shoot, I've left it too late," she said, looking over the depleted produce and baked goods.

Alva smiled and pulled out a brown paper bag from beneath the shelving. "I put aside a bag for you, Margaret."

Earlier, Carol had watched her mother fill the bag with half a dozen of the best tomatoes, a baker's dozen of corn, and a loaf of banana bread.

Margaret Gallagher pulled out her wallet, but Alva shook her head. "No, Margaret, please accept this with our thanks. You're always having Carol over and well, I appreciate it."

"It's no problem at all," Mrs. Gallagher said. "What's one more kid in my house?"

Both women laughed.

Margaret hesitated. "Are you sure?"

"Of course I am."

Before the other woman could protest any further, Alva picked up a second brown paper bag that contained Carol's overnight items.

"Did you remember my book?" Carol whispered.

Her mother frowned and whispered back, "I did, but I don't know why you need a book on a sleepover. Don't ignore Lottie to read your book."

"I won't."

She kissed her mother goodbye and with the paper bag beneath her arm, she hopped after Lottie and her mother. After climbing into the back seat with Lottie, Carol put her bag on the floor. As the station wagon pulled out onto Erie Street, she looked back and waved at her mother, who smiled and waved back.

Mrs. Gallagher had a few errands to run before she headed back to the Gallagher house. Carol and Lottie waited in the back seat while she ran into Milchmanns grocery. Fifteen minutes later, she appeared with two brown paper bags, full, one in each arm.

"One more stop and then we can go home," she said, looking in the rearview mirror at the two girls.

They crossed over Erie from Main Street and Carol watched the beach pass by. Mrs. Gallagher parked in front of one of the last houses on Star Shine Drive. It was the second to last house on the street, not as big as the others, but big enough. There were two stories plus a third floor of dormer windows which housed the attic.

The peeling yellow paint and the green shutters—some of which needed to be replaced—gave the house a shabby but impressive feel.

"Come on, girls, let's go inside and see if Delphine is home."

Carol frowned but Lottie leaned over to her and whispered, "This is where the lady from France lives. She makes chocolate. You'll like it here, trust me."

Unsure, Carol followed Lottie out of the car. She'd been down this street before but had no idea a Frenchwoman lived here. Now she was just plain curious.

As they followed Mrs. Gallagher around to the back door, Lottie whispered, "She's hard to understand sometimes because she speaks with a French accent, but her chocolate is something else."

Carol recalled her mother speaking from time to time of a Frenchwoman who'd taken up residence in Hideaway Bay after the war. Her mother had called her a war bride. Had her mother visited the chocolatier? And if so, why hadn't Carol seen any of the chocolate? She reminded herself to ask her mother these questions when she returned home.

Carol was the last one in through the back door. Immediately her eyes widened as she was greeted with the scent of chocolate and fresh-brewed coffee. Her mouth watered.

"Come in, come in," said a pretty auburn-haired woman in the kitchen. She had wide-set blue eyes in a heart-shaped face. Her smile was as generous as her figure. She was younger than Carol's mother. A baby sat in a high chair next to the kitchen table. In one hand, he held a rattle and in the other, he held a spoon. At times, he banged them against his tray. But every square inch of the countertops was covered in trays of chocolate.

Gape-jawed, Carol looked from one batch of chocolate to the next. She'd never seen anything like this before. She was used to wrapped chocolate: Hershey's, Butterfingers, and Baby Ruths. And at Christmas, her father always gave her mother a box of Fanny Farmer candy. But these were petite, delicate creations, each one looking more perfect and tempting than the next.

The Frenchwoman clapped her hands. "Your timing is perfect, Margaret. I'm trying out a new flavor. Will you try? You will, of course you will." Her speech was rushed as if she was afraid they might change their minds and leave.

Mrs. Gallagher smiled. "That last batch of orange chocolate was delicious. I enjoyed every morsel."

Lottie eyed her mother suspiciously and asked, "What batch of orange chocolate?"

Mrs. Gallagher and the Frenchwoman, who said her name was Delphine, exchanged a glance and then giggled together.

She swept past them, kissing the top of the baby's head as she went by.

"Ah, my sweet love," she cooed to the child.

At the far end of the kitchen, she took some chocolates off a rack on the drainboard, placed them on a delicate floral saucer, and carried them over to where the three visitors stood.

"Try," she prompted, putting the plate in front of them.

Carol looked over to Mrs. Gallagher, who nodded. Lottie showed no restraint, and she thrust her hand forth, took a piece of chocolate, and popped it into her mouth. Carol did the same, and Mrs. Gallagher put hers into her mouth and closed her eyes.

"Oh my, Delphine, that is exquisite," she said.

Carol let the piece of chocolate melt slowly on her tongue, experiencing the combined flavors of apricot and almond. She had never had chocolate like this before.

As she savored it, already wishing for a second piece, Delphine set a pan of melted chocolate in the middle of the table. She reached for a bowl of strawberries and gave Lottie and Carol a skewer each. She took Lottie's skewer and showed her how to pierce a strawberry and dip it into the melted chocolate, then handed it to Lottie. "Now let it cool down a bit before you eat it or you'll burn your tongue."

As Carol and Lottie gorged on chocolate-covered strawberries, Delphine showed Margaret the other confections she was making. Mrs. Gallagher sampled a few pieces and pronounced, "That coffee chocolate flavor is divine." She licked her fingers in approval.

They circled back to the table and Mrs. Gallagher asked, "How are things, Delphine?"

Delphine nodded. "It is good."

"I'll take a small box of those coffee flavored chocolates."

As Delphine carefully placed chocolate pieces in a small gold-foiled box, Carol helped herself to another strawberry and dipped it in chocolate.

They stayed up late that night.

Carol loved going over to her best friend's house. It was pure chaos, but everyone seemed so happy. Everyone, that is, except Lottie's oldest sister, Peggy. She was chronically miserable.

Carol followed Lottie up the creaking staircase to her bedroom. It was a small room with a big double bed with a lumpy mattress. Lottie shared the bed with her two older sisters, Peggy and Colleen.

As soon as the younger girls entered the room, Peggy, who was stretched out on the bed with a *Movie Play* magazine, said, "Get out, twerp" without even lifting her head from the page.

All the Gallagher children were dark-haired and blue-eyed like their parents. The oldest, Peggy, had the looks of Jean Simmons but was also in possession of a sharp tongue.

"I've got to get my stuff. Carol and I are sleeping downstairs tonight."

At the mention of Carol's name, Peggy looked up and narrowed her eyes at her. "What are you doing hanging around my sister? I thought you had better sense than that, Carol."

"Lottie's my best friend," Carol said.

"Sounds like poor judgement to me," Peggy said, returning her attention to the magazine.

"Where's Colleen?" Lottie asked, digging through a bottom drawer for a nightgown.

"How do I know? I'm not her keeper. Probably out with that knucklehead," Peggy muttered, flipping a page in her magazine.

With a huff, Lottie slammed the dresser drawer, but Peggy ignored her. When they walked out of the room, Lottie leaned in and pulled the door shut with a slam so hard it shook.

"You better not be slamming that door again, Loretta Mary," her mother yelled from the kitchen.

"Why is it my sister is a jerk but I always get in trouble," Lottie grumbled as they ran down the stairs.

A small room off the kitchen served as Mrs. Gallagher's sewing room. With Carol's help, Lottie moved all the furniture to the perimeter of the room to clear a space for them on the floor. The two girls laid out blankets on the floor and set their pillows on top. The small windows were wide open, but there was no relief from the stifling heat. Carol's clothes clung to her, and her bangs stuck to her forehead. Outside the window, the crickets were loud and obnoxious.

From the kitchen, Carol could hear the muted sounds of the radio and Mrs. Gallagher singing along on occasion. Mr. Gallagher was out back, working on the car. He would not come in until dark. Lottie had told her once that her father loved being outside. Carol thought he should have been a farmer.

Lottie drew the drapes but left the windows open, and she and Carol changed into their nightgowns. Carol relished the feel of the light cotton material on her skin.

They went to the kitchen, where Mrs. Gallagher set down a snack of saltines covered in peanut butter and grape jelly with a glass of milk.

"Can we get glazed donuts in the morning, Ma?" Lottie asked.

Her mother shook her head. "That's only on Sunday mornings."

After their snacks, the girls settled down in the sewing room.

"Tell me my future, Carol," Lottie said, lying on the blanket on the floor and pulling an old sheet up to her chin.

Carol was disappointed that Lottie already wanted to go to bed.

"Do you want to play a game?" Carol said.

"Nah. Tell me my future," Lottie persisted.

"All right, then," Carol said, getting comfortable.

This was a game they played often, though Carol was better at it than Lottie was.

"You're in your twenties and you're working on Madison Avenue in New York City. You have a job as a secretary to a very important man at a big company. He treats you like one of his daughters and constantly tells you how smart you are. You wear the prettiest, most stylish clothes right out of Vogue."

Beside her, Lottie sighed. Carol knew of Lottie's desire to go off to just about anywhere and have a career.

Carol frowned, thinking. "It's Tuesday night, so tonight's the night you see Brad. You only see him on Tuesdays."

Lottie bounced up. "Oh, tell me about Brad."

"Brad used to play football in college. He's got broad shoulders and a dimple in his chin."

"A dimple?" Lottie said.

"Yeah, you know, like a cleft?"

"I don't, but keep going," Lottie said, settling back down.

"He left a single pink rose on your desk with a note saying 'Dinner tonight?'" Carol said. "And every Tuesday night, he takes you for dinner and cocktails at a restaurant overlooking Manhattan. Sometimes, if the weather is warm, he takes you for a carriage ride in Central Park."

"Ohh," Lottie gushed, pleased.

Carol went on about Brad, how he was always bringing her little gifts, like charms for her bracelet. As she was in the middle of this, Lottie dozed off.

Carol waited a few minutes to make sure Lottie was asleep before she quietly stood, tiptoed over to the table next to a chair and flipped a lamp on. She pulled her book out of her bag, settled in Mrs. Gallagher's overstuffed floral chair, and opened her book and started reading.

After breakfast, Mrs. Gallagher suggested the two girls go down to the beach.

"But not too long, or you'll get burnt to a crisp," she said.

She retrieved some old bath towels from the cupboard and handed them to the girls, who tucked them under their arms. Carol carried her bag with her.

"What's in the bag?" Lottie asked, taking the bag from Carol and digging through it.

"Lottie!" Mrs. Gallagher chastised. "You don't ever go through someone else's things without permission!"

Lottie was not embarrassed. She simply shrugged and said, "Carol doesn't mind."

"Let's ask Carol," Mrs. Gallagher said.

"I don't mind," Carol said. She didn't. Lottie was her best friend.

"Might want to leave the bag behind," Lottie advised. "Won't need a book on the beach."

Carol had a grim set to her lips. She'd hoped that while Lottie was watching all the boys on the beach, she could settle in with her book. She loved Lottie but she was boy crazy. It was all she talked about. Carol liked boys but from a distance or in a book.

Wearing only their bathing suits and sandals, they left the house and headed to the end of the street, turned left, and walked in the direction of the beach. Carol had a bit of money with her that her mother had given her before she left the house. She planned on getting her and Lottie ice cream cones at the Pink Parlor later.

"Do you ever think about getting married?" Lottie asked.

Carol snorted. "No, I'm only twelve."

"I think about it all the time," Lottie said dreamily.

"You do?"

Carol knew Lottie liked boys, but she didn't know she was already thinking about matrimony. They were still in elementary school.

"But I thought you didn't want kids," Carol pointed out.

"Oh, I don't! After living in my house with all my brothers and sisters, I don't want any kids. I only want a handsome husband," Lottie said. "I'd like a mink coat and cocktails at six."

"I want to be a librarian," Carol said.

She glanced at her friend out of the corner of her eye. It was the first time she'd verbalized her dream to anyone. She'd been thinking about it on and off for the last two years, wondering what you had to do to become a librarian. Was it one of those deals her father tended to go on about, where you had to know the right people? If that was the case, she'd be out of luck; she didn't know anyone.

"That makes sense, Carol. You're always reading books!" Lottie said.

She didn't scoff at her dream or make fun of her or tell her she was being silly or stupid. Her best friend in the whole world thought her dream to become a librarian was sensible.

Carol looked up to the cloudless blue sky that seemed to go on forever. The warmth of the sun hit her in the face. It felt good and she smiled, happy.

By early afternoon, they left the beach as it had become unbearably hot. They'd gone in the water several times but by the time they reached their towels laid out on the sand, they were hot again.

After deciding it was time to pack up and go, they picked up their towels, shook out the sand, and tied them around their waists. Their wet hair hung in hanks and their faces were red with sun. After they slipped on their sandals, which were tight because their feet were wet and sandy, they hobbled off. Carol ignored the pinch of the sandal strap digging into her ankle.

"Come on, let's go to the Pink Parlor," she announced.

"I didn't bring any money," Lottie said, dismayed.

"I've got plenty for both of us," Carol said.

Lottie broke into a smile and linked her arm through Carol's. "Let's go then, what are we waiting for?"

The Pink Parlor was packed. There was a line out the door. A large group of boys stood in front of them. Carol homed in on one of the boys, who appeared to be the center of the attention of the group. He was a couple of years older than her, and she figured he went to the high school. He had dark hair and the bluest eyes she'd ever seen. His laugh was easy and his friends seemed to defer to him. To Carol, he was like a character in a book.

Unable to take her eyes off him, she elbowed Lottie. "Who's that?"

Lottie followed her gaze. "Oh, that's Roger Harrison. You know that mansion up on the cliff? The one with the white pillars in front of it? That's where he lives. His family is rich. He was away at boarding school but came back to Hideaway Bay for high school."

Carol marveled at her friend. "How do you know all this?"

Lottie shrugged. "He's in Jimmy's class." She referred to her older brother. Realization dawned on her and she grinned. "You like him, don't you!"

Carol felt flustered and she stammered, "No, no, it isn't that. I-I-I've never seen him before—"

Lottie continued to smile. "Don't worry. I won't tell anyone." When she spotted the look of panic on Carol's face, she held up her pinkie. "Pinkie promise."

Carol wrapped her pinkie around Lottie's and repeated, "Pinkie promise."

Later that evening, Carol sat on the stool next to the bathtub as her mother rubbed Noxzema on her sunburned shoulders.

"I've told you a hundred times that you can't stay in the sun too long."

But Carol was only half paying attention, for since the stop in the Pink Parlor, she'd thought about nothing else except a boy named Roger Harrison.

Chapter Twelve

1956

"I was thinking of going over to the library before it closes. Did you want to go with me?" Alva asked, removing her apron. She pulled her scarf and coat off the hook by the back door. She wound the scarf around her neck and slipped on her coat, buttoning the big black buttons on the front of it.

"Not tonight, I can't, too much homework," Carol said. She was seated at the kitchen table, grudgingly doing her assignments. She would have preferred to go to the library.

They had developed a habit of going to the library together once a month, usually on a Saturday and sometimes, an occasional trip on a weeknight if they had time. Alva would have liked for it to be more often, but it was all she had time for. Carol went more regularly herself but lately, nothing on the library's shelves appealed to her; she felt as if she'd read everything. Besides, Lottie's sister Colleen had given her a paperback novel she was engrossed in called *Forever Amber*. It had opened Carol's eyes and was now safely tucked beneath her bed.

"Are you sure?"

Carol nodded. "Yes. I'm going to go to the movies later with Lottie, if that's all right."

"You seem to be going to an awful lot of movies these days," her mother remarked.

Carol shrugged. "I love going to the movies."

It was a little more than that. What she loved was that her crush, Roger Harrison, worked at the cinema. It was worth the fifty cents if only to lay eyes on him.

"What are you going to see?" Alva asked, patting her pockets for her gloves.

"That new one with Grace Kelly. *High Society*," Carol replied.

"She's so beautiful I could watch her in anything."

"Me too."

"Are you sure you don't want to go to the library with me?" Alva asked again.

Carol looked over at her. "I'm positive."

Alva hesitated at the back door.

"Next time," Carol promised. She returned her attention to her schoolbooks.

Lottie was a no-show for the movies later that evening.

Carol paced back and forth on the snow-covered pavement in front of the movie theatre. It was unlike Lottie to not show, and she hoped everything was all right.

It was bitterly cold outside, and Carol kept moving to keep warm. She bit her lip, debating whether she should return home or go inside by herself. Would that be strange to see a movie alone? She really didn't know.

It was also a Tuesday night in January, and there weren't many moviegoers. In fact, Carol had seen no one. She couldn't blame them; it was freezing outside. If she had any sense, she would have stayed at home too.

"Are you going to walk back and forth all night or are you coming in to watch the movie?"

Carol jumped at the sound of the voice behind her. Turning, she spotted Roger Harrison with that beautiful dark hair of his, standing in the doorway, hands on his hips. He wore the uniform of the cinema: a red short-waisted coat with a white shirt and black tie and black pants. There was a cowlick in the front of his hair that looked as if it required some effort to tame. But it was his facial features that Carol was entranced with: Cheekbones so sharp they looked as if they could cut paper. A jaw so square it appeared to have been made from granite. And eyes such a pale blue they were almost translucent.

She didn't say anything at first, too stunned to speak. Roger Harrison was actually speaking to her!

"What's it going to be? In or out?"

"I-I-I'm coming in," she said and briskly walked up to the ticket window.

After all, Grace Kelly had just announced her engagement to a real-life prince, and she wanted to see her up close on the screen. To see what you needed to possess to capture a prince.

Roger proceeded into the ticket booth and said, "That'll be fifty cents." He took her coins and handed her a ticket.

He flashed her a brilliant smile and said, "You're in luck, you've got the whole place to yourself tonight. Movie's about to start. Did you want something from the concession stand?"

"Yes, please."

She followed him to the snack counter and studied the back of him, committing it to memory. The way his hair curled at the nape of his neck. The broadness of his shoulders and how they seemed to push against the fabric of his uniform. She watched, enthralled. She didn't think she'd ever seen anyone as beautiful as Roger Harrison.

Roger was the only employee she could see at present. She supposed there wasn't a need for a lot of staff on a weeknight in the dead of winter. That would be different on the weekend when the place would be packed. Old Mr. Bauman would have a counter person, another running the projector, and his wife, Mrs. Bauman, selling tickets behind the glass window out front.

"Hey, it's Carol, right?" Roger asked, slipping behind the counter and standing in front of her.

"That's right," she said.

She smiled, secretly pleased that he knew her name. She was a year behind him at school. He was a senior, captain of the football team, captain of the debate team, but she wasn't popular at all. She had tried starting a book club but that had not gone over well. No one her age wanted to read books except for a handful of people. And by the start of the school year, she'd lost interest in clubs when she became interested in him.

"I've seen you around school."

He'd noticed her.

"What will you have?" he asked.

"Um," she said, tapping her fingernail on the glass countertop.

"Don't get the Milk Duds, they stick to your teeth," he said.

She could feel the heat rising within her beneath his scrutiny.

He leaned forward, resting his arms on the counter, cutting the distance between them in half. He lowered his voice, his eyes never leaving her face. "I don't think I would like to kiss a girl who had candy stuck to her teeth."

Carol's face burned. She didn't have to look in a mirror to know her cheeks had gone scarlet.

"Would you?" he asked, his voice barely above a whisper.

Lifting her face slowly, she regarded him for a moment and said, "Well, I certainly wouldn't want to kiss a girl whether she had candy stuck to her teeth or not."

His eyes widened and he broke into a grin. The laugh that escaped his mouth filled the lobby.

"But I'll have a Coke and some popcorn," she said, pleased she'd gotten that reaction from him. Feeling a bit bolder, she added, "with extra butter, please."

"You really like the movies, don't you?" he asked, sliding the paper carton of hot popcorn across the glass countertop to her. The smell of hot butter wafted off the popcorn.

She didn't know if he was making fun of her or simply making a statement of fact. If he only knew the real reason she came to the movies so often.

As she walked to the theater with its plush red seats, she forced herself not to look back and stare at Roger.

But she felt his eyes on her and was glad she'd worn her favorite skirt.

She picked an aisle seat halfway up, removed her coat, and got comfortable in her chair. With a glance at her wristwatch, she saw there was only five minutes before the movie started.

She was surprised to see Roger coming into the darkened theater; she'd assumed he was supposed to be running the projector.

He stopped at the end of her aisle, his hands in his pockets. "Hey, Carol, I wondered if you wanted to come to the projector room with me. You know, keep me company while I run the movie."

She didn't have to think about it. She stood, gathering her things. Roger relieved her of her coat and carried it to the screening room.

The room was located at the top of a dimly lit, narrow staircase. It was small and cramped with an equally small window looking out on the darkened movie theater. The projector stood on a stand.

Roger hung her coat over the back of one of the chairs.

He demonstrated how to put the large film reel on the wheel and start it. It made a constant rattling noise once it started, and the film emanated from the lens in a milky blue stream of light.

"Are you still going to show the movie even though there's no one in the theater?" Carol asked.

"Sure, you want to see it, don't you?" he asked. "You paid for your ticket."

She nodded quickly. "Yes, I do."

"Get comfortable on that stool over there," he said with a nod.

While the film played, Carol was acutely aware of Roger behind her. The cramped space of the small room heightened her senses. Her nerve endings tingled so much she was almost certain they emitted a low buzz. She half watched the movie and half watched what he was doing.

Carol started going to the movies every Tuesday night. She lied to her parents and told them she was meeting Lottie, but she always went alone. It was the highlight of her week, being alone with Roger in the projection booth. It was on the third visit that he kissed her.

It was just as she'd imagined it would be. Like she'd seen it in the movies. He'd reached out and grazed his thumb along her cheek, whispering, "I want to see if your skin is as soft as it looks." He stared at the place where his thumb touched her, mesmerized, not blinking, focused on the back-and-forth movement. Without warning, he leaned in and laid his lips on hers. His breath was sweet and warm and tasted like Coca-Cola. She leaned into him, sighing against his mouth. He tilted his head for a better fit. Carol got lost in all that kissing and touching, and her body felt like hot liquid, languid and sweet. She never wanted it to end.

When she pulled on her coat to leave, there was a smile on her face. Her chin and the area around her mouth were chafed from all the kissing but she was proud of it; it was evidence that he'd kissed her. That it was real.

He walked her to the door and said, "I'll see you next Tuesday night?"

She nodded but had to admit to a little disappointment that he hadn't asked her out on another night.

For the next three months, Carol hardly picked up a book. Never in her life had she seen so many movies. Some she saw two, three, or four times. But every Tuesday night, she was in the projection booth with Roger. He was better than any character in a book she'd ever read. She couldn't get enough of him. Never before had she so looked forward to going to school. Not that she had any classes with him. But she passed him in the hall, and his locker was directly behind hers on the opposite wall. When she'd run into him in the hallways, he was polite, friendly, and would chat a few minutes with her. And he'd end every conversation with, "See you Tuesday night."

Years later, Carol would admit that she got caught up in something that was much bigger than herself. That she'd been sucked into a whirlpool and went along willingly, went with the flow, so to speak. Because that first kiss soon led to other things, namely unintended consequences.

Chapter Thirteen

"What? You're pregnant? Are you sure?" Roger asked. He slumped against a small wooden table in the projection room and muttered, "Oh no. Not *this*."

There was a small muscle at the corner of his perfectly curved mouth that appeared to be working overtime. And those beautiful blue eyes, so pale and light as to almost appear ethereal, at that moment were dark and stormy.

"I-I-I don't know what to do," Carol stammered.

She wasn't afraid; she was terrified.

"Well, don't ask me," he said, folding his arms across his chest.

"But it's your baby too," she said.

She took a step toward him, looking for relief. Looking for comfort. Looking for assurance. He slid half a step away from her, still leaning against the desk.

"There's nothing I can do," Roger said.

Her heart broke. She dreaded telling her parents. But if he'd marry her, then perhaps that would soften the blow.

"We'll have to get married," she said hurriedly. Wasn't that what people did when they found themselves in the family way?

His expression turned darker. "I can't marry you. I'm going away to college in the fall."

"That's when the baby's due!" Carol cried.

He stared at the ground. When he didn't say anything, she panicked. In the books she'd read, the ones her mother didn't know about, unmarried girls either had to give up their babies or they were forced to seek abortions.

She tried again. "But if we got married, we could—"

"I won't marry you, Carol," he said, shaking his head.

Her eyes widened and her mouth dropped open.

"Why not?" she asked, the volume of her voice dropping.

"It's just not going to happen," he said with a shrug and a smirk.

There was coldness in those beautiful eyes, something she'd never noticed before.

"What am I going to do? I can't have a baby! I'm only sixteen! My parents will kill me," she cried.

"I don't know. But it's your problem, Carol." He stepped away from the desk and opened the door. "I think you should leave now."

She was too stunned by his rejection to protest, to shout, to demand that he do the right thing and *help her*.

When she reached the door, he whispered. "Do not tell anyone this is my child. I will deny it."

She slanted her head, gape-jawed, staring at him in disbelief. She ran out the door, down the stairs and away from him, bursting into hot, fat tears.

In her entire life, Carol had never seen her father so angry. It was beyond anger. It was rage.

"Who is the father of this child you're carrying?" he demanded again.

She stood in the kitchen with her parents. The air was tense. Her mother sat at the big farmhouse table with its worn surface, her face buried in her hands, crying, and her father stood there with his hands on his hips, his lips pressed so tightly together they'd turned white. A scowl furrowed between the slant of his dark brows.

"I can't say," Carol stammered. Feeling as if her legs would no longer hold her up, she pulled out a chair from the table and sank into it.

It hadn't taken Alva long to figure out exactly what was wrong with her daughter. After three weeks of Carol vomiting nonstop in the morning, she'd gotten her a cool compress and asked quietly, "You're not with child, are you?"

Carol, hunched over the toilet bowl and full of panic at being found out, shook her head, but when she burst into tears, her mother understood that to be a "yes." Alva gasped, threw her hand to her mouth, and stepped back, stumbling, reaching out for the wall to steady herself.

But now this was different from her mother's initial hurt and shock, Carol knew. Her father's face was tight and red, and his rage scared her. Would he hit her? It had been a long time since she'd been spanked as a child, and it was usually her mother who'd been the disciplinarian, but she was uncertain about her father in this state.

"What do you mean you can't say?" he asked.

She shook her head, her brown curls bouncing around her face.

Carol wasn't sure what she wanted to do with her baby. She hadn't gotten that far. All she knew was she didn't want to be pregnant—that was the one thing she was sure of. She wanted to go back to the way it was before she started fooling around with Roger Harrison. She wanted to go back to the days when her head was always buried in a book. Reading had been so *safe*.

Suddenly, her father paled, the anger leeching out of him. "Do you know the father?"

"Yes! But I can't say who it is!" she said, her voice a plaintive wail.

She didn't want to be questioned on the identity of the father. She'd never say. Roger had made it very clear that if she named him, he'd deny it and then people would assume the worst of her. That not only had she gone and gotten pregnant but she was a liar too. He was from a well-heeled family. They'd never believe her over him. Never. Besides, how could she prove he was the father?

"Tell me his name and I'll get this sorted out right now," Her father said in a voice that was not to be denied. "You're going to have to marry him."

Marry him? Roger had already made it clear there'd be no marriage. "But I'm only in high school."

Her father cut her off. "Yes, doing adult things!" The timbre of his voice sliced through the dense air of the kitchen.

Carol hung her head and cried, her shoulders shaking. Big fat tears plopped onto the table, making dark stains on the wood grain. Her mother thrust a clean handkerchief in her line of vision.

Alva lifted her head from her hands, her expression stricken, and swiped at her eyes and nose with a handkerchief. "Do you want to marry this boy?"

"She has no choice! How's she going to hide a pregnancy and then a baby?" Tom cried.

Carol hated herself for distressing her parents like this. If only she could go back in time and do things differently. Or not do them at all.

"Why won't you tell us who the father is?" her father demanded, his voice rising.

"Because I can't prove it, and he's already told me he'll never admit it."

"What?" her mother asked in disbelief.

"What kind of man does not take responsibility for his actions?" her father said.

Carol could only shrug.

"So not only have you found yourself in the family way, but you've been abandoned by the father of the child," her father recapped. His voice was tinged with anger.

"Tom," Alva pleaded.

"Don't 'Tom' me, Alva!"

This was followed by a tense moment of silence. Carol wished someone would say something.

"There is another option," Alva said quietly. She fiddled with her handkerchief in her hands.

"And what is that? Because there aren't many, and I hope you're not going to suggest a back-alley visit somewhere," Tom Anderson said.

"Give me a little credit," Alva snapped.

"Then what is it?"

"She can go live with my sister until the baby is born."

Carol's head snapped up. "With Aunt Lina?" That was worse. Aunt Lina was the younger but shriller version of her mother.

"I'm listening," Tom said.

"We could send her down to Lina's and tell everyone Lina needed help."

That was true, Carol thought. Her aunt had just had her fourth baby in as many years.

"What about school?" Tom asked.

"I'm thinking about that part. She can't miss a whole year but maybe she could be tutored at home," Alva said.

"And how would we pay for that?"

Alva shrugged. "I'm not sure yet."

"And when she has the baby, then what?"

"She'll have to put it up for adoption," Alva said. "There are a lot of families out there who would be willing to adopt a brand-new baby."

Carol felt invisible, as if she weren't even in the room. Part of her was relieved to let the adults work it out, but the other part wanted some say in her future and what to do with the baby growing inside her.

"Put it up for adoption," Tom repeated.

"Yes."

"I'll need to think about this," he said with a defeated sigh.

Before he stepped out of the room, he turned toward Carol and said quietly without looking at her, "You've disappointed me like no one else ever has."

And he was gone.

Carol laid her head on the table and cried.

Chapter Fourteen

By the end of her third month of pregnancy, Carol was shipped off to her aunt's house in Pennsylvania. Her mother had wanted to go along if only to see her sister, but her father had vetoed that, and an argument had ensued between them.

The back-and-forth bickering ended abruptly when Tom shouted, "This is not a social call, Alva. I'm dropping her off and turning around and coming home."

Carol swallowed hard. It all sounded so cold. Her father had hardly spoken to her since her pregnancy had been revealed. Her mother spoke to her only to relay information or assign chores. "Peel the potatoes." "Set the table." "The path to the barn is covered from last night's snowfall."

It was determined that her baby would be arriving at the beginning of October. As it was almost May, she wouldn't miss that much school, and the remainder of the school year would be done at her aunt's home with a tutor.

Departure day arrived, and she went over early in the day to see her grandparents and say goodbye.

"I don't know why you have to go all the way to Pennsylvania to help Lina when I could use some help myself," her grandmother said.

Grandma Anderson sat in a rocker, several blankets on her lap, her right arm shriveled and contracted at her side.

Carol's grandparents hadn't been told of her pregnancy. She couldn't decide if it was because her parents were concerned about their advanced age or if it was because they were mortified at the truth.

There was some truth to what her grandmother had said. Nearing seventy, she'd become frailer with each passing year. Her hair, once gray, had now gone white. She shuffled when she walked, grabbing onto things like the edge of the counter or a table or the wall with her left hand, which wasn't her dominant hand, to maintain her balance. Carol's grandfather, meantime, appeared as hale and hearty as ever.

"Lina has four young 'uns, and Lina isn't as sturdy as Alva," her grandfather said thoughtfully. "She'll be glad to have an extra pair of hands around."

But the elderly Mrs. Anderson wasn't convinced, and Carol often wondered if her grandmother suspected the true purpose of Carol's trip to Pennsylvania. She hoped not; she'd never be able to look her grandmother in the eye again. Grandma Anderson had always been so kind to her, and she couldn't bear to see a look of disappointment in her eyes too.

Shame was an awful thing; it destroyed you from the inside out. But she supposed she had no one to blame but herself.

The three-hour car ride to Pennsylvania was completed in total silence. They'd taken her mother's car as Tom had said the truck wasn't meant for such a long drive. Her father looked straight ahead and did not once throw a glance her way or even engage in conversation. Carol felt both conspicuous and invisible.

She'd packed a small suitcase with a few clothes. Her mother had gone to Goodwill in Buffalo and had bought a couple of second-hand maternity outfits for her. They seemed too big, but her mother assured her they would fit in no time. She'd packed a couple of books in her suitcase and wondered briefly if there was a public library within walking distance of her aunt's house. But she quickly dismissed that idea. She certainly couldn't go walking around her aunt's town, unwed and pregnant. No, she'd have to remain hidden until the baby was born.

Aunt Lina and Uncle Ralph lived in the northwestern part of the state. Uncle Ralph worked for a manufacturing firm that made radiators. He was a big, burly man who liked cold beer and a good joke.

When they pulled up to the modern-looking low and long brown-brick ranch, Carol was relieved to see that her uncle's car was not in the driveway. He worked shiftwork. The last thing she wanted was a welcoming committee of knowing looks and hushed voices.

There were still small piles of snow over the lawn. The lawn itself was nothing but mud and muck.

Her father hauled her suitcase out of the trunk and marched to the front door. Wordlessly, Carol followed him, resigned to her fate. The big picture window on the front of the house was smudged on the inside with little fingerprints. As if on cue, two little heads popped up in the window and waved. Carol smiled involuntarily at them. She couldn't remember the last time she'd smiled, certainly not in recent memory.

Her aunt opened the front door before they reached it. On her hip was her most recent baby, a boy named Frank. He was a chubby baby with drool on his chin.

"Hello, Tom," was all Lina said. She glanced at Carol, her inspection traveling down to Carol's belly, and Carol was glad she had on her heavy winter coat.

"Lina, how are you?"

"Fine, Tom."

Lina opened the door wider to allow them in. Tom stepped back, and Carol advanced through the open door and stood next to Lina.

"Aren't you coming in, Tom? A bite to eat before you get back on the road?"

Tom Anderson shook his head, looking at Lina but intently keeping his eyes directed away from his daughter. "No, thank you, Lina, I want to get back on the road and get home before dark."

"Suit yourself."

He looked at Carol. "I'll see you in September." And he turned on his heel and walked toward the car.

Carol panicked and chased him. "Dad, please!"

He stopped but did not turn around. Carol scooted around in front of him, her eyes full of tears, her chin quivering. "Dad?"

When he said nothing, she threw her arms around him. "Dad, I made a mistake, I'm sorry, I promise to be good. Please don't leave me here."

Her father wrapped his arms around her, squeezed her tight, kissed the top of her head. "It will be all right, I promise," he said, his voice breaking. And with that, he cleared his throat and disengaged himself from her clinging embrace, side-stepped around her, and walked rapidly to the car.

Carol began to follow him, her steps stuttering, and then stood, watching him drive away, her arms hanging loosely at her sides.

When the car disappeared from sight, she turned slowly and headed into the house. She closed the door behind her and removed her coat. Her suitcase stood by the front door.

Aunt Lina's three older kids were lined up on the sofa from oldest to youngest, staring at her. Like their parents, they were brown-haired and brown-eyed. Lined up like that, they looked like steps on a staircase.

"Here, you might as well practice," Lina said, handing off the baby to Carol, who hadn't even hung up her coat yet.

Lina was the younger, leaner version of Carol's mother, even after four babies in five years. She was all sharp angles.

"I'm giving my baby up for adoption," Carol said quietly.

Lina regarded her. "Whether you're giving it up or keeping it, I need help." And she disappeared into the kitchen, leaving Carol alone with a baby who had a terrified expression on his face. Moments later, he let out a shriek, and big fat tears soon appeared.

In the months she spent at Lina's, Carol learned an important thing about herself: she loved babies and little kids.

As the weather grew warmer, she was able to take her little cousins outside into the fenced-in backyard, where there was a swing set. When they tired of that, she would sit with them beneath the only tree in the yard that provided any shade and make up stories for them. They would watch her, their little faces earnest, hanging on every word, or sometimes roll around in the grass, laughing at a silly story she'd made up.

She kept the children out of her aunt's hair and her aunt, who suddenly had a lot of free time she hadn't had in years, made more trips to town, but she always brought back a new paperback for Carol and a new Little Golden Book for the children.

Carol loved those kids as if they were her own and the baby, Frank, became quite attached to her. She couldn't imagine leaving them come October.

In those rare moments when she had time to think, her heart felt heavy. She wished she could keep her baby. She didn't want to give it up for adoption. Her feelings grew stronger with each flutter and then with each kick and movement. In her later months, she felt cumbersome, top heavy, and although she wished it were over with, there was a part of her that wished she could stay pregnant forever so her baby would always be with her.

But summer flew by as summers always do, and when the calendar pages flipped to September and then October, she knew her days were numbered, and it wouldn't be long before she'd be handing off her child to be raised by strangers.

Keeping her baby simply wasn't an option.

Chapter Fifteen

"She'll need to go to the hospital," the midwife declared, standing up from the bed and stepping back after her examination.

Carol tried to process what the midwife was saying, but the pain that gripped her lower abdomen was something else—it felt as if her womb was being wrung out and was ready to burst forth any moment. Having grown up on a farm, she knew about the birthing process, she just hadn't known the amount of pain involved.

Plus she'd been unwell since yesterday. She'd felt illness coming on. Not like a flu or a cold but general malaise.

"Please let this be over with," Carol whispered, her mouth dry. Her bangs clung to her damp forehead.

Her mother had driven down earlier in the week, close to Carol's due date, to be there. In the few months since she'd left, her mother had aged. There was more gray at her temples and the lines on her face appeared more pronounced. She stood at the side of the bed and mopped Carol's brow with a cool washcloth.

"Can you open the window?" Carol asked.

It was unbearably warm in the small bedroom at the back of the house. The bedsheets felt damp and there was a sour smell about the room.

"The window is open, Carol," Lina said. She stood at the foot of the bed with the mid-wife. Both wore concerned expressions.

Carol looked from her mother to Lina to the midwife. The midwife stepped out of the room.

"What's wrong, Mother?" Carol asked.

Her mother sat down on the side of the bed, next to Carol, the mattress dipping slightly beneath her weight. She took her hand and squeezed it. "Nothing's wrong," she said, her voice unnaturally high. "This baby is taking a little longer to deliver, that's all. You might have to go to the hospital."

Carol tried to gauge her mother's expression, but another contraction gripped her, feeling like a vice on her womb, and she let out an agonized scream.

"Is she supposed to be this hot?" Alva asked her sister. "She's burning up."

Lina walked around to the other side of the bed so she was across from her sister. She leaned over and pressed her palm to Carol's forehead. With a frown, she said, "She's got a fever."

The midwife stepped back into the room. "I've called for an ambulance. She needs to be in the hospital."

"But she's going to be all right, isn't she?" Alva asked, her voice shaky.

"Of course she's going to be all right, Alva," Lina said with forced brightness. "Women have babies every single day."

"But she's still a girl," Alva protested.

Despite the pain, Carol felt as if she were fading, as if she were viewing the other women in the room with her through a gauzy veil. She felt as if she were sliding along the edge of blackness. She'd welcome the darkness. She wanted to slip right into it.

In the distance, sirens wailed.

"Oh, thank God," Alva breathed out.

Carol didn't remember much after that. Men arrived wearing uniforms, their voices and footfall loud in the small house. The last thing she remembered was being removed from the bed and strapped to the stretcher.

Something was definitely wrong. You didn't need for it to be spelled out to pick up on it. She was glad her mother was there. Her mother was a take-charge type of person. She'd figure it out.

She could hear her mother's voice, but she seemed like she was far away. "I need to go to the hospital with her."

"I'll drive you, come on," Lina said.
"But what about the kids?"
"Ralph is here, isn't he?"

When Carol woke, she had a pounding headache and was no longer in the back bedroom of her aunt's house that she'd occupied for the past five months. Groggy, she slowly moved her head to look around the room. She was the lone occupant. The walls were high and painted an ugly shade of green, and a large window let in an inordinate amount of pale light. Her bedding consisted of white sheets and a white blanket. She tried moving but groaned. She was sore all over. A tube ran from her arm to a glass bottle hanging from a pole beside her bed.

Even though she'd only just woken up, she felt tired and looked around again, realizing she was alone in the room.

Her memory returning, she lifted the sheet and peeked at her belly. It wasn't as big as it had been. She felt it, pressing her fingers into the flesh. It wasn't hard like a rock either; it was soft and squishy. She'd had her baby. She wondered if it was a boy or girl. Then she wondered if it was alive.

The door opened and her mother pushed through, peeking her head around the corner. She turned and spoke over her shoulder in a whisper, "She's awake."

Alva pushed the door open and entered, followed by Tom, who held his hat in his hands.

"Dad?" Carol tried to sit up, but it cost too much effort and with a groan, she sank back down onto the bed, putting her hand to her forehead. Her head pounded.

Her mother hurried to her side, setting her purse on the chair next to the bed. "Don't sit up, Carol. You gave us quite a fright." She laughed, but it sounded forced and brittle.

Carol turned her head on the pillow to look at them. They stood next to each other. Her father looked ashen, but Carol was glad to see him. She hoped he would speak to her.

"Why am I in the hospital?"

"You had a serious infection. You've been here for a week," her mother said.

"I have?" Carol asked, unable to comprehend the fact that there were missing days in her life. She folded the edge of the sheet and then unfolded it, thinking, almost afraid to ask because they weren't saying anything. But she had to know.

"Is the baby . . ." Her chin quivered. Obviously, she'd had the baby, but she knew nothing more than that.

Her mother stepped closer to her, her eyes filled with tears. "You had a boy, Carol."

"Is he all right?" she asked. How could he be if she'd been out of it for five days?

Her father spoke up, his own eyes wet, his countenance brightening. "He's a little champ."

"That's good," Carol said, closing her eyes and pressing her palm against her heart. "Can I see him?"

"Yes, of course. I'll let the nurse know," her mother said.

Within minutes, the newborn was brought to her. Her father and mother had helped her sit up in the bed, propping a pillow behind her. Although she felt dizzy and weak, she was determined to hold her baby.

The baby was wrapped in a standard-issue hospital receiving blanket. When the bundle was handed to her, she gasped.

She studied his plump, pink face and counted his ten fingers and toes. The hair on top of his head was baby fine and brown like hers. She traced around his face gently with her finger, marveling at him. It was hard to believe he was a part of her. It beggared belief. In an instant, she fell in love with him.

Finally, she had to ask, had to know although it tore her heart out. "When do I have to hand him over to the adoption agency?" She supposed she should hand the infant back to her mother while she still could. Before she became too attached and wouldn't be able to give him up.

Her mother had come down to visit her at her aunt's once before, back at the start of the summer, and they had visited an adoption agency. All the paperwork had been discussed and gone over. The agency said they handled adoptions from northwest Pennsylvania, southwest New York state, and northeast Ohio. Carol had been struck by the number of mothers who didn't want their babies. But maybe they were teenaged girls like her who'd gotten into trouble. Maybe they didn't want to give up their babies either but had no choice. At the time, Carol had felt detached during the meetings, as if they were discussing someone else and someone else's baby to be given up.

"That's what we'd like to talk to you about," her father said, turning his hat around in his hands, fiddling with the brim.

Alva had not taken her eyes off the infant in Carol's arms.

Carol waited but held on tightly to her baby.

"Your mother and I want to adopt him," her father said.

"What?" Carol tilted her head to one side and pursed her lips, thinking she hadn't heard correctly.

"If your father and I adopted the baby, we'd raise him as our own child," her mother said. "He'd be an Anderson. He would live with all of us on the farm."

This presented immediate problems to Carol. "What would he call you?"

"What do you mean?" her mother asked, her smile disappearing.

"Would he call you Granddad and Grandma?"

"Well, no, of course not," Alva said. "He'd call us Mother and Dad."

"But I'm his mother," Carol protested.

Her father circled around to the other side of the bed so he could get nearer to her. "He couldn't come home as your son, you know that. His life would be miserable as a child born out of wedlock."

There it was. The cold hard facts. Illegitimacy. It was an ugly truth. There'd been a girl in her fourth-grade class whose parents, rumor had it, had never married, and the teasing and name-calling had been brutal and relentless. And all that bullying had been based on nothing more than rumors.

Carol leaned back and looked up at the ceiling with its water stain the color of tea. "Oh God, I don't want that."

"Carol, do you want to keep the boy?" her father asked.

"Oh, yes, definitely," she said.

The thought of not knowing if he was loved or cared for made her sick to her stomach.

"Then this is the only way," her father said. "Your mother and I will adopt him, and he'll have the Anderson name."

"But what would I be to him?" Carol asked.

"You'd be his sister, his older sister," her mother said with a smile.

It wasn't ideal, but at least she could bring him home with her. She wouldn't have to give him up. She'd be there with him, even if it was in the capacity of sister. There was relief in that. Almost joy. He'd come home with her.

"You need to name the baby," her father said.

"Oh, I hadn't thought of that." She stared at the infant.

"Why don't you name him Richard," her mother suggested brightly.

Carol scrunched up her nose. "No, I don't like that name."

Alva went to say something but closed her mouth.

"No, I'd like to call him Ben, short for Benjamin," Carol said firmly.

"But don't you think—" her mother started.

Her father shook his head almost imperceptibly, communicating wordlessly with his wife.

Carol did not miss the pained expression on her mother's face and remembered all she'd put her parents through these past months. Finally, she said, "Benjamin Richard Anderson."

"That's a lovely name for a little boy," her mother said, her eyes filling with tears.

"Yes, it is," Tom agreed.

Alva tentatively held her arms out, and Carol handed her Ben. She was finally going home, and she was taking her baby with her.

Carol had been home two weeks when there was a loud knock at the front door. Her mother jumped up from the kitchen table. Ben was asleep in the bassinet in the living room and the baby had been a little fussy, so Carol knew her mother was anxious not to have him disturbed. They'd barely sat down for the noontime meal.

When the shrill, high-pitched voice of the grocer's wife, Elvira Milchmann, filled the air, Carol practically winced. The woman's voice rose and fell sharply on certain syllables like stray bullets from a machine gun.

From the living room, she heard her mother say, "We only just got him to sleep."

Elvira Milchmann lowered her voice, but it was still loud. Carol hoped it wouldn't wake Ben.

There was a grim set to her father's mouth as he chewed his dinner.

Alva brought her through to the kitchen and Elvira paused in the doorframe, apparently surprised to see Carol and her father seated at the table.

"Oh, I'm sorry, I didn't think you'd be in the middle of your meal," she said. She had begun to pull off her driving gloves but stopped.

"Sit down, Elvira, I've got tea and a nice apple pie," Alva said.

"My goodness, Alva, when did you find time to bake a pie with a new baby in the house?" Elvira took the chair directly across from Carol and set her purse on the vacant seat next to her, laying her gloves on top of it. She held up a box wrapped in patterned paper: storks carrying baby boys in blue blankets. "Just something for the little one."

"Thank you, Elvira," Alva said with a smile.

As Alva served her a slice of apple pie with a square of sharp cheddar, Elvira said, "When I heard you'd adopted a baby boy, I had to come out and see it for myself."

Carol's parents exchanged a glance, but her father continued to eat his dinner in silence. Alva poured amber-colored tea into a china cup for Elvira.

"Of course, I can't understand why you would want to start all over at your age," Elvira said with a brittle laugh.

Tom stopped chewing but still said nothing.

Elvira kept talking. She took a sip of her tea and sighed. "But I suppose, different strokes for different folks."

Carol's eyes darted from her father to her mother and back again. Her mother's hands shook as she refilled her father's teacup, and her father kept his head bent, concentrating on clearing his plate.

"Why we adopted a baby at our age is no one's business," Tom said tightly.

Elvira's head spun in Tom's direction. "I'm sorry, Tom, I meant no disrespect." She took a sip of her tea and set the cup back on the saucer, squaring it up with the edge of the table. Without looking at anyone, she continued to fiddle with her teacup and saucer and said pointedly, "Of course, people might draw the wrong conclusions."

"What do you mean?" Tom asked sharply.

"Oh you know, just that Carol was away for a while and then came back and suddenly the two of you have adopted a baby," Elvira said, now looking at Tom.

Carol's skin burned on the inside. Was this what the townspeople were saying? Had they figured it out despite all their care?

"What is being said?" her father demanded. His voice was icy and if Elvira Milchmann wasn't afraid, she should have been. Despite the second summer they were experiencing at the end of October, Carol shivered.

"Nothing, nothing at all," Elvira answered quickly. "But you know how people can be malicious with their gossip."

"I do," Tom said, chewing his dinner but not taking his eyes off Elvira.

Alva stood there almost frozen, her hand on her throat, fingers splayed, but saying nothing. In the light of the kitchen, Carol could see the fine hairs on her mother's arm standing up.

"How's Bertie McCall?" Tom asked suddenly.

Elvira blinked. "Bertie McCall? How would I know?"

"I was only wondering. There might be some talk about how you're always sweet on Bertie, saving the best cuts for him. Giving him a little extra," Tom said with a wolfish smile.

Carol watched, enthralled, as this verbal fencing continued between the grocer's wife and her father.

"Who is saying such things?" Elvira demanded, the parentage of the new baby now forgotten.

Tom shrugged. "You know how malicious people can be with their gossip."

For a split second, Elvira stared at Tom, her expression steely-eyed. Then she quickly looked at her watch and said, "Oh my, would you look at the time! I hadn't realized it was so late. I must get back to the store. Jerry must be wondering what happened to me."

She stood up quickly, knocking her gloves and purse on the floor.

Tom jumped up to retrieve them, handing them to her. "I've enjoyed this visit, Elvira. But I too must get back to work. Thanks for dropping by." He made his way toward the back door.

Elvira nodded, her mouth set, her lips no longer visible. "I'll leave you to enjoy your new baby, Alva. Again, congratulations." She paused. "There would have been nothing I would have liked more than to have a child with Jerry. But I suppose with him being so much older, it simply wasn't God's will."

Tom, lifting his hat off the peg, said, "Sometimes there's nothing wrong with the seed, it's the field that's barren." He set his hat on his head. "Good day, Elvira."

Without another word, Elvira raced through the living room, not even stopping to take a last look at the sleeping baby in the bassinet and slipped through the front door.

Elvira Milchmann never set foot in the Anderson household again.

Chapter Sixteen

1963

Carol arrived home, eager to see Ben. One of her favorite parts of the day was driving home from work, knowing that he would be there at the end of that journey.

After graduation from college, she'd taken a job at the downtown library in Buffalo, about an hour's drive from Hideaway Bay. It would have made more sense to stay and live in the city, but she insisted on commuting. She couldn't leave Ben, there was no way.

Carol slowed her car as she approached the house.

Ben was driving his toy tractor around the front yard, the one Tom had bought him for Christmas. Ben, now aged seven, had been thrilled with it. The bright red of the tractor had not yet begun to dull despite its constant use.

As she pulled around the side of the house, she waved out the window and called his name, her face breaking into a big smile at the sight of him.

"Hiya, Carol," Ben said, smiling back.

She parked her car at the back of the house next to her father's pickup truck and her mother's new Buick. She walked quickly around to the front of the house and as she passed Ben, she leaned in and tousled his hair. She had to resist the urge to sweep him up in a big embrace. Her mother constantly reminded her that she had to temper her affection and exuberance with Ben, that she was his sister and not his parent. But in her heart, she would always be his mother.

Carol smoothed out the bottom of her skirt and sat down on one of the porch steps. She set her purse aside and clasped her hands around her knees, happy to watch Ben drive his tractor back and forth in front of the house.

In a certain light and with some of his expressions, she was starkly reminded of Ben's father, Roger Harrison. In fact, he had some of his father's features. It didn't bother her because if Ben resembled the Andersons too much, tongues would wag. And besides, Ben was being raised with love, and she was certain he'd turn out a better man than his father. She'd make sure of it.

"Watch this, Carol!" he said, beaming, turning the tractor at a sharp angle, leaning a little to go with the turn.

Carol clapped. "You're doing great, Ben!"

He rode toward her, put up a hand in a wave, and took off again. He raised his right hand, lifted a fist, pumped it in the air and yelled, "Toot, toot!"

Laughter filled her. One of the most pleasurable things for her was watching him growing up and enjoying life. He was such a happy, sunny child.

The screen door opened behind her, and her mother emerged, wiping her hands on her apron.

"Is he still on that tractor?" she asked with a smile, shaking her head. "He loves that thing."

"I know," Carol said.

Her mother leaned against the porch railing, put her hand up, and shielded her eyes from the late-afternoon sun.

"It's amazing how the love of farming is already showing straight through him," Alva said. "He follows your father *everywhere*!"

"I know he does," Carol said.

"I'll sit out here with him." Alva pulled one of the porch rockers closer to the railing so she could see over it.

"I don't mind. I haven't seen him all day," Carol said. She twisted the gold bracelet on her wrist. It had been a

ONE LAST THING BEFORE I GO   181

college graduation gift from her parents. It was delicate with stars and a crescent moon hanging from it. The lavishness of the gift from her parents—plain, ordinary people—had surprised her, and she cherished it.

"Go on in and wash up. Supper's almost ready," Alva said. "We're just waiting on your father."

Carol's eyebrows knitted together, and she stood, her smile strained. Her mother always seemed to be shooing her away from Ben. Alva did not appear to notice her annoyance. On the way in, Carol slammed the screen door behind her.

This way of living could not go on any longer. The situation had become intolerable. She was going to have to talk to them after dinner. It was time to make a move. She dreaded this upcoming conversation, but it was time.

During dinner, Carol pushed her food around on her plate. Every time Ben called her mother "Mom" or her father "Dad," it was like a stab to her heart. Would he ever call her "Mom?"

Ben was an exuberant, cheerful child. He talked nonstop throughout dinner. At one point, Tom leaned over with a laugh, tapped Ben's plate with his own fork, and said, "How about a little less talk and a little more eating?"

Ben grinned. "Okay, Dad."

Tom laughed to himself and scooped up mashed potatoes and gravy with his fork. "How are you going to get big and strong if you don't eat your dinner?"

Ben stared at Tom, mesmerized. He idolized the man.

"You've hardly touched your food," Alva said with a nod toward Carol's plate.

"I guess I'm not hungry," Carol said quietly, staring at her plate and the food that had gone cold on it. Her stomach did somersaults. She hadn't been this anxious since her parents found out she was pregnant.

After a bit, Ben put his head down and cleaned his plate. Alva and Tom looked at each other and smiled.

"You're a good boy, Ben," Tom said. "I think Mom might have a chocolate chip cookie for you."

"Oh boy!" Ben said excitedly.

Alva stood, carried the dirty plates over to the sink, and returned with a plate of homemade chocolate chip cookies.

"Just two now," Alva said, unable to contain her smile.

"Aw, Mom, only two?" Ben said.

Alva nodded, smiling indulgently at him. "If you're good, you can have a glass of milk and another cookie before you go to bed."

He stared at her, rapt, nodding excitedly. He took a bite out of the cookie and a chocolate chip fell to the table, and he leaned down and sucked it up with his mouth. Alva looked horrified, and Tom struggled to suppress a grin.

"Where on earth did you learn that?" Alva asked, both alarmed and amused.

"From Jerry Merton at school. He does it all the time at lunch."

Alva scowled. "We don't need to vacuum the crumbs off the table with our mouths."

With that, Ben burst out laughing, then finished off the cookie and gulped the milk down.

"Not so fast, you'll get a stomachache," Carol said with a laugh.

"If you're finished, you may go," Tom said.

Ben slid off his chair and skipped out of the room.

"I don't think that child is ever in a bad mood," Alva said, watching him disappear from view.

Tom pushed back his chair.

"Um, Mother and Dad, I was hoping to talk to you about something," Carol said, her voice shaky, trying to summon what little courage she had.

Her parents looked at each other, and Tom pulled his chair back in.

"What is it?" Alva asked.

"I'm thinking of living in Buffalo, closer to my job," she said.

The truth was she'd already found an apartment about a twenty-minute ride from the downtown library. It was only a one-bedroom unit, but it was bright and sunny. When the landlady, an older widow of Polish descent, had found out Carol was a librarian, she was delighted, and the two of them had a ten-minute discussion about books. The only hesitation had been when Carol mentioned her son would be living with her. The landlady had narrowed her eyes and asked, "Are you a divorcée?" Carol had not missed the religious pictures and the statues and the lit votive candles all over the place. Their presence confirmed her decision to lie and say she was a widow. Immediately, the elderly woman made sympathetic noises, and wouldn't let Carol leave without taking a loaf of her homemade babka. The bag sat on Carol's bed. She couldn't bring it down to the kitchen; how would she explain it?

For a moment, neither one of her parents said anything.

"But why?" her mother finally asked.

"Because I'm dreading the drive back and forth in the winter. Right now, it takes me a little more than an hour, and that's if the weather is good."

"Can't you get a position closer to home? Have you looked into the library at Hideaway Bay?"

A position at her hometown library would be ideal but the current librarian, Miss Peckinpah, showed no signs of retiring. She wasn't even near retirement age. Carol would grow old herself waiting for a slot to open.

"There's nothing available down here," Carol said. She swallowed hard, unable to look at either of her parents. "I'm planning to take Ben to Buffalo with me."

There was dead silence. The type of silence that is heavy and ominous and weighs you down.

"What?" her mother cried.

"Let me remind you that we are his parents," Tom said. "Legally."

Carol lowered her voice, afraid that Ben might be somewhere in earshot. "But I am his mother."

"Carol," her mother pleaded.

"How would that work?" her father asked. "Would you prance around Buffalo as an unwed mother?"

Carol reddened. Would they ever forgive her for the mistake she'd made? Although they adored Ben, who was the product of that mistake, sometimes their goodwill did not seem to extend to their daughter.

"Well, I wouldn't *prance* around as you say," Carol said tightly, trying not to feel offended but failing. She had a cover story. Actually, she had a couple. That was the thing with reading, it sharpened your imagination. "I'd say I was his sister or his mother and that I was a widow."

"That would be insulting to the widows out there," her father barked.

Carol shrank in her seat, feeling smaller.

"You selfish girl," her mother raged. "After all we've done. We took Ben into our home and our hearts and raised him as our own."

Carol didn't want to point out that as they loved him so much, it didn't seem much of a hardship for them.

"We put you through college so you could get a good job to support yourself someday, and this is how you repay us?" Alva said.

Tom did not raise his voice or shout. He simply asked, "Have you given any thought to how this might affect Ben?"

When she remained silent, her father said, "This is his home. *We* are his parents."

"But I'm his mother," Carol whispered.

"You gave up that right when you signed him over to us," Tom said quietly.

Carol burst out crying, surprising her parents.

As an unwed mother, there had been no way she could keep her baby, and although she was grateful to her parents for adopting him so he would always be near her, she wanted to be his mother. His *real* mother. It had occurred to her that moving Ben up to Buffalo, away from the only life he'd known with her parents and grandparents and the farm, might be traumatic. But the romantic in Carol pushed thoughts like these aside, focusing on a bright and happy future with her son.

"Carol, I don't think you've thought this through," her father said. "I can understand your desire to leave and live your own life. And maybe you should move to Buffalo. Start fresh somewhere else."

How could they not see that she'd never leave Ben? She wasn't going to move away to Buffalo by herself without Ben. How did she make them understand that she wanted to raise Ben as her own? It couldn't be done in Hideaway Bay. Everyone had accepted the story of Alva and Tom adopting a little boy and to Carol's knowledge, no one had ever suspected the truth. Not even that busybody, Elvira Milchmann, had ever said anything more.

"But she doesn't have to leave," Alva protested. She looked at Carol. "You don't have to go. You can continue to live here with us and Ben. Hideaway Bay is your home."

"I want to be Ben's mother," she said again, with a pleading look at her father.

"It's too late for that," her Tom said. "Your options were quite limited when you found yourself in the family way at the age of sixteen."

Carol cringed at her father's words.

"Ben was going to have to be given up for adoption if he didn't come home with us. At least he's with us. Be grateful for that."

Carol began to perspire and felt like she might vomit. Would Ben never know she was his mother?

Chapter Seventeen

Carol put aside her idea of moving to the city and taking Ben with her. She decided to put a positive spin on things. At least her child was with her, and she did owe her parents a debt of gratitude for making that possible.

On one of the last weekends of summer, Carol packed a picnic basket and took Ben to pick up Lottie and her kids to go to the beach for one last day of swimming. Carol wasn't a good swimmer, but Lottie's husband, Dennis, had taught Ben to swim when he'd been teaching his own kids. Ben loved the water almost as much as he loved the farm.

Lottie piled her two girls, who were four and three, into the back seat next to Ben. Despite her desire as a young girl to move away and have a career she met Dennis Moloney in their junior year and couldn't wait to marry him right after high school. She plopped herself down in the front seat, her belly so big it almost reached the dashboard. She was hoping for a boy this time. She let out a long breath.

"Are you all right?" Carol asked.

"Yes, another month and this will be over with," she said. "I don't know if this is a boy or a girl, but it feels more like an aircraft carrier."

With that, Carol burst out laughing, glanced in her side mirror, and pulled away from the curb.

It was late morning by the time they arrived at the beach. Carol spread out the old blanket her mother had given her and put one of her shoes in each corner to keep the blanket from moving. Lottie did the same with the other two corners.

Carol watched with concern as her friend labored to move around.

"Why don't I take the kids in the water, and you can sit and relax."

"That sounds wonderful, thanks Carol," Lottie said, collapsing onto the blanket. She sat up, legs stretched out in front of her, and rubbed her blooming belly with one hand.

Carol walked to the shore with Ben and Lottie's girls. As they neared the surf, the three kids bolted, running and screaming, into the water, kicking and splashing. Carol stepped in. It was like bathwater. On the horizon, frigates and trawlers could be seen. The shallowest of the

Great Lakes, Lake Erie had benefited from a long, hot summer.

Ben had a farmer's tan. His neck and arms were brown, but you could see by the pale, white skin on his back and his feet that he spent most of the summer in a T-shirt, shorts, and socks. The girls were evenly tanned as Lottie had a small kiddie pool at her house.

"Swing me, Carol, swing me," Ben said, jumping up and down in front of her, water splashing everywhere, including right into Carol's eye. She blinked and lifted Ben up, swinging him until he was giddy, and tossed him into the water. Lottie's girls clambered around her, yelling, "Pick me, Carol, pick me!"

When she was done throwing them around until they were exhausted but wearing big smiles, she told all three of them to hang on to her and she waded out to deeper water, up to her chest. The three kids clung to her neck and back, Lottie's youngest perched on her hip. The water was refreshing. She loved being with the kids and was sad that she'd never have another one of her own. Ben's birth was so traumatic that it had left her scarred and unable to bear any more children. Her mother relayed this information to her when she was eighteen in a quiet voice. At the time, it meant nothing to her, she was so glad to have Ben with her.

By the time they reached the shore, the three kids had quieted down until Ben piped up and said, "I'm hungry."

Smiling, she said, "I think Mother may have packed something nice in the picnic basket."

He took off at a run back to the blanket, sand flying and Lottie's girls following him.

Carol reached the blanket and sank onto it next to Lottie, who sat up at their arrival. She could smell the Coppertone in the air. Nearby, someone had a transistor radio playing. All she could hear was the tinny, staticky sound of it. She couldn't make out what song was playing. She made a note to bring her own transistor the next time they came to the beach.

Ben was bent over the wicker hamper, digging through it.

"Here, let me, Ben," Carol said. "I've got chicken or ham sandwiches. What kind do you want?"

Ben took chicken and the girls opted for ham. Carol pulled out three sandwiches wrapped in wax paper and handed them out. "Sit on the edge of the blanket and eat your sandwiches so they don't get sandy."

The kids plopped down and Carol turned to Lottie. "Lottie, I've got one ham sandwich left and one chicken. What'll it be?"

"Chicken if you don't mind. I'm so sick of ham," Lottie said.

Carol handed it to her and opened a couple of bottles of Coke, pouring it into three plastic cups and handing one to each child. Then she opened two more bottles and gave one to Lottie. She got comfortable next to her friend and unwrapped her sandwich.

"Thanks for feeding my kids," Lottie said wearily.

"Mother packed it. Said you wouldn't be in the mood to pack lunches for everyone," Carol answered.

"She's right about that."

They ate in companionable silence and when they finished, Lottie pulled a Hershey's bar from her purse. "Here, take half. It's my contribution. But don't let the kids see because I've only got the one."

Carol took her half and began breaking off pieces and popping them into her mouth.

"Do you remember years ago when your mother took us to that house on Star Shine Drive? Where the Frenchwoman who made the chocolate lived?"

Lottie nodded her head enthusiastically. "Delphine. The chocolatier. You know, I still think about her chocolate from time to time."

"Whatever happened to her?" Carol asked. "One day she was there and then she wasn't."

The house on Star Shine Drive had been abandoned for some time now. It was a shame because it had a great view of the beach across the street. But now it was all boarded up.

"No one knows. She just disappeared," Lottie said. "My mother tried to find out what happened, but no one knew anything."

"Huh. That's too bad," Carol said, staring out at the horizon.

Lottie struggled to get up and Carol said, "I'll get it. What do you need?"

"No, stay put. I need to stretch my legs," Lottie said, finally standing. "Did we ever think it was going to be this hard when we were in high school?"

Carol chuckled. "No, I don't think we did."

Lottie nodded. "That's what I thought." She gathered the used waxed paper and empty plastic cups from the three kids and laid them on the blanket. "All right, kids, time to build some sandcastles." The kids jumped up. Lottie pulled out three stacked plastic pails with matching shovels in the colors of green, yellow, and orange. She set the kids up away from the blanket and gave them each their own pail and shovel, then returned and sat down slowly next to Carol.

"Why did you put them so far away?" Carol laughed.

The three kids were in their line of sight but almost out of hearing range.

"So they're out of earshot."

Carol looked at Lottie, thinking that was a strange thing to say.

Lottie busied herself folding the wax paper from their sandwiches. She tucked that away and then opened her bag, looked over the three children and whispered to Carol, "Do you want some chocolate?" She pulled out a chocolate bar and discreetly broke it in half and handed one half to Carol.

Carol laughed. *Was that all?* "Still hiding chocolate?"

"Something I learned from my mother," she said. She broke off a bit of chocolate and popped it into her mouth.

She didn't look at Carol when she spoke. "Carol, can I ask you something?"

"Sure, go ahead," Carol said, wondering what was up.

Lottie looked at her, her dyed blond hair framing her face, the freckles across the bridge of her nose darkened with exposure to the sun, her blue eyes dark and expressive. "Ben is your son, isn't he?"

Carol could feel herself blanch, felt all the blood draining from her face. Her heart rate picked up and despite the heat, her hands became clammy.

Lottie immediately reached for her. "Carol, this is Lottie you're talking to. Your best friend forever," she said softly.

Carol felt the sting at the back of her eyes and lowered her head, unable to look at her friend. As she debated internally whether to tell her friend the truth, she was aware on another level of Ben's voice in the background, laughing and talking to Lottie's girls. Finally, without looking up, she whispered, "Yes, Ben is mine." The relief that came with admitting that out loud made Carol lie back on the blanket. She put her arm over her eyes as the tears spilled over.

"I thought so," Lottie said.

Carol swallowed hard, trying to pull herself together. "How did you know?" she managed to choke out. She lifted her arm slightly from her face to peer at her friend.

Lottie shrugged. "I guessed a while ago. You treat him like a mother would treat her child. I first suspected something when you went away to your aunt's in Pennsylvania."

"Oh, that long."

"Why didn't you tell me?" Lottie asked.

Carol did not miss the hurt in her voice.

"I was afraid," she said, a big lump of emotion lodged in her throat.

"I guess it wasn't easy," Lottie admitted. "I mean, I'm married and it's hard. And you were only sixteen."

Memories slammed back at Carol: the relentless fear of what was going to happen and the feeling that she had no control over the situation. It was a feeling she hoped never to experience again in her life.

"You must have been so scared," Lottie said.

"I was," Carol said.

Lottie handed her a paper napkin from her purse. "It's clean," she said with a laugh.

Carol smiled, sat up, and wiped her eyes and blew her nose. "I was supposed to give him up at birth."

Lottie looked at her with an anguished expression.

Carol shook her head. Those days surrounding Ben's birth were a blur. "I ran into problems giving birth and—well, it's lucky we both survived."

"Oh no, I'm sorry, I didn't know," Lottie said.

Carol shrugged. No one knew except her parents and her aunt and uncle. "Because of it, I won't be able to have any more children."

"Oh, Carol," Lottie said, her shoulders sagging.

"When I came to, my parents said they would adopt Ben."

"Thank goodness," Lottie said.

"In a perfect world, I'd be able to raise Ben as my son," Carol said quietly.

"Yes, that's how it should be. Society simply hasn't caught up yet. But at least he's with you in the same house, and your parents seem to adore him."

"They do," Carol said.

Since Ben had come into their lives, it was as if the sun was a little warmer and a little brighter.

"Was it Roger?"

Carol nodded.

"Does he know?"

"Yes," Carol said, and she relayed the tale of the threats he'd made.

Lottie became indignant. "Why that no good—"

"It's all right now, though it was scary at the time," Carol said.

"Wait 'til I see him," Lottie said. "I'm going to give him a piece of my mind."

Carol panicked. "Oh no, you mustn't. No one, and I mean no one, can ever know."

"I won't tell anyone, I promise," Lottie said.

Carol sighed, relieved. It was nice to have this out in the open with her best friend. She could talk to Lottie in a way she couldn't talk to her parents.

"Remember when my cousin Edna got pregnant?" Lottie said. "Her parents forced her to give the baby up for adoption. *What would the neighbors think?* And she hasn't been right since." Her lips thin, she muttered, "It's criminal to make a mother give up her child if she doesn't want to."

"Yes it is," Carol agreed.

They both went quiet. Carol looked out at the horizon, watching a sailboat glide along the purplish navy water of the lake.

"I wonder if I should take them back into the water," she said out loud. She looked over her shoulder, smiling at the three kids shoveling sand into their pails.

"We have to go," Lottie said, her voice sounding strange: worried and fearful.

Carol turned to her friend as Lottie grimaced, clutching her hand to her side. "What's wrong?"

"My water broke," Lottie said. "Baby is on its way."

Carol jumped up and gathered their things, throwing everything haphazardly into the bag. Lottie made her way to the car, bending over each time a contraction hit her. Hurriedly, Carol piled the kids and the bags into the back seat and drove Lottie straight to the hospital, leaving them all sitting there in the car while she ran in and got a wheelchair and some help. An orderly came out with the wheelchair and before Lottie was wheeled away, Carol promised she'd call her husband and keep the kids with her at the farm.

Carol reached down and wrapped her arms around her friend and whispered, "Don't worry about a thing, Lottie. I'll take care of the girls. Just concentrate on yourself and your new baby."

Lottie grimaced as a contraction rolled through her but managed to pat Carol's arm in thanks.

Chapter Eighteen

1966

By the summer of 1966, Carol had fallen into a rhythm between work and home. She'd been at the downtown branch of the library for almost four years, and what free time she had she spent devoted to Ben. It didn't leave much time for dating, but she didn't mind.

Around the time of Ben's tenth birthday, Miss Peckinpah, the Hideaway Bay librarian, asked for a transfer to a library closer to her sister up in Batavia as her sister had fallen ill and Miss Peckinpah wanted to take care of her. Carol immediately put in for the position of head librarian at the Hideaway Bay branch and crossed her fingers. But it wasn't meant to be, and another woman with more seniority was awarded the position.

By now, Carol's grandfather was well into his eighties, and her grandmother had passed. Her grandfather suggested he take Ben to the fruit-and-veg stand so he could learn the business. At first, she was hesitant because this would be on Saturday mornings, which was her day off, but she was reminded again that decisions about Ben weren't hers to make, and her parents heartily agreed to it. But at Carol's suggestion, he was only allowed to be up there for four hours and when noon rolled around, she was usually waiting for him in her parked car. She'd take him for a burger and fries and then either stop at Lottie's or take him to the movies for the afternoon.

Ben's biological father had moved out of the area, so Carol was able to confidently walk around town with Ben without fear of running into him. She loved going to the movies with Ben. She took him to see all the kids' movies. She did all sorts of things with him: taught him to roller-skate and how to ride a bike, bought him a basketball and a football. Watching him grow up made these some of the happiest years of her life.

Winter arrived with more snow than usual. From her vantage point near the windows of the downtown library one afternoon, all Carol could see was a blanket of white outside. As it was after five, darkness had already descended, and she didn't treasure the prospect of the drive home to Hideaway Bay in weather like this.

Her colleague, Janet Rimmer, stood next to her, her arms crossed over her chest. "Ugh, look at it out there."

"I know," Carol said fretfully. "I've got another hour before I leave."

"My brother's coming to pick me up," Janet said.

Carol thought she was lucky to have someone to pick her up. Internally, she debated as to whether it was safe to drive home.

She'd worked with Janet since she started at the library back in 1962. Janet was a nice girl, and sometimes they had lunch together or shared a break. She had a boyfriend she was going steady with and more than once, she'd said she hoped there would be a ring at Christmastime. Carol hoped that for her as well.

When the hour was up and the library was shutting down, Carol walked with Janet down to the main floor. The security guard, Howard, was starting his rounds to lock up the building.

"Drive safe out there, ladies, it's terrible," Howard said.

"Thanks," Carol said.

"Goodnight, Howard," Janet said at the same time.

Just inside the front door, Janet's older brother, Todd, waited for his sister. He wore a heavy coat, galoshes over his shoes, and a gray and black striped scarf around his neck.

Carol had met Todd Rimmer on more than one occasion, usually in passing, as he too worked downtown and always gave Janet a lift home to the house they shared with their mother in South Buffalo. Carol sometimes wished she had someone to share her drive with. It was a long, tedious ride back and forth on the thruway from Hideaway Bay to Buffalo.

She liked the look of Todd. He wasn't that tall, but he was solid, and he had sandy brown hair he wore short, and hazel eyes. But it was his face she was drawn to; it was kind.

"How's the driving out?" Carol asked.

"Awful. You can't see your hand in front of you for all the snow coming down," he said.

"Carol has to drive all the way to Hideaway Bay tonight," Janet said.

Todd scowled. "You can't do that, Carol, it's too dangerous."

But what choice did she have? She knew no one in the city, and she couldn't stay here in the library. She was about to say as much when Todd said, "Come home with us and you can stay at our house."

She hesitated. But one look out the window where she couldn't see the buildings across the street told her not to chance it. There was a section of the thruway to

Hideaway Bay that was isolated and remote. And she was terrified of sliding into a ditch and not being found. She had Ben to think of.

"Look, if it's clear in the morning, I'll drive you back to the city to pick up your car," Todd said.

"Todd's right, Carol, you shouldn't drive in this," Janet piped in. "You can call your parents from our house."

"Are you sure you don't mind?" Carol asked, feeling as if it might be a great imposition.

"Not at all," Todd said. His confidence put her at ease.

"What about your mother?" Carol asked, unsure. She certainly didn't want to impose.

Todd and Janet exchanged a glance and laughed.

"Don't worry about Mother, she'll be happy to see you. She loves to fuss over people," Janet said.

"Come on, let's go before it gets any worse," Todd said. "We're going to have to take South Park all the way home."

―――♦―――

The drive to the Rimmers' family home in South Buffalo was fraught with terrible conditions: almost zero visibility with the blinding white snow, and slippery roads that caused the back end of Todd's car to fishtail more than once. Each time it did, Carol grabbed onto the seat and the door to brace herself.

She sat in the back seat, while Janet sat in the front with her brother. She was glad she'd worn her heavy wool coat and thick gloves. The back seat of the car was freezing, the kind of cold that made your bones ache.

As Carol gripped the edge of the seat, she studied Todd as unobtrusively as possible. He seemed confident behind the wheel despite the awful driving conditions. He remained alert and drove slowly, and when the car did fishtail or slide, he kept his composure. After a while, she decided she liked his profile: he had a broad forehead, high cheekbones, and a square jaw. He was, she decided, almost perfect. *Probably too good to be true*, she thought, trying to see out her window. She suspected there was a girlfriend, probably some fresh-scrubbed, cheerful girl next door. Someone without a child. Carol glanced down at her gloved hands in her lap, thinking she could never be those things. She was a thinker, and she was serious-minded. She almost snorted at the thought of being described as "the girl next door." Maybe if that girl had a son out of wedlock.

"Did you see that car?" Janet asked, interrupting Carol's internal monologue. "He's gone into the ditch."

"I did. Let me pull over and see if they're all right."

Gently, Todd steered the car over to the side of the road.

As he got out of the car, Janet called after him, "Be careful, Todd."

He nodded.

Carol and Janet watched him through the windshield and the heavy, falling snow. He trudged through the snow, walking in the path other tires had created. He rapped on the car's driver's-side window.

It was apparent that the car would not be able to be moved from its current position. It sat at a forty-five-degree angle on its passenger side in the ditch. Todd spoke to the driver, who remained unseen. Then he pointed to his car, and the driver's-side door opened into the air and a tall man hoisted himself out using both his hands. Then he and Todd reached in and pulled out a petite woman in a dark wool coat and galoshes, her hat crooked on her head, looking a little worse for wear.

The tall man put his arm around the shoulder of the woman and said something to her. She clutched at his side and nodded her head. They followed Todd to his car. The door to the back seat opened and the woman looked in, saw Carol, and hesitated. Her eyes were a dark brown but there was a startled look about them. The man beside her encouraged her and she slid in, glanced at Carol, and gave a small smile, which Carol returned. The big man got in beside her and slammed the door shut. The three of them sat shoulder to shoulder in the back seat.

Todd climbed back into the front seat and turned halfway, looking at Janet and then at Carol. "This is

Steve and Mary. They don't live too far from us, so we'll give them a lift home. Steve, Mary, this is my sister, Janet, and her friend Carol."

Steve said, "Hi," but Mary remained quiet. The petite, dark-haired woman was trembling, and in the dim interior light of the back seat, Carol could see that she was awfully pale.

"It's not a good night to be out driving," Steve said.

Carefully, Todd pulled back out onto the road.

"We went into a skid and the car wouldn't stop," Mary said, her voice quaking.

"It must have been terrifying," Carol said sympathetically.

Mary nodded.

"Sorry, folks, hold on again," Todd said, after they'd driven only fifteen minutes. Ahead, on the opposite side of the road, a man was trying to lift the back fender of a car as his friend stepped on the gas pedal, but the back wheels kept spinning, making a loud squealing noise, slushy snow flying.

"Let me see if I can give them a hand," Todd said.

"I'll help," Steve said.

The two of them jumped out of the car, made their way across the street, and shouted above the squall to be heard.

"When we get home, I'm not going out until the spring thaw," Mary said beside Carol.

"I don't blame you," Janet said.

"Do you live in the area too, Carol?" Mary asked.

"Carol lives down in Hideaway Bay," Janet answered for her.

Mary turned her head and cried, "You're not driving down there tonight in this weather?"

"No." Carol shook her head. She hoped she could get home the following day.

"Good, although Hideaway Bay is one of my favorite places. I love the beach there," Mary said. "What's it like in the winter?"

"Bleak," Carol said with a laugh.

She thought of the beachside town. The colorful awnings were all taken down until spring and by January, the beach would be covered in big piles of snow and ice.

"But I bet it's still beautiful."

Carol had to agree that it was.

Todd and Steve stood at the back fender with the stranger and as his friend pressed on the gas pedal, the three of them lifted the back end of the car, getting it out of its rut. The two guys yelled their thanks above the howling wind. With a wave from Steve and a thump on the back of the car from Todd, they drove off slowly.

The drive was painstakingly slow for the next hour, and the conversation was almost nonexistent. Everyone seemed tense and it was cold.

"Our house is right there," Steve finally said, pointing to a two-family home on the corner.

Beside Carol, Mary visibly relaxed as her home came into view.

Todd pulled up at the curb as the snow in the driveway was knee-deep.

"Do you have a shovel?" Todd asked, looking over his shoulder at them.

"Aw, don't worry about it, Todd. We can't thank you enough," Steve said.

He opened the door, and a blast of frigid air filled the car with a few drifting, heavy snowflakes. From the back seat, Carol watched as Steve scooped Mary up and lumbered slowly through the snow until they reached the side door of the house. He did not set Mary down until they stepped inside.

Carol stared out the window long after Todd pulled away, thinking how romantic it was that someone would look after you like that, attend to your needs, *knowing* what they were without having to be told. She thought Mary was a lucky woman.

When they'd left the library, Janet had said the ride to the Rimmer home should only take twenty minutes. Now, almost two hours later, Carol was beginning to lose the feeling in her feet. Her toes were numb.

A few minutes after dropping off Steve and Mary, Todd slowed down in front of an Arts and Crafts–style bungalow with a deep porch and extended roofline. A lamp in the front window cast an amber glow on the porch. Carol thought it looked inviting.

"Afraid we'll have to get out here," Todd said. "I'll have to shovel the driveway first before I can pull the car in."

Carol followed Janet and Todd up the driveway, tramping through the deep snow. That was the problem with winters in Western New York: the snow was always higher than the top of your boots. Carol hoped Janet would lend her a clean pair of socks.

She followed Janet up the front steps, slipping on the bottom one but righting herself immediately.

"Tell Ma I'll be in shortly; I need to clear the driveway," Todd said.

Janet snorted. "You won't be in shortly. I'll change and come out and help you."

"No, stay inside and keep warm," Todd instructed, and he disappeared around the side of the house.

Before they reached the top step, the front door swung open. An elderly woman with short silver curls filled the doorframe, pulling her cardigan tight around her against the cold. Light spilled out from behind her. She opened the storm door and held it for them.

"There you are. I was getting worried," she said, her voice anxious.

"Ma, the driving is awful, you can't see anything," Janet said, stepping inside.

Her mother stepped back to allow them to enter. Carol followed Janet's lead and stamped her feet on the mat, the snow falling off in clumps.

"I brought Carol home from work. It was too far for her to drive to Hideaway Bay," Janet explained to her mother, shrugging out of her coat and hanging it on the stand by the door.

Mrs. Rimmer looked at Carol. "Do you drive there to Hideaway Bay all by yourself?"

Carol nodded.

"Oh no, you couldn't take the chance to drive there tonight," she said. "It would be too dangerous. You'd get killed."

Carol removed her hat and hung it over her coat. She stuffed her gloves into the pocket of her coat and looked around nervously.

"Carol, did you want to call your family and let them know you're okay?" Mrs. Rimmer asked. There was a deep furrow between her brows as if she'd spent the afternoon worrying.

With palpable relief, Carol said, "If that's not too much trouble."

"Of course not, they must be so worried," Mrs. Rimmer said. "Let me show you where the phone is and then

Janet can supply you with whatever you need. Maybe a pair of pants and some dry socks?"

"Thank you, that would be wonderful."

There was a black rotary phone tucked into a small alcove between the kitchen and living room. The house was warm, and something smelled good from the kitchen. Carol's stomach growled in response.

"I made stew earlier," Mrs. Rimmer said. "It'll taste better tomorrow but at least it's hot and will fill you up. I'll be in the kitchen if you need anything."

"Carol, come upstairs after you're done," Janet said, heading up the staircase. "I'm the first room on the right."

"Thank you," she said.

She'd been nervous coming over. The only house she'd ever stayed at was Lottie's. But Janet and her family were so nice it was easy to relax.

Her mother answered on the second ring.

"Mother?"

"Carol? Is that you? Thank God! Where are you?" her mother asked. And then in a muffled voice, she said to someone in the background, "It's Carol."

"I went home with Janet from work. I'll stay here tonight."

"Oh, thank God," Alva said. "We've been so worried about you. We tried to call the library and tell you to stay in the city, but it had already closed. They've closed down the thruway out here."

"Really?" Carol asked, surprised. She could only remember the occasional time when they closed the thruway due to inclement weather, usually snow. "The driving was terrible here. It took us forever to get to Janet's house. A lot of cars off the road."

Her mother made a *tsk-tsk* noise.

"I'll stay here overnight, and Janet's brother will drive me back into the city in the morning if the roads are clear," she said.

"That's good. Stay put. No one should be out in this weather. Can you call us in the morning?" Alva said.

"Yes, of course. You can tell me how it is down in Hideaway Bay," Carol said.

"All right then. I'm relieved to know you're safe. We'll talk tomorrow—"

"Wait, Mother," Carol said. She turned around in the tiny alcove, faced the wall, and lowered her voice. "How's Ben?"

Her mother laughed. "He's fine. Delighted with all the snow of course. Your father brought down the old sled from the barn. Do you remember? The one you used to use when you were little?"

Carol smiled; she did remember.

Ben was warm and safe and home and in good hands. "All right, Mother, thanks." She hung up the phone and stared at it for a moment, realizing that this would be the first night she'd spent away from Ben since the day he was born. They would not be under the same roof at nighttime. Her stomach recoiled, and she pushed the thought out of her mind. There was nothing to be done about that.

Janet lent her a sweater, a pair of pants, and a pair of socks, and she began to feel slightly better. She pulled her comb out of her purse and ran it through her hair. Once she changed and freshened up, she followed Janet downstairs.

Todd came in through the back door, his cheeks ruddy with cold and his face glistening from melted snowflakes.

"That's done," he said. "I put the car in the driveway. Probably will have to shovel again in the morning."

"Never mind that. Wash your hands and sit down. It's time for dinner," his mother said, setting a Dutch oven on a trivet in the middle of the table.

At Janet's invitation, Carol sat in the seat next to her. Mrs. Rimmer removed the lid of the Dutch oven to reveal a steaming beef stew loaded with chunks of meat, potatoes, carrots, onions, and dumplings. Carol couldn't wait to eat it, but she didn't know if that was because it smelled so good or because it looked so hot.

ONE LAST THING BEFORE I GO

Todd soon joined them and sat across the table from Carol. His hair was smashed from his winter hat, his complexion still red from exposure to the elements.

Mrs. Rimmer ladled stew onto plates and handed one to each of them. She brought over a loaf of fresh-baked bread, sliced it up, and passed it around on bread plates.

Carol hadn't realized how famished she was until she spooned in that first mouthful of stew. It had a rich, hearty taste and Carol had to refrain from closing her eyes and groaning. As soon as she spread butter over her slice of bread, it melted. She took a bite, savoring the warm, yeasty flavor, and enthusiastically took a second slice when offered.

She refused a second helping of stew, thinking she was ready to burst, but she couldn't refuse when Mrs. Rimmer offered her a slice of warmed apple pie.

When they were finished, Janet and Mrs. Rimmer cleared the dishes. Carol jumped up to help but they insisted she remain seated. That left her alone at the table with Todd.

"Carol, did you always want to be a librarian?" he asked, finishing a second slice of apple pie.

"I don't remember when I first thought I'd like to be a librarian," Carol answered, "But I've always loved books."

She always thought of her life as split down the middle: before Ben and after Ben. And it wasn't until after Ben was born and it was decided she should go to college that she seriously began to work toward becoming a librarian. It had been a wise choice as far as she was concerned. How lucky was she to be surrounded by books at her job? Aside from the fact that she was so far away from Hideaway Bay, she considered her job almost perfect.

She became aware of Todd studying her and squirmed under his gaze. She was not used to the attention of a man. Since Ben's birth, she'd dated no one. Men had asked, but she'd always refused, too afraid, and always with Ben in the back of her mind.

But now, this man across from her with the hazel eyes and kind face had stirred within her an interest she'd not had in a long time.

"What is it you do, Todd, if you don't mind me asking?" Carol said.

"I'm an accountant for a firm downtown," he said.

"Do you like it?" she asked.

"I love it," he said. "Except for tax season when it gets pretty busy."

Carol laughed.

They made small talk until Janet rejoined them at the table.

"We should play cards or something," Janet suggested.

"Good idea," Todd said, standing up and pushing back his chair.

Janet and Carol followed Todd through to the living room. From a front hall closet, Todd pulled out a card table and set it up in a corner of the living room as their mother sat in an easy chair.

"Did you want to watch something on television?" Mrs. Rimmer asked.

"No thanks, Ma. We're going to play cards," Todd said. To Janet he said, "Get the folding chairs out of the closet."

Carol helped her friend remove three wooden folding chairs with leather seats and carry them over to the card table.

Once everything was set, Todd took a deck of cards out of a drawer in the walnut sideboard.

Mrs. Rimmer sat in her easy chair, watching *Gomer Pyle*. Carol thought of Ben, who was hooked on *Star Trek*. That's what he looked forward to every Friday night.

It was almost midnight by the time they put away the cards and the table and chairs. They'd snacked on Mr. Salty pretzels and drunk Squirt out of green glass bottles. It had been one of the most pleasurable evenings Carol could remember in a long time. Snow continued to fall outside the window, but she hardly noticed with the attention Todd paid her. She learned that he had no girlfriend and for a moment she felt hopeful, but then she reminded herself that her life was in Hideaway Bay with Ben. This thought tempered her enthusiasm over the prospect and promise of Todd, and restraint was called for for the remainder of the evening.

By the time they all headed upstairs, Carol was almost sad that she'd have to leave in the morning.

As she climbed into the spare twin bed in Janet's room in a flannel nightgown borrowed from her colleague, she moved her legs around to warm up the sheets. Janet unfolded an extra blanket, shook it out, and spread it out over Carol.

"Thank you, Janet," Carol said.

"There's more blankets in the cedar chest if you need one during the night."

"Thanks, but I'm fine."

Janet turned off the ceiling light and got into her own bed, pulling up the blankets around her shoulders. In the darkness, she whispered, "I think my brother likes you."

This said out loud startled Carol. Had it been that noticeable? What must Janet think of her?

Quickly, she said, "I'm sure he was only being polite."

Janet giggled in the dark like a schoolgirl. "I don't think so. I've never seen him act like this before. Usually when I bring friends home, he's polite but not as solicitous as he was with you this evening."

Carol frowned. Had he treated her different? How would she know? But then she reminded herself that she was a mother with a young son back home in Hideaway Bay. She turned over to face the window on the other side of the room. She stared at the falling snow in the glow of the streetlight and yawned. It was too bad she was going home in the morning, but there it was. She told herself it was stupid to worry about Todd Rimmer when she'd probably never see him again.

The snow still hadn't let up by the next morning, and according to the forecast, it was expected to continue. They listened to the radio as they sat at the kitchen table eating fried eggs, bacon, and toast with jam, washing it all down with hot tea. According to the announcer, there was a driving ban in place.

Carol was torn. She wanted to stay and get to know Todd better, but she missed Ben desperately. As soon as breakfast was finished, she called the house phone down in Hideaway Bay, anxious to hear Ben's voice and see how he was doing. She was disappointed to hear that he was outside with her father, being pulled on the sled.

"He's having the time of his life," Alva crowed. "They've been sledding all morning."

There was a small stab to Carol's heart at the thought of missing Ben's enjoyment. "I'll be home as soon as I can."

"No rush. By the looks of things down here, no one is going anywhere soon," her mother said.

"I'll call later tonight."

"We'll talk to you then, Carol. Call after dinner," Alva said. "Ben will be inside."

When Carol hung up, Mrs. Rimmer asked, "Carol, did you give your mother our telephone number, in case she wants to call you?"

"No, I didn't."

"Give her a call back and give her the number," Mrs. Rimmer said.

Carol redialed her home phone and her mother picked up on the first ring. "Hello, Mother, it's me again. Mrs. Rimmer thought it would be a good idea if you had her phone number."

"Let me grab a pencil and some paper," Alva said, and jotted down the number.

"Come on, Carol, let's go outside," Janet said after Carol finished her call. She held Carol's jacket out to her.

She supposed she would like to get outside and get some fresh air.

Carol still wore the clothes Janet had lent her the previous night. She wound her scarf around her neck and pulled her gloves from the pocket of her coat.

The air was brisk, and her breath came out in wispy streams in front of her. Janet went first down the front steps. Todd had shoveled off the porch. Up and down the street, neighbors were out shoveling their driveways and the sidewalks in front of their houses. Todd had finished clearing snow from the driveway for a second time in less than twenty-four hours and now worked on the sidewalk in front of the house.

"Let's build a snowman," Janet said.

"Okay," Carol said.

She'd built one with Ben the previous two winters using a carrot for the nose and two large black buttons for eyes. He'd squealed with joy, though, when Carol's father built an igloo using an old diaper pail to make the blocks.

As they rolled snow over to the front of the yard to create the base of the snowman, Carol watched Todd out of the corner of her eye. He'd made quick work with the shoveling, making it look like child's play. At one point, she looked over to catch him staring at her and she looked away, feeling the heat creep up her neck and into her face.

Todd put the shovel away in the garage and he joined them, helping make the base bigger. By midafternoon, they'd built a rather large snowman and had trampled through the snow to the house next door to help the kids, who were about Ben's age, build a snowman in their own front yard.

Carol bent over to roll some snow together and when she stood, she was smacked in the face with a snowball. She stood there momentarily stunned, then burst out laughing. As she wiped snow away from her face, she caught Todd grinning and rolling more snow in his hand. Not to be outdone, she quickly packed some snow in her hand until it held shape, and she lobbed it around the snowman at Todd. He ducked and it sailed over his back.

"Oh, shoot," she said with a laugh, scooping up more snow. This time, she looked before she stood up, but the snow had already landed on the top of her head.

"Carol, you're slacking." Todd laughed.

"Oh you," she said. "I'll show you." She grabbed some snow and chased him, but he remained out of her reach. He stopped, turned, and said with a laugh, "Maybe you could check out a book on how to win a snowball fight. You know, strategies and such."

"Ha-ha." She dropped the snowball at her feet and asked. "Truce?"

"If you say I win."

She walked toward him, hand extended. "Okay, you win."

He stepped toward her and as he extended his hand, she bent over quickly, grabbed snow, and threw it in his direction. It hit him smack in the middle of his face. He blinked, snow clinging to his eyelashes and eyebrows.

Carol stepped back, giggling, covering her hand with her mouth. "You might want to check that book out yourself."

As he advanced toward her, she took a step back, still laughing. "You know, to brush up on your own strategies. Especially the section on surprise attacks."

He reached for her wrist, and she let him, deciding she would like very much to see where this led to. Behind them, Janet continued to build the snowman, working studiously on it, conspicuously ignoring them but smiling to herself all the same.

He'd just circled his hand around her wrist when the front door of the house opened and Mrs. Rimmer stepped outside to the edge of the porch, an apron covering her cardigan and slacks.

"Carol?" she called, her expression serious.

Carol turned to her, still smiling. "Yes?"

"You have a phone call," Mrs. Rimmer said, and she rubbed her arms and stepped back into the house.

For a split second, Carol wondered who could be calling her here at the Rimmer house. But it could only be her mother, of course, who would never call if it wasn't important. Her thoughts turned to Ben, and she ran to the house, creating another path through the snow.

Inside, a blast of warmth and the smell of vanilla and sugar hit her. Her pants were caked with snow up to her knees. Her nose ran and she wiped it with the back of her gloved hand. There was a brush on the boot tray, and she used it to brush the snow off her pants before she toed off her boots. Not wanting to keep her mother waiting, she didn't bother removing her coat.

She reached the tiny alcove and picked up the phone. "Mother?"

"Carol," her mother said, and her voice broke into a sob.

Carol's heart stopped, or at least that's what it felt like, and she was gripped with fear. She could hear her mother sobbing on the other end of the line. There was a brief awareness within her that she and her mother were on opposite sides of something awful, her mother knowing and her not knowing.

Summoning some courage, she whispered, "Mother, what is it?" But in her mind, all she could think of was Ben, and she prayed he was all right.

"It's your father."

"Dad?" Carol asked, not comprehending. What could possibly be wrong with him?

"He's dead."

Chapter Nineteen

"What do you mean, he's dead?" Carol knew what every word of that sentence meant, but she was having difficulty understanding it.

"Dead?" she repeated, hating the way that sounded coming out of her mouth.

Her mother cried some more, sniffled, and confirmed with a gulp, "He's dead."

"How?" Carol cried.

All sorts of scenarios filled her mind. Had he been in a car accident? Was it the tractor? Did something happen on the farm? Had he fallen and banged his head? For hadn't that happened to Mr. Lime's father last year—eighty years old and he'd decided to clean out the gutters, but the ladder fell out from under him and he landed on the concrete path on his head. He was dead by the time they found him.

"He was outside pulling Ben in the sled. They'd been out there for a long time. Ben came running in and said Dad had grabbed his chest and fallen over. When I went outside, he was facedown in the snow." Alva sobbed harder now. "I sent Ben over to Granddad's, and between Granddad and me we managed to drag Tom into the house. I couldn't leave him out there in the snow! It was so cold."

"Was he alive?" Carol asked, still not believing those words were coming out of her mouth in relation to someone she loved.

"I—yes—I don't know," Alva wailed. "We called the doctor, but he couldn't get to us. Said he was snowed in. Granddad was too shook up to get him in the tractor, so I called the Svensons."

Her mother was referring to their lifelong neighbors, the farming family across the highway from them.

"Sven drove his tractor into town to pick up the doctor but by the time they got to the house, it was too late. The doctor said there was nothing more that could be done."

So many thoughts raced through Carol's mind. The first one being Ben.

"How is Ben? Where is he?" Her father was the only father he knew.

"He's shook up. But I've sent him upstairs to his room. Ann Svenson is here to keep me company."

"I've got to get home," Carol said.

"How? There's still too much snow out there."

"I don't know how. I'll figure it out." Carol's mind whirled. She supposed she could get a taxi or pay someone to drive her. She had money on her, and if that wasn't enough there was more in her sock drawer at the house.

"I don't want you to get hurt," Alva fretted.

"Mother, I will find a way to get home today," she said firmly. It might take all day, but she'd get there. Even if she had to walk every step of the way.

They said their goodbyes and Carol promised to call her as soon as she knew when she was leaving. She remained for a moment standing in the tiny alcove, her shoulders shaking, hardly able to believe what her mother had told her.

Her father dead? That seemed unfathomable. He'd been so alive when she left for work the day before. Her mind raced back to yesterday morning, remembering their brief conversation at the breakfast table, trying to discern if there were any clues about his impending death that she might have missed. She could recall none. Then her mind fast-forwarded to this morning. She'd been outside making snowmen and engaging in a snowball fight with Todd Rimmer while her father was falling over into a snow-covered field while Ben watched. She felt slightly sick. Guilt unsteadied her, and she rested one hand on the wall for support.

Finally, summoning some inner strength from deep inside her, she turned around and came face to face with all three of the Rimmers.

Mrs. Rimmer's face was etched with deep lines and furrows, her lips pressed together. Janet's eyes were wide, her lips slightly parted.

It was Todd who spoke. "Everything all right at home?"

The words wouldn't come. How would she say that out loud? That horrible thing. That her father was dead. She shook her head, her eyes filling, and pressed her fist against her mouth, her teeth biting into her hand. On top of everything else, the humiliation of breaking down in front of strangers.

"Carol?" Todd prompted.

"My father's dead," she said, her voice quivering. Her voice sounded strange to her: disembodied and strangled.

"Oh!" Mrs. Rimmer gasped.

That startled Carol into action. She rubbed her fingers along her forehead, thinking. "I've got to get home. I'll need to call a cab."

"You can't leave now, you won't make it, the roads are awful," Janet said.

Mrs. Rimmer put an arm around her shoulders and guided her to the kitchen. "I'm so sorry for you, dear. It's a terrible shock, I know. Let me get you a cup of tea."

But Carol didn't want tea. She wanted to go home. What couldn't they understand? She needed to get back to Hideaway Bay. For Ben. For her mother. Ever polite, Carol let herself be guided and sat in the chair Todd pulled out for her. But courteous as she was, she wasn't letting go of the idea that she was going home. That day.

Mrs. Rimmer rushed around the kitchen, filling the kettle with water and turning on the stove. "Cut a slice of cake for Carol," she whispered to Janet.

Todd sat down at the table next to her and turned his chair sideways so he faced her, his right arm on the table and his left arm leaning off the back of the chair.

"What happened?" he asked.

She was aware of Mrs. Rimmer and Janet listening as they went about making tea and cutting cake. She didn't want food. She wanted to go home.

"Had he been ill?" Mrs. Rimmer asked, bringing four teacups down from the cupboard.

"No, he dropped dead in the field."

Mrs. Rimmer stopped what she was doing and turned to look at Carol. "That's awful."

Yes, it was, wasn't it? she thought. She wanted to wail. She wanted to scream. But she had to sit there and wait for tea and cake and be polite and demure while grief pulled her under.

"He was pulling Ben in the sled, and he just fell over," she said, staring at a spot on Todd's pants at the knee. The pants were wet from snow. He should change, get more comfortable, not sit there with her with his pants soaking wet from the knee down. "And the doctor couldn't get there right away because of all the snow . . ." Her voice trailed off. If he had dropped over in the heat of summer, in that field that would grow high with green silky stalks of corn in August, would the doctor have made it out in time then? Or had he been dead as soon as he hit the ground?

And what about her grandfather? He was in his eighties. What kind of shock had it been for him?

Mrs. Rimmer and Janet set down plates of cake and cups of tea, and Carol bounced out of her seat.

"I've got to go. May I use your phone? I'll call a cab," she said, frantic.

"There'll be no cab to take you," Mrs. Rimmer said.

"Have some tea, Carol," Janet said softly.

"I don't want any tea, I want to go home." Her voice broke.

Todd was at her side. "I'll drive you home, Carol."

"You will?"

He nodded.

"But Todd—" his mother started.

He shook his head.

To Carol he said, "Let's have something to eat, then you can get your things together and we'll leave while it's still light out."

She couldn't believe his kindness. Her eyes filled again, not with sorrow but with gratitude. "I'll pay you."

"Don't be ridiculous." He reached out and laid a hand gently on her arm. "Let's have something to eat, because we don't know how long it'll take us."

Carol nodded, glad that someone else was going to be in charge, if only for a short while. That someone else was going to be kind and guide her.

She sat down but didn't remember much after that. She ate what was put in front of her and drank the hot, milky tea.

Afterward, Janet led her upstairs to gather her things. Later, Carol wouldn't even recall carrying her dishes over to the sink. Weeks later, she would send a kind note to Mrs. Rimmer.

Once she'd used the bathroom, she followed Janet back down the stairs. Carol had offered to change back into her own skirt, blouse, and cardigan, but Janet wouldn't hear of it.

"You'll be freezing by the time you get home, so don't worry about the clothes," she said.

While they were upstairs, Mrs. Rimmer had put cold sandwiches in a brown paper sack and filled a Thermos with hot coffee. Tears sprang to Carol's eyes for their kindness. She hugged Mrs. Rimmer and Janet goodbye but pulled away first because she was on the brink of tears escaping.

Todd came into the house, ready to go.

"Car's brushed off and I'm ready if you are, Carol," he said. He waited by the door as his boots were caked with snow.

Carol nodded. "I'm ready, thanks." She wrapped her scarf around her neck and felt around in her pockets for her gloves. She pulled them on and turned and thanked Mrs. Rimmer for her hospitality.

Mrs. Rimmer took her gloved hands in her own and said, "My deepest sympathy, Carol, on your loss."

Carol couldn't look at her because if she did, she knew she would cry. With her head down, she nodded quickly, her chin quivering, and watched as one lone tear fell and landed, round and perfect, on her glove.

Before she could have a major meltdown and collapse into a pool of grief, she hurried out the door, which Todd held open for her, and carefully made her way down the front steps.

Todd opened the passenger door for her, and she slid in, the seat beneath her cold. She was too anxious to get home to care.

She put her elbow along the door as they set off and stared out the window at the never-ending mounds of snow. Todd didn't make small talk, and she was grateful as she didn't have any energy for trivialities. She went over and over in her head her last meeting with her father, unable to make any sense of it. How did so much change happen in such a short period of time? Yesterday morning he'd been alive and today he was dead. It didn't make sense. She felt blindsided. She worried about her mother and Ben. How were they coping? She couldn't wait to get back to them. Every time tears threatened to spill over, she pressed her hand to her mouth to tamp them back down.

"Carol, you don't have to be ashamed to shed a few tears in front of me," Todd said quietly.

She looked at him. His kindness made her want to weep.

"I'll try not to do that to you," she said, her voice cracking.

She knew some people were uncomfortable with others' show of strong emotions, especially tears. Tears came from the depths of the soul, some seat of anguish, and it sometimes made those witness to them feel helpless and uncomfortable.

"I don't mind," Todd said. "How you feel is normal."

The driving was so slow it was almost painful. More than once, Carol was tempted to ask Todd to try and go a little faster, but she knew the road conditions didn't warrant reckless driving. She was truly grateful to him for going out of his way to get her home. Hideaway Bay wasn't exactly around the block from the city of Buffalo. She only hoped they'd get there before dark.

Surprisingly, the thruway was open, and the roads had been salted and plowed. But after the Hamburg exit, snow began to fall furiously again, and they were the only car on the road. Their conversation dwindled as the sky grew ominously darker, and Carol preferred not to distract Todd with endless prattle.

Finally, she saw the sign for Hideaway Bay, and she was filled with relief.

"Have you ever been here before?" she asked.

"Yes, we came out here to the beach a few times when I was growing up," he said. "I don't remember much about the town, but I remember the beach."

The conditions were much better out here, but there had been a significant amount of snowfall since Carol had been home the previous morning. The western sky over the lake was colored pale pink and mauve and lavender. The bare, dark trees stood in stark contrast against it.

Carol pointed to the long driveway off the highway that would lead them to the farmhouse where she lived. Her stomach started to do somersaults over what she might find. A part of her hoped she had just dreamed the whole thing and when she opened the door, her father would be there waiting for her.

Someone had plowed the driveway and Todd drove slowly over it, the packed snow crunching beneath his tires.

"You said your family are farmers," he said, looking around.

"Yes," Carol said. "My Granddad lives over there." She pointed to the tidy redbrick house across the fields, just visible against the snow. "His grandfather started the farm."

The old white clapboard farmhouse was almost indistinct from the snow-covered landscape. Carol loved the way the farm looked in the winter: everything covered in snow with the big red barn and the greenhouses out back. She thought of the fields sleeping beneath all that cold and ice, taking a rest until planting season. On a farm, all the seasons were beautiful.

The area in front of the house was disfigured with tire tracks and footprints. Someone had shoveled off the steps and floor of the front porch.

Todd opened the car door and Carol stepped out, tucking the short strap of her purse over her arm and looking up at the house, hesitant. Did it appear different now that her father was gone?

"Come on, Carol, it's best to get it over with," Todd said. He took her by the elbow and guided her gently up the steps.

At the front door, she closed her eyes and took a deep breath. When she opened them, she was aware that Todd was watching her. There might not be another time to speak to him privately. She turned her head toward him with one hand on the door handle.

"I want to thank you for driving me home," she said. "It means a lot to me." As long as she lived, she would never forget this kindness of his.

He shrugged, sheepish. "It was important for you to get here."

She gave him a small smile and opened the door.

She noticed two things when she stepped into the living room. The house was quiet, there was no noise. And it was cold. Almost freezing.

Frowning, Carol pulled off her gloves and scarf, hat and coat, and set everything on the chair by the door. She indicated that Todd should do the same. She was sure he'd want to get back on the road, but she'd give him something to eat and refill his Thermos first.

Slowly, she made her way to the back of the house, to the kitchen. She stood in the doorway for a moment. Her mother sat at the kitchen table with her head in her hands. Ben sat next to her, staring into space. Trails of dried tears were evident on his young face. Neither said anything.

Carol's heart broke.

"Mother. Ben," she said quietly.

Her mother's head snapped up and Ben jumped out of his chair, a smile forming on his lips.

"Oh, you made it," Alva said, her eyes and nose red.

Immediately, Carol took Ben in her arms, wrapping him in a tight embrace. She felt his small arms slide around her waist, and he laid his head on her chest and cried.

"Shh," she said, her voice constricted. She smoothed the hair on the top of his head.

Alva stood but her gait appeared shaky and Carol, still holding Ben to her, made her way over to her mother and wrapped her right arm around her. Her mother laid her head on Carol's shoulder and sobbed.

She soothed them until they were able to speak without crying, then disengaged from the embrace, squeezing Ben to her once more to reassure him.

She turned to Todd and said, "Mother, Ben, this is Todd Rimmer, he drove me home."

"Todd, this is my mother, Mrs. Anderson, and my... brother, Ben."

"Thank you so much for bringing Carol home," Alva said, shaking Todd's hand. "We really needed to be together today." Her voice quivered as she spoke.

The counters in the kitchen were covered with all kinds of casserole dishes and pots and trays of baked goods. No kind of bad weather would prevent the citizens of Hideaway Bay from being good neighbors.

Carol turned to Ben and pushed his hair off his forehead. "Have you had anything to eat?"

He shook his head.

"I'm so sorry, Ben," Alva cried, sinking back down into the kitchen chair. "I wasn't thinking."

Ben put his hand on Alva's shoulder. "It's all right, Mom."

"Sit down, I'll fix you all something to eat," Carol said. "Mother, when was the last time you ate something?"

Alva seemed distressed by the question and then she said, "I don't remember."

"The house seems kind of cold," Carol said.

Her mother appeared confused. "Does it?"

"Don't worry about it," Carol said. "I'll take care of everything."

"Do you have a furnace or boiler that needs coal?" Todd asked.

"Down in the cellar," Carol said. She grabbed an apron off one of the hooks by the back door and reached behind her back to tie it. "There's a pile of coal on the floor."

But she hesitated, not wanting him to have to go into the cellar. "But don't worry about it. I can do it."

Todd shook his head. "No, this is something I can do."

"All right," she said.

She indicated that he should follow her. She turned on the light switch at the top of the cellar stairs. A bare bulb at the foot of the stairs shone light all around in the darkness. Metal shelves filled with jars of canned goods lined the wall.

"The furnace is to your right. Can't miss it. There's a coal shovel and bucket right next to it."

"Got it."

"And watch the bottom step, it's weak. Dad keeps saying he's going to . . ." And she stopped, realizing that her father was never going to fix that bottom step. Tears filled her eyes.

Todd reached out and laid a hand on her arm. "It's going to be like that for a while until you get used to the idea."

She nodded quickly, not trusting the sound of her own voice, but she doubted she'd ever get used to the idea of her father being gone.

"Okay, let me get this thing going," he said, and he made his way carefully down the narrow steps into the cellar.

Carol turned her attention back to the kitchen. Her mother continued to sit at the table, numb, as did Ben.

"Ben, would you like to go watch some television?" she asked.

"Is it all right?" he asked, looking at Alva.

"Yes, it is," she said.

He was too young to absorb so much grief at once.

"I'll call you when everything is ready," Carol said.

He took a look at Alva, hesitant, but pushed his chair in and ran off to the living room. Within minutes, Carol heard the familiar sounds of horses and guns going. Ben had been raised on a steady diet of westerns with her father.

She was glad for things to do. The distraction was a blessing. She lifted lids and tin foil covers from all the casserole dishes. There was a variety of food. Elvira Milchmann had sent over a cooked ham. The Hahns had sent over two lemon meringue pies—their pies were legendary. There was also macaroni salad, scalloped potatoes, potato salad, sliced roast beef, ambrosia salad, green bean casserole, Swedish meatballs, a pan of brownies, a platter of sugar cookies, a pan of biscuits and gravy, and goulash. She was touched by the outpouring, but it would take them weeks to eat all this food.

She turned the oven on to preheat it and took a bit from each dish, putting the food in an oven-safe dish and popping it in the oven. She checked the range in the corner of the room. The fire would have been lit in the morning when her father got up, but it had gone out. Carol took kindling from the metal bucket at the side of the stove and a piece of rolled-up old newspaper and threw them into the hole. She lit it with a long match and left the cover off for a moment to keep an eye on it.

Todd came up the stairs, brushing dirt off his hands. They were black from the coal dust. Heat from coal was great, but the dust that came off it was not.

"There's a sink out back if you want to wash your hands," she said.

"The place should be heating up soon."

"Thanks," she said.

Out of the corner of her eye, she watched her mother. She hadn't moved since she sat back down. Carol made her a cup of tea, set it down in front of her, and prompted her to drink it.

"What can I do?" Todd asked.

"Nothing. Why don't you sit down and relax," she suggested. He had a long drive back to Buffalo ahead of him.

"Would it be all right if I used your phone to call my mother and let her know I'm here?"

Carol blushed, embarrassed that she hadn't thought of that. "Of course, go right ahead." She showed him where the rotary phone was on the desk in the hall between the kitchen and the living room. The television was so loud you couldn't hear yourself think. While he dialed his home number, Carol stepped into the living room and turned down the volume knob. Ben was stretched out on the floor on his belly, elbows bent, face resting in his hands.

She hurried back to the kitchen, trying not to listen to Todd's conversation with his mother on the phone. She checked the dishes in the oven, and everything was heating up nicely. Her stomach growled.

She could hear Todd talking to Ben in the other room, his phone call with his mother finished.

The phone rang and she went to answer it.

"Hello?"

"Is this Mrs. Anderson?" asked a male voice.

"No, this is her daughter, Carol," she replied.

"Carol, it's Wendell Reidy of Reidy's Funeral Home. Let me express my condolences on the death of your father," he intoned. He had a stentorian voice that made Carol think he should be doing Shakespeare plays instead of burying the dead.

"Thank you, Mr. Reidy," she said.

"Usually, I'd have your mother come in tonight to make the funeral arrangements but with the weather, we could leave it until tomorrow," he said. "May I speak to her?"

Carol leaned back to glimpse at her mother through the kitchen doorway. She remained seated, staring blankly at her teacup, which remained untouched.

Carol said quietly into the phone, "Mr. Reidy, she can't come to the phone. If you tell me the time, we'll be there."

She wrote down the time on a notepad and said goodbye to the funeral director. There was a note lying next to the phone. Her heart slowed when she recognized her father's handwriting. There was a name and a phone number written on it. Her eyes filled as she stared at it, studied it, the familiar scrawl of her father's handwriting that she would see no more. Carefully, she folded it into quarters and tucked it into her pocket. That was worth saving.

Her grandfather arrived at the back door, looking every one of his eighty plus years. His pallor was gray, and he looked shaken. Carol hugged him and he gripped her tightly. She introduced him to Todd, and he nodded. He made his way around the table, stopped at the chair where her father usually sat, tapped on the back of it, and proceeded to the next chair, sitting down with a sigh. Since Carol's grandmother had died, her grandfather had joined them every night for his dinner.

Carol called Ben, and he ran into the kitchen and sat next to Granddad. It was the only time the elderly man smiled.

"How're you holding up, young man?"

"I'm okay, Gramps," Ben said with a shrug.

"That's because you're made of sturdy stuff," he said.

As she served a cobbled dinner made up of things dropped off by generous neighbors and friends, Todd said, "I'll head home right after dinner if it's all right with you."

Alva looked at him as if she hadn't seen him before. "It's getting late. You should stay the night."

"No, I couldn't impose on your hospitality," he said. "My mother said the roads are passable in the city and the weather has improved. I'll take my time."

"Are you sure?" Alva asked.

"I am, thanks, Mrs. Anderson," he said. He looked at Carol. "Besides, it's really a time for you to be alone with your family."

Carol hadn't said anything. In a way, she was embarrassed that she hadn't encouraged him to stay. She liked him. A lot. But tonight, when everything was cleaned up and Ben was put to bed, she wanted to be alone with her grief and thoughts of her father.

After dinner, Todd stood and said goodbye. Alva appeared more aware and thanked Todd for bringing Carol home. Then she insisted Carol go down into the basement and bring up some canned jars for Todd to take home to his mother as a thank-you for the hospitality she'd shown Carol.

He said goodbye and Carol walked him to the front door. It was as black as pitch out. Carol drew in a deep breath. It was going to be a long night.

At the door, he slowly pulled on his coat and scarf as if he was reluctant to leave.

"Would you call me when you get home, so I know you made it all right?" Carol asked.

He nodded. "Does Janet have your number?"

"She does."

There seemed to be hesitation and Carol blurted out, "Maybe you should stay."

He smiled at her. "I appreciate the offer, Carol, but your family doesn't need an outsider hanging around."

"You're not an outsider," she said softly, her gaze downward.

"To you, I hope not," he said.

Her gaze bounced up and she was pulled in by the warmth and kindness in his eyes.

"I'll call as soon as I get home," he said.

He pushed through the front door and headed down the porch steps. He waved one last time before sliding into his car. She watched the car make its way slowly down the long, wide driveway, its red taillights bright against the darkness.

She returned to the kitchen to wash the dishes.

"He's a fine young man, Carol," Granddad said.

"Yes, he is," she agreed, and she turned on the tap in the big white basin sink and squirted in some dish soap.

Chapter Twenty

1971

Carol used a comb to separate a small section of her hair, applied some Dippity-do, rolled it around a pink foam roller, and clipped it shut. She did her whole head as Todd watched her from the bed. Wearing a white T-shirt and boxers, he leaned against the maple headboard.

She couldn't remember when she'd ever been as happy as she'd been these last two years since she and Todd got married. She'd finally gotten the job as librarian of the Hideaway Bay Library, and he'd agreed to settling in the little beach town, only putting his foot down when she brought up the idea of living with her mother. He'd shaken his head and said no, he wanted their own place. They bought a little brick home within walking distance of the library, and Todd found a job as an accountant with a manufacturing firm a ten-minute drive down the highway. She'd told him she was unable to have children due to a childhood illness and Todd, being the gentleman, hadn't pressed for details, saying it didn't matter, that it wasn't a dealbreaker. She stopped and saw Ben every day after work and had him sleep over at their house on the weekends.

She wrapped a hairnet around her head to keep the rollers in place. Finished, she set her comb down next to the mirror tray that held bottles of her favorite perfumes: Emeraude, Chanel No. 19, Dana Tabu, and Prince Matchabelli Wind Song.

She turned off the small light on top of the dresser, then slid into bed, relishing the cool sheets. Carefully, she laid her head on her pillow, not wanting to smash her rollers too much. Beside her, Todd was grinning.

"What's so funny?" she asked.

He made a gesture with his finger around her head. "I can hardly resist you with all those rollers in your hair."

"The price of daytime beauty, my love," she said with a smile. She leaned over and placed her lips on his, kissing him. He reached up and caressed her arm.

Carol turned off the bedside light and settled in on her side of the bed, pulling the blanket up and closing her eyes. She wondered if there was any cream cheese in the fridge for a recipe she wanted to try the following night.

She couldn't keep the stuff in the house as Todd liked it on Ritz crackers.

"Carol, I want to talk to you about something," Todd said, switching on the light on his nightstand.

"Now?" she asked, opening her eyes.

"Yes, it's important," he said quietly.

She lifted herself up, leaned against the headboard, and looked over at him. "Is everything all right?"

"I've been offered a job," he said.

"You have?" She didn't even know he'd been looking.

"Yes."

"I thought you were happy at the plant."

"I'm not."

This was news to her. Well, maybe not. She knew he wasn't crazy about it, but he didn't complain. She hadn't thought he disliked it enough to go looking for another job.

"I want to take it," he said.

"Well, if it makes you happy, then you should take it."

Without taking his eyes off her face, he said softly, "It's in Chicago."

"Chicago?" She laughed. Was this some kind of joke?

With a sinking feeling, she asked, "You're not serious, are you?"

Todd slipped his arm behind his head, leaned against it, and tapped the top of the headboard with his finger. "I might be."

Carol blinked several times, trying to process this new information.

From the start, when they began dating after that terrible snowstorm that had claimed her father's life, she had made it clear that she wanted to live in Hideaway Bay. No other place interested her. Her mother needed her, she'd told him. And there was a kernel of truth to that. But what she didn't tell him was that she needed to be as close as possible to Ben. She'd never leave him.

"But we've created a life here in Hideaway Bay," she said.

"I know, but I'm ready for some change," he said with a dissatisfied sigh.

"Is it only your job you're disenchanted with?" she asked, almost afraid of the answer. Maybe it was something more than job dissatisfaction. Small-town life wasn't for everyone.

"Partly. I'm bored with it," he said. "I've learned everything I can there, and I've been promoted as far as I'm going to go."

"And that's not enough for you?" she asked.

She knew she'd spend the rest of her life at the Hideaway Bay Library, and that thought made her very happy. Why couldn't he be content at his job?

"No, I don't want to spend my whole career at the plant," he said firmly.

"I think you're getting too big for your britches," she said, her voice tight. "There are a lot of men out there who'd give their right arm for that kind of job security."

"I know, but that isn't me. I can't stay in this job and not get stagnant. I'm already bored."

"Can't you get a hobby or something outside of work that would stimulate your mind?" she asked, groping. She toyed with the hem of the green, orange, and yellow floral bedspread in her lap.

He snorted. "A hobby is for evenings and weekends. I'm looking for satisfaction in my job."

Carol was determined to find a solution.

"Why don't you look around and see if there is another job. Something else that doesn't involve moving to another part of the country."

"I've been looking for the last six months," he admitted.

Carol was shocked. "I didn't know that. You never said."

She didn't know if she liked this feeling of being in the dark. Of him not sharing this. Had she been tooling along these last few months, blissfully ignorant, thinking she and Todd were happy, only to find out that the seeds of dissatisfaction had rooted and were pushing through the soil?

"What about Buffalo?" she asked, desperate.

There certainly would be lots of jobs for accountants up there. Granted, the daily commute would be tedious, but he'd have to make the best of it.

"It's too far. I wouldn't like a steady diet of that in either bad weather or good," he said. He reached over and began to trace lazy circles along her arm. "I wouldn't want to spend a minimum of two hours every day commuting."

Words—something she loved—escaped her. At a loss, she said, "I don't know what to say."

"I don't want to live in Hideaway Bay forever," he said.

There it was. This was a problem. Her heart felt like lead.

"But I don't want to live anywhere else," she said quietly. "I can't leave."

He sighed again. "Your mother seems quite a strong woman."

That was true. After the initial shock of her husband's death, Alva had bounced back, determined if not to overcome her grief, then to wrestle it to the ground and pin it down. She'd thrown herself into raising Ben, volunteering at his school and joining all sorts of groups in town. She was president of the gardening club. She was a member of the committee responsible for the beautification of the war memorial and the grounds, and she played bridge on Monday nights. Carol suspected her mother threw herself into all these things so she wouldn't have to think, wouldn't have to deal with the fact that she was now alone.

"I couldn't leave Ben," she said weakly.

"I know you're close to him, but Ben is not your responsibility."

Carol hesitated, on the brink of revealing the truth about Ben's parentage. She should have told him.

Tell him now, a voice prompted her.

But the fear was there that it would mar their idyll. That he'd leave her. Even now, the memory of her father dropping her off at Aunt Lina's and driving off without so much as a backwards glance haunted her.

She'd just opened her mouth to say something when Todd spoke.

"Ben will be all grown up and going off on a life of his own soon," he said. "I'd like us to have a life of our own."

And the opportunity was lost. She sank down a bit further into the bed, her head and shoulders still resting against the pillow propped up against the headboard. But now she had a greater problem on her hands other than her secret about Ben: she didn't want to lose her husband. But there was no way she could be happy in Chicago or anywhere else, not so far away from her child. She'd be heartbroken.

If they remained in Hideaway Bay, Todd would be unhappy. If they left, she would be heartsick. For the first time in their short, happy marriage, a big black cloud rolled over the horizon, engulfing and ominous.

"We don't need to make any decisions tonight," he said, yawning. "I feel better now that I told you." He turned off the light on his nightstand, bathing the room in darkness.

She wished she could say the same. She slid down into the bed, righted her pillow, and turned on her side, her back to Todd. He crept closer, throwing his arm over her and pulling her close to him. Within minutes, she heard his familiar, light snore. She blew out a short breath between her lips, hoping he wouldn't mention this again, but doubt filled her. For the rest of the night, Todd slept soundly, but Carol lay awake, wide-eyed and alert, trying to figure out a solution to their problem. By dawn, she'd come to the conclusion that there might not be one.

After going back and forth about it for weeks, with the pressure from the company for Todd to make a decision as to whether he wanted the job or not, they compromised: Todd would take the job in Chicago on a trial basis, and they would fly back and forth to see each other. It wasn't ideal, but it was the best solution they could come up with. The problem was that both of them were miserable with the compromise.

Chapter Twenty-One

1972

Carol stood with her hands on her hips in the middle of her den, looking around. She'd redecorated in the last year, something to keep her busy while Todd was living in Chicago. By herself, she tore down the wallpaper, using her mother's suggestion of a vinegar mix. Then, she ripped up the old gold carpet. In their place were maple paneling and bookshelves and an orange shag carpet. Gone was the little black-and-white television with the rabbit ears, replaced with a brand-new RCA console. She was pleased with the look. Not only were the colors warm and cozy but the books made her feel comfortable, as if her best friends were in the room with her.

Todd was due in on a late-afternoon flight and would arrive in Hideaway Bay in the evening. Throughout the day, she kept checking her watch, fretting and counting down the hours. Then she'd close her eyes, take a deep breath, and exhale.

He'd been gone a year; that had been the arrangement they'd agreed on. They'd taken turns flying back and forth between Chicago and Hideaway Bay.

It hadn't been easy, Carol would be the first to admit. It was the lack of day-to-day living together that affected them the most. When there had been a blinding snowstorm in Chicago and Todd had been stuck in his apartment, unable to get to work, Carol had walked to the library and the weather had been cold and crisp and sunny. When a bird had gotten stuck in the chimney, she had to hire someone to get it out despite Todd's protests to wait until he got home. It was something that couldn't wait that long. When he spoke about his life in Chicago and the people he worked with, she had a hard time picturing them. It was as if the two of them were in different chapters of the same book.

She missed him so much.

And she hoped he'd feel the same way about her and want to come home. The only problem was he loved his new job. It was exciting and every day was different, and he'd already had one promotion since he arrived.

But she was counting on the fact that he loved her more than he loved his work.

They spoke every night on the phone and they both had the long-distance telephone bills to prove it. Over the phone, they never discussed their future, both agreeing that those conversations were best had in private, together, and face to face.

By the time he arrived at the house, Carol's stomach was in knots. She hadn't been this nervous since their first date. He strode up the path in a stylish pair of slacks, a turtleneck, and a corduroy blazer. She tilted her head, narrowing her eyes. His conservative style of dress had changed.

When he walked in, he dropped his overnight bag and pulled her into his embrace. She settled in. Being in his arms always felt like home.

"Is that new cologne you're wearing?" she asked.

"Do you like it?" he asked, pulling back and brushing his finger along the side of her face.

She nodded. "I do. What made you change it?" He'd been wearing Aqua Velva for years.

"Just wanted something different."

"I like it," she said with an uncertain smile, trying to navigate all this new territory.

Would she have noticed these changes if he'd remained in Hideaway Bay, or would they have been more gradual? More subtle?

"And you've done something with your hair. No more rollers?" he asked with a grin.

She shook her head. "Nope. This is the new style. It's called a shag." She turned her head in profile and raised her eyebrows and grinned.

Todd smiled. "I like it on you. It's sexy." His eyes drifted to the necklace with the teardrop emerald that hung around her neck. He'd given it to her for their first Christmas together as newlyweds and she wore it every day, along with her thin gold wedding band and the bracelet her parents had given her.

She laughed and pulled him along with her to the den off the kitchen. "I want to show you what I've done."

But he stopped in the kitchen. "Wow, what did you do here?" he asked, looking around.

It was hard to get her head around the fact that he hadn't been home in six months. There'd been a big project at work and he couldn't make it home to Hideaway Bay, so Carol had been going out to Chicago to see him.

"I keep busy by remodeling," she said.

"I'll say."

The kitchen had been upgraded with Harvest Gold appliances, including the rotary phone with the extra-long cord hanging on the wall. The cabinets were dark laminate with wrought iron handles.

Todd looked around, speechless, and then stepped into the den. He blinked and said, "I no longer recognize my own home."

Carol's mouth opened slightly. "That wasn't what I was going for."

He gave her a quick smile to reassure her. "I know. I didn't mean anything by it."

An uncomfortable silence bloomed between them.

"A lot of things have changed," he said quietly. "Your hair, the kitchen, the den . . . our marriage."

Immediately, she went to him and slid her arms under his, pressing her palms against his back and laying her head on his chest. She was relieved when he wrapped his arms around her.

"But we haven't changed. We're still the same people and we love each other," she whispered.

He didn't say anything, and that hurt her.

Sunday afternoon, Carol made Todd's favorite dish: lasagna. She hadn't made it since he'd lived in Hideaway Bay full time. It didn't make sense to make a big pan of pasta just for herself. And although she could have shared it with her mother and Ben, her mother turned her nose up at it, saying she preferred plain, no-nonsense cooking.

After Todd finished his second serving, Carol stood and turned on the kettle.

"I've got chocolate cake, too," she said.

Todd leaned back and patted his stomach. "I'm pretty full but I'm going to force it, because I love your chocolate cake and who knows when I'll get a chance to have a slice again."

Even though her heart sank at the implication of his words, it was the opening she needed.

"Todd, we should talk about our future before you go to the airport," she said.

Although she trembled, she felt brave for saying it. No sense in not bringing it up. She cut two slices of cake, put them on plates, and handed Todd the bigger piece.

"Thanks," he said.

After the tea was made, she joined him at the table.

It was time to be practical, no matter how much it hurt.

It didn't escape her that Todd said nothing.

She sat down, sliced off a piece of cake with her fork, and put it into her mouth. But her stomach was a jangle of nerves, and the rich chocolate and sugary frosting caused her stomach to revolt. She pushed the plate away and took a sip of her tea, immediately feeling better.

Todd was having no problem eating the cake.

"We can't ignore our situation anymore," she said quietly. "We agreed that at the end of the year living apart, we would reevaluate our decision."

"I know," he said, licking his lips. He set his fork down. "I've been dreading this conversation."

This comment did not inspire confidence in Carol. "Why?"

Todd didn't answer her right away. He fiddled with his fork, then pushed his chair back and crossed one leg over the other, his ankle jiggling. With each delay, the panic in Carol raised up a notch.

"Because I think we're in the same place we were last year." He did not look at her when he spoke. His stare was fixed on some imaginary spot on the table.

Carol wanted him to look at her. To look her right in the eye.

"The truth is, relocating to Chicago was a good move for me. I have a future there," he said.

He spoke so quietly that Carol had to strain to hear him. She noticed he'd used "I" instead of "we."

"But what about us?" she asked, afraid of the answer.

He leaned forward and took hold of her hand. "Come to Chicago, Carol. I think we'd be very happy there."

She shrank back, pulling her hand from his. "Todd, I told you, I can't leave Hideaway Bay."

He sighed, exasperated and frustrated. "Why?"

"Because my mother and brother are here, and this is my home! I happen to love my job here at the library."

"Come on, Carol, a lot of people leave their families," he said. "And you'll be able to get a job at a library in Chicago."

"I don't want a job at a library in Chicago," she said. "I want to live and work here."

"Well, I don't," he said evenly. "Hideaway Bay is a small town and to be honest, I find it suffocating."

"Oh," she said, dejected. She could think of many adjectives to describe Hideaway Bay, but "suffocating" wasn't one of them.

"I won't be coming back to Hideaway Bay, or Western New York for that matter," he said.

"And I won't be going to Chicago," she managed to choke out.

They sat there in silence for a while, neither looking at the other. When they finally stood up, they held each other and sobbed.

PART 3

Present Day

Chapter Twenty-Two

Jackie

Between the time she left Carol's house and that first morning she was due to meet Ben and Carol at the field, Jackie knew she had a lot of research to do on sunflowers and how to grow them. She'd scour whatever information she could find on the internet and immerse herself in whatever videos were available about growing not only sunflowers but any kind of flower, cut or otherwise. She waited until Anna was tucked into bed, and then she made herself a cup of coffee and settled down with her laptop on the sofa.

From the bedroom, Anna called, "Can we get a dog?"

"No," Jackie responded.

"What about a kitten?" Anna pressed.

"No, now go to sleep," Jackie called back.

Anna grumbled something Jackie couldn't hear. That's just what she needed in her life: a pet. As if she didn't have enough to do.

The more she thought about growing sunflowers, the more she warmed up to the idea. Aside from the extra money that would allow her to take Anna to Disneyworld, it would be a good experience for Anna. Jackie didn't allow herself to get too excited though. She kept any possible runaway emotions in check. It was too hard to climb back when things came crashing down.

Before she got started, she surfed Facebook, needing to do something mindless. She hadn't posted in a long time. What was she supposed to post? *Here's a photo of Anna and me, struggling to move on after Jason? Trying to rebuild our lives?*

She landed on a post of a friend she'd gone to high school with. The other woman had posted twenty-one pictures of their beach vacation over Easter break. There was a photo of her and her husband wearing khaki-colored pants and white T-shirts against a dusky beach, the sky smudged with lavender, pink, and pale blue. Unashamed, Jackie scrolled through the woman's other photos. There were the kids, and there was also a pair of golden retrievers back home in what looked to be a brand-new four-bedroom house.

Exasperated, Jackie closed that browser page without bothering to sign out.

"Okay, YouTube, show me what you've got," she said quietly, typing "sunflower growers" in the search bar.

It didn't take much to go down that rabbit hole. She watched one video after another and sometimes, the same video two or three times, jotting down notes in a spiral-bound notebook. When she eventually glanced at the clock on the wall, she was shocked to see it was almost midnight. She yawned and stretched, getting up from the sofa and powering down her laptop for the night.

She went through her nighttime routine, shutting off lights and making sure the front and back doors were locked. Holding her key fob, she pointed it out the window at her car until she heard the familiar beeps that assured her it was locked.

Her last stop before her bedroom was Anna's room. She pulled up the blanket that Anna had kicked off and covered her with it, then bent and kissed her daughter on the forehead. On her way out, she left the door open and a night-light on in the hall.

She washed her face and brushed her teeth before pulling on her nightgown. She crawled into bed, collapsing on the comfortable mattress. She was feeling a level of excitement she would never admit to, not even to her parents. She suspected it had to do with all those videos of tall, majestic sunflowers reaching toward the sky and swaying gently in the breeze. It was intoxicating, all those golden sunny fields with row after row of sunflowers as far as the eye could see. Her eyes closed and she could feel herself drifting down into sleep. She was a good tired.

Stepping outside into the May morning sunshine, Jackie inhaled a mixed smell of wet earth and the briny spring essence from the lake that appeared after the snow had melted and winter had deposited its waste along the shore.

Her parents had offered to watch Anna while she met with Ben and Carol, but she'd decided she'd bring her along. It might be best to get her used to the idea of growing the sunflowers; after all, they were going to be spending a lot of their summer out in the field.

She pulled her car into the parking lot by the produce stand, the loose gravel crunching beneath the tires. Mimi Duchene was there at the stand. Jackie knew her to see her, and returned the girl's friendly wave.

She unbuckled Anna from her car seat and the little girl jumped out of the car, sporting a small pink backpack on her shoulders. She pushed her sunglasses up on her nose, looked around and asked, "Where are the sunflowers?"

With a smile, Jackie replied, "They're not here yet. We have to plant the seeds and help them to grow."

Anna processed this and frowned, saying, "Oh."

"Who's that?" Anna said, pointing to Mimi.

"It's not polite to point at people," Jackie said. "That's Mimi."

Mimi spotted Anna and waved. As there were no customers, she came out of the stand and walked over to them. "Hi. I'm Mimi Duchene."

"I'm Jackie Arnold, and this is my daughter, Anna."

Mimi squatted down on her haunches and said, "I really like your sunglasses. They're so cool."

Shy Anna appeared, lowering her head, pointing her toe into the gravel and smiling. But she said nothing.

"Can you say thank you?" Jackie asked.

"Thank you," Anna whispered.

Mimi laughed. "You're welcome." She stood and addressed Jackie. "If you need anything, Kyle Koch and I tend to be here most afternoons after school and the weekends, working the stand."

"Thanks, Mimi, I appreciate that. I'm here to meet Ben and Carol," Jackie said, looking around but seeing no sign of them approaching.

"He's usually pretty punctual," Mimi said. "I wouldn't worry. He'll be here soon."

Jackie nodded.

Her attention was distracted by a car pulling in from the highway. Expecting to see Ben and Carol in the front seat, she was disappointed when it wasn't them. Had she gotten the time wrong? The date? That wouldn't look good.

An elderly couple parked in an accessible parking spot close to the stand.

"I better get back to work, it was nice meeting you both," Mimi said with a smile, and she hopped off back toward her place at the stand.

"You too," Jackie said.

When Mimi was out of earshot, Anna said, "She's pretty."

"Yes, she is. Come on, let's check out this field," Jackie said. She held out her hand and Anna slipped her smaller one into it. Jackie always loved the feel of her daughter's hand in hers.

They walked along the edge of the field, staring at the two acres in front of them. The area had been sectioned off with wooden stakes whose tops were covered in strips of fluorescent orange tape, which oscillated in the gentle breeze.

Seeing how big the field actually was made Jackie swallow hard. Her confidence wobbled.

What have I gotten myself into?

Anna stopped every so often, bored. She bent down to look at her shoe. She took off her sunglasses and then put them back on. She took off her backpack to look through it. It must have been hard for a four-year-old to understand what there was to look at in a field of dirt and grass. Jackie was having a hard time envisioning it herself.

She didn't want to walk all the way to the back end of the field as she was afraid Ben and Carol might show up and didn't want to keep them waiting. Despite all the videos she'd watched, she realized she really hadn't a clue as to what she was doing, and wondered if they could get someone else at such short notice. She doubted it.

She was stuck.

Just as a sense of panic began to fill her, another vehicle pulled into the lot and Jackie squinted to see if it was Ben and Carol.

It looked like Ben's truck, but only one person got out.

"Come on, Anna, I think Mr. Anderson is here."

She headed back in the direction of the stand and when Ben put up his hand in a wave, she picked up her pace, Anna running to keep up with her.

"Hey, Ben," she said as she reached him.

"I'm sorry I'm late," he said.

"I thought I had the time wrong," Jackie said.

"No. Carol had a bad turn this morning and I had to wait for the hospice nurse to come out," Ben said. "I couldn't find my phone to send you a text."

"Oh, I'm sorry to hear that," Jackie said. "Is Carol all right? We can reschedule."

Ben waved his hand dismissively. "Nah, that's all right. The nurse is with her. I won't be able to stay long. I've got all the seeds and equipment in the truck. We can unload it and store it in the shed."

"That's fine," she said.

If Carol was having a difficult morning, she would not burden her with quitting. She wasn't going to add to the woman's troubles. She was going to have to suck it up, figure it out, and grow the sunflowers.

Ben looked at Anna and said, "You must be Anna!"

Anna nodded her head vigorously and smiled, showing off her baby teeth.

"Are you ready to get to work and plant some sunflowers?" he asked, clapping his hands.

More nodding.

They followed Ben to the galvanized-steel storage shed behind the stand and waited as he unlocked the combination lock and opened the door. The shed looked brand-new, unlike the whitewashed stand, which had been there for as long as Jackie could remember.

"Before I forget, Jackie, you'll need the code to the combination lock here," he said. He paused, patted his pockets, and frowned. "I have no paper on me. Do you?"

She shook her head.

"It's nine, six, five, seven," he said. "Can you remember that? It's my wife's birthday. September sixth, nineteen fifty-seven."

How sweet. Jason used to use her birthday and their anniversary for all his passwords. She'd forgotten about that. She wondered how many other things she'd forgotten.

"Don't forget, now," Ben said.

Jackie stirred. "I'll remember," she assured him. She repeated the number several times silently to herself, committing it to memory.

She helped Ben unload the tools and several bags of seeds.

"Carol ordered a variety so it might be best to mark where you plant each."

"Okay," Jackie said, making a mental note.

Panic set in when stuff was unloaded that she didn't recognize, but she was too embarrassed to ask. The biggest object was something with two low wheels and a handle that looked like a cross between a bike and a wheelbarrow. She had no idea what that was for and parked it in the back of the shed, out of the way.

"That's everything," Ben said. "I'll leave you to it."

"You're leaving already?" Jackie said, trying to disguise the panic in her voice.

"I've got to get back to Carol. Once the field is ready, you can get started on planting the seeds."

Jackie's glance bounced around the field. "Oh yeah, right . . ." she said, her voice trailing off. What was required to get the field ready? She hadn't researched that.

Before she could protest or ask the questions she didn't even know she needed to ask, Ben waved goodbye and hopped in his truck. He was pulling out of the parking lot when the first question formed on Jackie's lips.

"How do I start?" she asked no one in a whisper.

"What did you say, Mommy?"

Jackie blinked several times and muttered, "Nothing worth repeating. Come on, Anna."

She walked back to the field and stared at it.

It was grassy. How had she not noticed that and asked how she would plant seeds in a grassy field? It would have to be overturned. But how? She didn't know one piece of farm equipment from the next. All the videos she'd watched had been about planting and growing the flowers. She felt well-versed in that. But she hadn't done any investigation into the prepping of the field. In the videos, all the seeds had been planted in fine dirt, not clumpy soil or grassy fields.

"Come on, Anna, we need to go to the store," she said. She supposed she could get a spade or a shovel. She didn't even know the difference between the two. Hopefully, someone at the hardware store would be able to help her out.

The hardware store up on the highway was crowded, but an employee who went into his life story about being a bored retiree at home was eager to help her out and told her for turning over grass to create a garden bed, she'd be better off using a shovel. Happy with her purchase, Jackie left the hardware store with her newly purchased piece of equipment, eager to get back to the plot behind the fruit-and-veg stand.

Thinking about all the physical labor that was going to be involved, Jackie dropped Anna off at her parents' house, feeling guilty for doing so.

"Don't feel guilty," her mother said as if reading her mind. "It's a lot of work and she'll get bored at times."

"That's what I'm afraid of," Jackie said with a sigh. "But I don't want to take advantage of you and Dad. You're already watching Anna three days a week."

"Nonsense," Helen said. "You know we'll help any way we can."

"Thanks, Mom. I don't know what time I'll be back," Jackie said, brushing her bangs off her forehead with the back of her hand.

"Don't worry about it. Do what you have to do," her mother said firmly.

There was no sense in putting it off, she might as well get back to the field and get started.

Chapter Twenty-Three

Carrying the shovel with her, Jackie went to a spot by the nearest stake, a little nervous and wondering how long it would take her to turn over the grass on a two-acre plot.

Thinking she'd start at one end and work in clean lines, she tipped the shovel into the earth, but it wouldn't budge. The dirt beneath the grass was stone dry. She placed the pointy edge into the ground again and this time, she stood on it, putting all her weight onto the top of the shovel. The tip moved about an inch. She tried again and again. She tried inserting the shovel at different angles but with no success. By now she was red in the face and sweating profusely. There'd been unladylike grunts and groans, and there'd also been a lot of expenditure of energy on her part and not much to show for it. Nothing, in fact. For a minute she stood there, looking across the staked-out field, feeling like a failure. If she couldn't turn over this one slice of land, how was she going to do the rest of it?

Finally, she gave up and abandoned her newly purchased shovel on the field. With her hands on her hips, she stared at the plot of land and bit her lip. Initially, the size—two acres—had seemed doable. In theory. But now, after wrestling with trying to overturn one square foot of topsoil with a shovel and unable to do it, it seemed a little more daunting. Overwhelming. Behind her, cars whizzed by on the highway. Several times, drivers turning down Erie Street honked and waved to her, calling out her name. All the while, she waved and smiled through gritted teeth. Nothing like being front and center for every citizen in Hideaway Bay to see how miserably you were failing at fulfilling a dying woman's wish.

Eventually, she sighed, picked up the shovel, and walked back to her car.

Back at the hardware store, she went up and down the aisles until she found the employee who'd sold her the shovel. He was at the back of the garden center outside, removing trays of red impatiens from a pallet. Jackie explained to him that the shovel wasn't quite cutting it, that she needed something stronger to move the earth to create a garden bed.

"Maybe a rototiller?" he asked, rubbing his chin with his forefinger and thumb.

She'd been afraid he might say that but found herself nodding anyway.

Again, she questioned her ability to complete this project, and if it hadn't been for her desire to take Anna to Disneyworld and for her daughter to experience something growing from seed to bloom, she'd go home right now and go back to her simple, orderly life. But here she was, renting a rototiller, something she had never used before.

When the store employee, whose name was Howard, took the time to give her a demonstration, she was buoyed by his kindness and anxious to get started. He helped her get the piece of machinery into her trunk. Then she had to by a bungee cord to secure the trunk lid because it wouldn't close all the way, and even though it was a short ride down the highway, it was too dangerous to drive with the trunk lid open and flapping.

When she returned to the field, she was relieved to see that Mimi wasn't busy at the stand, and she asked her if she would help her lift the rototiller out of her car.

Between the two of them, they managed to get it onto the ground. Jackie thanked her, and Mimi said goodbye and trotted back to the stand.

The actual use of the rototiller seemed much easier in the hardware store when Howard had given the demonstration. Operation of the machine required a lot of upper body strength, which she didn't have. She promised herself as soon as the field was turned over, she could go home, soak in a hot bath, and then open a bottle of wine. And she might even ask her parents to keep Anna overnight. She kept that thought in the forefront of her mind like a carrot dangling on a stick.

She'd finally begun to get the hang of it when she heard a vehicle pull up behind her. Tom Anderson in his brand-new shiny pickup truck. She groaned loudly. *Oh no, what is he doing here?* She didn't want him to see her struggling. He'd see in an instant that she didn't know what she was doing.

Tom jumped out of his truck and ambled over to where Jackie stood, next to the rototiller. She wished her face wasn't red and glistening with sweat. She wished her hair hadn't frizzed with the exertion, but there was nothing to be done about that. There was only so much you could control in life. There were too many variables.

He walked with his hands tucked into the front pockets of his jeans. He wore sunglasses, so it was hard to read his expression.

"Jackie, what are you doing?" he asked. He couldn't have been much older than her, but despite his youth, heavy lines tracked along his face. Instead of detracting from his handsomeness, they only added to it in a rough, rugged fashion.

"Um, prepping the field." She'd thought that was obvious.

"Didn't Dad tell you? I'm going to prep the field," he said. He removed his sunglasses, folded them, and put them in his shirt pocket.

She looked for any evidence that he was about to make fun of her or criticize her, but she found none.

Her shoulders sagged. "No, he didn't mention it. He must have forgot."

"I'm really sorry about that. He's distracted with Aunt Carol."

"I understand," she said truthfully. There had certainly been times in the last three years she'd been distracted by the events in her life.

"Well, let's leave Dad out of it for a moment and I'll tell you what I'm going to do," he said. He shook his head. "Again, I'm really sorry you've gone through all this trouble."

Now she felt bad that he felt bad. "It's all right. Now what were you saying about prepping the field?"

"I'll have to kill all the grass and weeds," he said, sweeping his hand across the two-acre plot. His arm was faded tan and muscular, with ropey veins running along the length of it.

She tried not to stare but couldn't seem to help it.

Tom was speaking, and Jackie turned her attention to what he was saying.

"Then I'll plow the field to break up the soil." He paused and looked at her, his eyes locking with hers. "When that's all done, you can plant the seeds."

"When will that be?" she asked.

"A couple of days."

"Will you let me know when the field is ready?" Jackie asked.

"Sure. Look, we really appreciate you doing this for us," he said.

His gratitude embarrassed her, and she mumbled something about it being no problem at all.

"And we need to remember that you're not a farmer," he said with a roguish smile.

He wasn't being mean or critical. He was being nice, and Jackie could use some nice in her life.

She blew out a deep breath.

He frowned, the creases in his forehead deepening. "Hey, don't sweat it. You're growing flowers."

"But this is important," she objected.

He nodded slowly. "Yes, it is. But accept that all is not going to run smoothly. That things are going to go wrong despite the best intentions."

"That doesn't sound so optimistic," she said.

He shrugged. "It's based on experience. Things do go wrong. You just have to deal with them as they come up and move on."

Curious, she asked, "Is that your philosophy for life, too, or just farming in general?"

"Everything, I suppose."

"I will admit to you, Tom, I've never grown flowers before. I can maintain things once they're planted though," she said, thinking of the gardens Jason had created at their house.

"Then you're halfway there," he said reassuringly.

She laughed. "You make it sound so easy."

"It is, once you get the hang of it."

"I'm going to hold you to that," she said, smiling.

"I hope you do."

He hadn't shaved and his stubble was dark. She remembered how that felt: stubble against her own skin, like sandpaper. Not an unpleasant sensation.

Silence descended, and it threatened to loom and become awkward.

He glanced at the rototiller and then to her. "Did you rent that from the hardware store?"

"Yes, Howard at the hardware store assured me I'd have no problem using it."

"That Howard is a salesman," Tom said with a laugh.

Jackie had to agree with him. "That's for sure."

"Would you mind helping me get it into my trunk?" she asked. "I've got to have it back by tonight."

"I'm on my way to the hardware store now. I'll take it back for you."

"I couldn't ask you to do that," she said.

"You didn't ask. I offered."

"I don't mind taking it back."

"Neither do I, since I'm on my way there anyway."

Before she could say anything more on the subject, he wheeled the rototiller to the parking lot and lifted it up into the bed of the truck.

"Thanks, I appreciate it."

"No problem," he said. "I'll text you when the field is ready. Then we can meet out here to get started on the seeds."

"I can plant the seeds myself," she said.

"I'm sure you can. But it's a big field and I'll show you how to use the seeder."

As they went their separate ways to their vehicles, she didn't know what possessed her but she called out, "If you need me to remind you from time to time that I'm not a farmer, I can. And I will."

His laugh was hearty as he threw his hand up in a goodbye wave.

What are you doing? she chastised herself.

No flirting!

Chapter Twenty-Four

Before going to pick up Anna from her parents' house, Jackie was overcome with a craving for ice cream. And since the weather was reasonably warm for early May, she decided to stop at the Pink Parlor and purchase a hot fudge sundae with extra hot fudge. She didn't allow herself to feel guilty about going alone or not getting anything for Anna. As the only grandchild in the family, Anna enjoyed more than her fair share of sweets and other treats. Jackie only wanted a few more minutes to herself before she picked up her daughter and went home.

A few people stood in line for ice cream. As the months wore on and the mercury rose, the line would get longer until it snaked out the door. But for now, she had no trouble finding a seat at one of the cute white wrought iron bistro tables in the front section of the shop, near the window. She enjoyed her sundae, careful not to drip hot fudge sauce on the pink-and-white striped seat cushions, and sighed when she was done, it had been that delicious.

Afterward, she stood on the sidewalk for a moment, digging through her purse for her sunglasses. Instead of returning to the parking lot behind the ice cream parlor and retrieving her car, the spirit moved her to continue walking along Main Street, heading north until she reached the end of it, right where it crossed over Erie and turned into Star Shine Drive. She turned left, crossed the street, and stepped onto the wooden boardwalk that would take her to the beach.

The sun was a bright white orb in the sky but the lake, whose waters still ran cold, lent a nip to the air. Jackie zipped up her light jacket. The freshness of the spring air felt good. She tilted her head toward the sun, letting the warmth bathe over her face.

There were a few people on the beach, mostly walkers. No one in swimsuits yet; it was a little early for that. Smatterings of conversations floated toward her on the cool breeze blowing in with the incoming waves. A lone seagull circled and swooped, his wings spread, gliding and slicing across the cloudless blue sky.

She started walking, her course parallel to Main Street, keeping her distance from the surf as she didn't want to get her canvas sneakers wet. Further ahead, she spotted Lily Monroe and her dog, Charlie, a merle Great Dane.

The dog didn't venture far from Lily's side as she bent over and collected beach glass, dropping it into a bucket.

Despite her misgivings about the sunflower project, Jackie had to admit that the kindness of the Andersons went a long way. Her meeting with Tom earlier had lifted a weight off her shoulders. And although she hoped she didn't make any mistakes; it was nice to know they wouldn't hold it against her if she did.

"Hi, Jackie," Lily called out.

Jackie lifted her hand in a return salute.

Charlie, wagging his tail, loped toward her.

"Charlie!" Lily called but he ignored her, heading in Jackie's direction. Lily broke into a trot after him.

When he reached Jackie, she bent over and rubbed his neck. "Hello, Charlie."

"I'm sorry about that," Lily said, grabbing hold of his collar.

Lily looked well. She had her blonde hair clipped up and wore a jean jacket over a lemon-yellow T-shirt and a pair of jeans.

"Don't worry about it," Jackie said. "We all know that despite his size, Charlie is as gentle as a lamb."

"He's also very clumsy and doesn't know his own strength."

"There is that too," Jackie agreed. She'd seen the dog in action. Although a gentle giant, he was infamous for knocking things and small children over. Mothers with toddlers and preschoolers gave him a wide berth.

"How've you been, Jackie?"

Jackie nodded and gave her pat answer. "I'm fine."

"How's Anna?"

"Fine. She's with her grandparents today." She traced an arc with her shoe, shifting the sand.

"It must be nice to have a little time to yourself."

"It is," Jackie agreed. "How's business?"

"Brisk," Lily said with a sigh. "But it's amazing. I'm out here every day and it seems like the beach never runs out of glass."

Jackie glanced out toward the horizon. "It makes you wonder what else is out there."

Lily followed her gaze and agreed.

Jackie thought she should be moving on and picking up Anna. She almost felt like she was playing hooky.

"Any chance you'll sign up for the beach glass workshop?" Lily asked.

She didn't want to hurt Lily's feelings. The Monroe sisters were nice people and after Jason died, their grandmother, Junie Reynolds, had been so good to her, sending flowers and a card, even bringing over homemade soup. The kindness had not been forgotten.

"I don't know yet," Jackie said. "It sounds interesting, but my time is kind of booked."

"I understand, no pressure," Lily said.

Jackie smiled. "Thanks." She exhaled and said, "I better get going."

"Me too. Simon is going to wonder what happened to me," Lily said with a laugh.

They parted, and Jackie thought Lily was lucky to have someone who worried about her. She used to have that too, at one point in her life.

Chapter Twenty-Five

Carol

Morning was her most difficult time of the day and to Carol that didn't make any sense. You would think that after sleeping all night, you'd be at your best when you woke up. That you'd be refreshed, with a gradual decrease in energy over the course of the day. But that wasn't the case. In fact, it was the opposite for her. She found that after a slow start in the morning—she had no choice but to take her time and pace herself—she'd begin to feel less lethargic by noontime.

At Gail's suggestion, she agreed to a personal care aide five days a week to help her with bathing and her activities of daily living. She didn't bother to protest and say it wasn't needed, because it was. If she wanted to remain at home as long as possible, she needed to utilize all the available resources. Ben and Tom helped out. They were a godsend. Ben was over in the morning to make sure Carol could get out of bed, and Tom arrived in the evening to tuck her in for the night. During the day, Lottie and Dawn popped in and out to check on her. She was grateful for all their help.

The personal care aide's name was Melanie Morgan. She was a middle-aged woman who'd gone into this line of work after her kids were all grown and gone. With a laugh and a shrug, she'd said to Carol, "What can I say? I like taking care of people."

Within a few days, they had developed their routine. Melanie didn't arrive until noon at Carol's request. Melanie had been agreeable, stating that all the patients wanted the early hours, so coming at mid-day was no problem.

They did the same thing every visit: Melanie followed Carol and her walker toward the bathroom as their first task was washing up. For the present, a shower every other day was plenty, with hair-washing twice a week. Too much effort sapped Carol of her precious energy.

Today was not a shower day. Carol sat on the seat of her walker at the bathroom sink and washed her face and brushed her teeth. When she was finished, Melanie handed her a towel and then helped her get dressed. After, Carol always had to sit for a minute before standing up. Melanie reassured her, "Take your time."

Carol made her way back to the den as Melanie made her lunch and did some light housekeeping.

She looked out the window. The sky was an endless blue, and she knew that tomorrow was the day that Jackie Arnold was planting the sunflower seeds. She closed her eyes and imagined what it would look like when they all began to sprout.

"Do you want anything?" Lottie asked from the kitchen, unloading the groceries from the bag.

"I'm fine. Melanie was here earlier, and she made me a grilled cheese and some tomato basil soup," Carol told her. What she didn't tell her friend was that she was only able to eat half of it. Her appetite wasn't what it used to be.

Lottie stood in the kitchen doorway and held up a half gallon of ice cream. "I got you some butter pecan. I know that's your favorite."

"Thanks," Carol said. She'd have a very small bowl before bed. It was only a few tablespoons; it was all she could manage.

She heard the freezer drawer open and close as Lottie put the ice cream away. Her friend returned and said, "How's it going with the sunflower field?"

"They're planting the seeds tomorrow," Carol said proudly.

She wished she were strong enough to drive over and park the car and watch. But that would take too much out of her.

"Jackie's little girl is real cute," Lottie said.

Eventually, after Lottie put the groceries away, she came and sat in the den. But she bounced back up. Carol wished she had half her vitality.

"Did you want tea or coffee or something else?" Lottie said. "I can make lemonade or iced tea."

"No thanks, I'm good. Sit down for a moment."

Lottie sat in the chair closest to Carol.

Carol frowned and half-turned in her chair to look for something on her table.

"Do you need something, Carol?" Lottie asked, anxious to be helpful.

Carol smiled. "Nope, I have it," she said, reaching for the items in question.

Since she was young, she'd never been one to wear a lot of jewelry, but she had some nice pieces. The emerald pendant necklace from Todd and the gold bracelet with the stars and crescent moon her parents had given her were the two pieces she treasured most. She handed these to Lottie now.

"Will I put them away?" Lottie asked.

Carol shook her head. "No. I want you to have them."

Lottie had nothing to say. She was too round-eyed and gawping. Finally, she recovered. "What? No way. Those are yours."

She handed them back to Carol, who pushed her hand away. "No, Lottie, they belong to you now."

Quietly, Lottie said, "I can't accept these."

Carol scowled. "Why not?"

"Because it's too much!" Lottie slid the pieces over on the table, but Carol pushed them back.

"Loretta Gallagher Moloney, if you don't take these, I will be very angry," Carol said firmly. She didn't want to be fighting about this. She'd made up her mind. These were her two most treasured pieces, and she wanted Lottie to have them.

Tears filled Lottie's eyes and she sniffled. Carol handed her the box of tissues.

"Thanks," Lottie said, pulling one from the box. "But, Carol, why?" She dabbed at her eyes with the tissue.

Carol rolled her eyes. Did she have to explain it? "Because you're my oldest and dearest friend. You're more than a friend to me. You're like a sister."

"You were a better sister to me than my own sisters," Lottie

Pretty soon they were both crying.

"We've been so close," Carol said.

They were twin flames really. Through thick and thin over almost eight decades, they had stuck by each other's side.

There was also a small provision for Lottie in her will, but she knew her friend would value the jewelry more than money.

"What about Melvin?" Lottie asked.

"I don't know yet," Carol said. She had put off finding a home for him. That was another thing she dreaded: parting from her cat. Melvin wasn't that old, only six, so he still had some life left in him.

"You know I'd take him in a moment," Lottie said.

"I know, but you need to think of Dennis." Lottie's husband had terrible allergies.

"Maybe I could get rid of Dennis and keep Melvin," Lottie joked.

Carol laughed. "You are too much, Lottie."

Carol had asked Ben and Tom to come by, and they arrived in the evening after the six o'clock news. David lived out of town, and this wasn't important enough to drag him home. Either Ben or Tom could pass on the message.

She was glad they were there; she was weary, and she'd have them help her to bed before they left. She could read for a little while before she went to sleep. There was no way she could stay awake until ten o'clock the way she used to.

First, she gave Ben an envelope containing her wishes for her funeral, including readings and psalms and songs chosen for the service. Ben looked grim but said nothing, only nodded. She informed them that her will was with Arthur Stodges at his office.

Tom interrupted. "Aunt Carol, we don't need to talk about this."

Carol held up her hand. "I know it's uncomfortable, but it would put my mind at ease if you knew some of my wishes. I've already given Dawn the outfit I want to wear at my wake."

Ben cleared his throat and studied the envelope in his hands.

"Also, I don't care what you do with the contents of the house," she said, directing this statement to Ben as he would inherit it. "But I ask that you give all my books away for free."

"Will do," Ben said gruffly.

"Dawn is welcome to my jewelry, but I've given the star and crescent moon bracelet and the emerald necklace to Lottie."

Ben swiped at an errant tear. "Aw shucks, I had my eye on that pendant."

This broke the ice, and they all laughed.

Chapter Twenty-Six

Jackie

Jackie and Anna were at the field, waiting for Tom. The warm weather continued but the sky was colorless, with no sign of the sun. Everything looked gray.

The field had been prepped as Tom promised. The grass was gone and the earth had been turned up, revealing rich, dark soil. How she had ever thought she could dig up the two acres with a shovel or even a rototiller was beyond her.

As she waited, she took delight in watching Anna running through a grassy patch along the side of the field, blowing bubbles through a wand. The iridescent bubbles floated up and off into the sky. It looked magical.

The rumble of an engine distracted her, and she turned her head and spotted the familiar pickup truck of Tom Anderson. This time she noticed something different: the logo of his fledgling business, the Hideaway Bay Vineyard, had been added to the side of his truck. He pulled in at the end of the field and Jackie walked in his direction.

"Come on, Anna," she called, "time to get to work."

Anna turned around and followed Jackie, waving the wand at her side, bubbles streaming out behind her.

"Hey, Jackie," Tom greeted.

"Hi, Tom," Jackie said, standing in front of him.

Anna clung to the back of Jackie's leg. She peeked around to stare at Tom.

Tom got down on his haunches, the ring of keys on his belt jangling. "And this must be Anna."

Anna smiled, nodding her head but remaining mute, squeezing her mother's knee with her grip.

"Say hello to Mr. Anderson," Jackie prompted.

"You can call me Tom," he said. And then, "May I call you Anna?"

More nodding but still no speaking.

He smiled and stood.

"I'm going to show you how to use the seeder. It's fairly straightforward and once you get the hang of it, you'll be fine. Let me go get it—I'll be right back."

He jogged to the storage shed behind the fruit-and-veg stand. Within minutes he was wheeling what she presumed to be the seeder in their direction.

So that's what that thing was.

It had a long, curved handle and two wheels, kind of like a bike, the back one smaller than the front. The frame was aluminum, and there was a chute and a chain between the wheels.

"Have you ever used one of these before?" he asked, parking it between them.

"No. I've never even seen one before," she admitted.

"Don't worry. They're easy to use. And again, if you have any problems, call me," he said.

She hoped she wouldn't have to call him; she was pretty sure he was busy enough with his vineyard.

"Step over here, so I can make sure the handle's not too high or too low."

She did as he asked and watched him bending over, his back in front of her as he adjusted the height of the handle. His shoulders were broad and tapered to a narrow waist.

Once it was adjusted to her height, he pointed to a large black tub at the base of the handle. "That's the seed hopper. You pour them in here and use this disk to space the seeds." He held up a round plastic disc and then inserted it into place inside the hopper. "The disk sets the seeds at specific intervals." He double-checked the markings and said, "For sunflower seeds, I'd say space them six to seven inches apart and plant them at a depth of one inch."

"That's what my research says as well."

The corner of his mouth tugged upward. "I'm impressed."

She felt a blush bloom out on her cheeks.

"Okay, how do I know the seed is being planted at a one-inch depth?" she asked.

"I'm going to set the ground opener to one inch," he responded. He bent down again, adjusted something on the bottom of the machine, and stood. Pointing to the front wheel, he said, "The front wheel creates the furrow, the seed drops through the chute there, and then the chain and back wheel cover it with soil. And then you're done."

"Presto."

He laughed and repeated, "Yeah, presto, just like that. Let's see how it works." He went to his truck and hauled a twenty-five-pound bag of sunflower seeds off the back of it.

"I've got three varieties here. I would divide the field up in three parts or you'll be going back and forth planting seeds and well, don't make it harder than it needs to be."

"Right."

"Ready to give it a try?"

"I am."

"Can I do it?" Anna piped in. She'd been quiet the entire time, her eyes steadfast on Tom as he explained how the seeder operated.

"You can help me," Jackie said.

Tom pulled a small utility knife from his pocket and slit across the top of the bag. "Anna, I'm going to give you the most important job."

Anna's eyes widened and she jumped up and down, clapping her hands.

Jackie and Tom laughed.

He opened the bag wide, took a handful of seeds, and threw them into the hopper. "Hold on, I've got a scoop you can use."

He disappeared into the cab of his truck and returned with an orange plastic scoop. He demonstrated to Anna how to scoop up the seed and fill the hopper with it. Anna filled the hopper with sunflower seeds as Jackie watched, amused.

"You've got a great helper, Jackie," Tom said.

"I agree!"

When the hopper was full of seed, Jackie took the handle and hesitated at the edge of the field. She pushed the seeder in a straight line down the field, watching it perform its magic. Anna skipped along next to her.

When she arrived at the end of the field, she stopped and turned the seeder around to start the next row.

Looking behind her, she could clearly see the row she'd seeded, flattened by the back tire.

Tom had walked over to the other end of the field.

"How much distance should I leave between the rows?" she asked.

"You're going to want to be able to walk between the rows, or else you'll end up having to cut a path. Best to do it now. I'd leave a space of between two and three feet," he suggested.

She nodded. It occurred to her that if a path needed to be cut, it wouldn't be her doing it. It would be Tom.

"I'll split the difference and do two and a half feet," she said.

"Perfect."

She wondered if he was always so amiable. If so, he was going to be easy to work for. She guesstimated the distance between two rows, looked over at Tom, who nodded, and started her second row. When she finished the third row, Tom waved over to her to let her know he was leaving.

Understanding, she waved back. He couldn't spend all day holding her hand, he had his own business to tend to.

Anna filled the hopper with seeds and insisted she could push the seeder herself. But when it proved too cumbersome for her, Jackie sensed a meltdown brewing and suggested, "Come on, we can do it together."

Anna put her hand on the stem of the handle while Jackie folded both her hands over the curved handle, and they started the fourth row.

Later that evening, after a quick meal at the Chat and Nibble, Jackie practically crawled into her house. Anna was unusually quiet, all the fresh air and jumping around outside having worn her out. It was going to be an early night for both.

She ran the water for the bath and set Anna in it. Anna yawned and didn't bother pulling out her bath toys. After her bath, Jackie combed her wet hair, got her a snack, and parked her in front of the television.

Anna settled in the corner of the sofa with her blanket and stared without blinking at a Disney movie.

Jackie went to the bedroom to strip off her clothes. The jeans and T-shirt she wore were covered in mud and dirt. Every muscle in her body ached, and she didn't know if she'd ever stand straight again. She wasn't a natural exerciser, but she was a big believer in fresh air. And although she didn't have a gym membership, she tried to get Anna out as much as possible. Her exercise routine usually consisted of walking behind Anna on her bike with training wheels as she cycled around a few streets in Hideaway Bay.

She tied the sash around her bathrobe and returned to the living room, where she found Anna fast asleep on the sofa. She carried her to bed and the child did not stir. Jackie settled her in, pulled up the blanket, turned off the light, and switched on the night-light in the hall.

Leaving the bathroom door ajar, she ran the water for a bath a second time. When the tub was full, with steam rising off the surface of the water, Jackie stripped off her robe and laid it in a pile at the door. She stepped into the tub and sank down into it, leaning back and groaning at the feeling of being embraced by hot water that smelled of eucalyptus and spearmint, her favorite bath salts. Every single muscle in her body, including the ones she didn't know she had, screamed in relief when submerged in the steamy, fragrant water. Immediately, she closed her eyes and smiled.

It had been a good day. The first one in a long time.

Chapter Twenty-Seven

Something woke Jackie in the middle of the night, and she turned on her side, peering into the darkness, trying to make out the numbers on the digital clock on the dresser. Squinting, she read one forty-five. She listened and realized the sound that had woken her was the rain pounding against the roof. There was something cozy about being all tucked up in your bed and listening to the rain outside. Smiling, she closed her eyes, her head sinking back into her pillow, and fell fast asleep.

That same clock blared five hours later, and Jackie sat bolt upright in bed, surprised she'd slept so well. It had been a long time since she'd had a good night's sleep.

Before she went through her morning routine of washing up and using the bathroom, she peeked in on Anna. The child was all curled up on her side, blanket up to her waist, hugging her pillow and still asleep.

As Jackie got ready for her day, she turned on the coffeemaker, and soon the house was filled with the aroma of freshly brewed coffee.

Jackie had the idea that she might take a drive out to the field and look at it. She wasn't expecting anything to have sprouted overnight, but still.

She gave Anna another half hour before she woke her, made her a breakfast of cereal and juice, and got her ready to go to her grandparents' house. Although Jackie could make her own hours, she liked to be at her desk by nine.

When she finally emerged from her house with a coffee in one hand and her keys in the other, Anna at her side, she glanced up at the sky. The warmth from the sun was feeble, but she was encouraged by the blue sky. She wasn't too concerned when she saw puddles everywhere. In fact, she noticed them, but didn't give them a second thought.

She drove off, noting the highway department dealing with a plugged sewer at the end of her street. Anna was quiet in her car seat behind Jackie, still not fully awake.

After dropping Anna off at her parents' house, she drove up Erie Street to the highway.

Ben and Tom stood at the edge of the newly planted field, arms crossed over their chests, their expressions grim. She wondered if she'd done something wrong, and suddenly she was sorry she showed up.

When she approached them, they turned to look at her. Neither smiled. Immediately, she wondered if something had happened to Carol but then dismissed it, thinking they wouldn't be there if that were the case. Her thoughts turned to her work yesterday; she must have made some kind of mistake, because they looked so glum. Her stomach clenched.

"Good morning, Ben. Tom," she said, attempting a demeanor of cheerfulness despite not feeling it. She pushed her bangs out of her eyes.

"Morning," Ben said.

"Jackie," Tom said.

"We take it you know what happened to the field," Ben started.

Now her stomach did a somersault. "No, what?" She scanned the area, seeing that it was covered in water. A little line of panic spread through her and blossomed. As the panic reached the end of her fingertips, she trembled.

"The field flooded," Tom said, placing his hands on his hips. At his neck there was a view of the white T-shirt he wore beneath his short-sleeved plaid shirt.

Were they blaming her? Was she supposed to know they were going to get all that rain? Was part of her remit to watch the weather forecast every night and divine whether it would have any bearing on the field? Maybe it was.

"I had no idea—" she said, unsure of what to say. What did they want her to do?

"It's not your fault," Ben said with a reassuring smile. "That field has adequate drainage. We might have gotten a little too much rain too soon last night."

"I should have paid a little more attention to the weather forecast," Tom said.

"They weren't predicting this much rain," Ben said.

Jackie stepped closer and stood next to Ben. Her mouth fell open. The field of rich soil where she'd spent most of the day planting seeds with the seeder and which had caused every muscle in her body to ache was now covered in water. Small black-and-white-striped sunflower seeds floated on the surface.

"Oh no," she cried, throwing her hand to her mouth.

All that hard work, now floating around on the surface of the field. And it seemed worse now. At least yesterday the field was plantable, but now it was awash in thick mud with seeds everywhere.

Her shoulders dropped and she slipped her hands into the back pockets of her jeans, feeling overwhelmed. She said nothing.

If there was a bright spot—and she'd have a hard time finding one—at least it hadn't been her fault. She certainly couldn't control the weather.

Sensing her despair, Ben turned and looked at her and gave her a kind smile. "Don't give up. It's a minor setback. In another day or two it should be ready for planting again."

"As long as it doesn't rain," Jackie said. She tried not to be pessimistic, but she couldn't help it. In recent years, it had been her default mode.

"I can replant the field," Tom volunteered.

Jackie shook her head. "No, thanks, Tom. I agreed to do this and what did you say to me? That sometimes things go wrong, and it's best to deal with it and move on?"

He smiled. "Something like that."

"Good. How will I know when to replant?" she asked.

"Let me check the field every day and I'll send you a text," Tom said.

"Okay. But it won't be for a few days?"

"No, the field has to dry out first," Ben said. He glanced at his watch. "I've got to go help Carol get out of bed. I'll talk to you later."

"Okay, Dad."

"Bye, Ben," Jackie said.

She stood with Tom in the field.

"I'm sorry about this, Jackie."

She waved his apology away. "No problem. Not that I'm an expert with the seeder, but I should have it replanted in no time."

"You seem to be taking it well."

She shrugged. "Like you said, things happen. Things go wrong. Best to just get on with it."

Chapter Twenty-Eight

Carol

She couldn't remember ever being this nervous. Not even when they told her the tumors were malignant and that the cancer had spread had she been so anxious.

Out of the blue, her ex-husband, Todd, had called and asked if he could come for a visit. She hadn't heard from him in years. Decades. Not since twenty years ago when he'd stopped by to see her when he'd flown in for his mother's funeral.

He'd remained in Chicago and never left. Through common friends, she'd sometimes hear what he was doing or what he was up to, and her first thought was always, *He should have been doing that with me.*

Although she'd retired from the library more than ten years ago, she still kept in touch with other librarians and met annually for lunch. That group included Todd's sister, Janet, who was also retired. Their friendship had waned due to Carol and Todd's divorce, but they remained civil and courteous to one another. She suspected it was Janet who had told Todd about her life-limiting disease. She'd missed the annual lunch due to illness that year, and her being sick had been no secret.

Todd was on time. But he'd always been punctual.

When Melanie left, Carol asked her to leave the front door open. When the doorbell rang, she called out, inviting the visitor in. She stood from her chair with great difficulty, cursing her dying body, wishing she wasn't so weak and tired, and that she could move faster.

Her heart was pounding, and her mouth went dry as he appeared in the den of the home they once shared. As soon as she saw him, her heart melted.

He wore a short-sleeved blue-and-red checked shirt and a pair of lightweight khaki pants. Like her, he had aged. Although his hair was now white and thin on top and there were jowls and age spots and deep lines much like her own, his hazel eyes were the same, and his expression was still full of warmth and kindness.

She'd put on her favorite headscarf for the occasion, the one that was a kaleidoscope of colors of blue, purple, pink, and turquoise.

"Carol!" he said, grinning broadly.

"Come in, come in," she said, waving him in.

He stepped in, looking around at the room.

"Just as I pictured you, surrounded by books," he said with a smile.

If he was shocked by her appearance, he didn't let on.

He greeted her by placing his hands on her elbows and kissing her on the cheek. With a shaky wave, she indicated that he should sit down.

She reached behind her, taking hold of the arm of the chair and sinking into the cushions with great relief. He made himself comfortable on the sofa, leaning back and laying his arm along the back of it.

The cat walked by, curious, gave Todd a look, decided he warranted no further investigation, and headed off to the kitchen.

Todd looked around at the well-stocked bookshelves. "I see your collection has grown. Impressive."

"My love of books was no secret," Carol said with a laugh. "Then or now."

"Janet told me you were ill, and I hope you don't mind my coming to see you," he said. His smile had disappeared, and his tone was sober.

Despite their divorce, she bore him no ill will. Any memories of Todd or ruminations about him were tinged with regret.

"How are you feeling?" he asked.

She shrugged. "Okay. My symptoms are well managed by hospice."

"I'm glad to hear that. But I am sorry about your prognosis," he said quietly.

"What are you going to do. It's just one of those things," she replied. Before the conversation turned maudlin, she asked, "Would you like something to eat or drink? I have iced tea." She hoped he still liked it. People's tastes were known to change over time.

"You remember." He smiled fondly.

"I do."

"I would love some, if it's not too much trouble," he said.

"I'm afraid I'll have to ask you to bring it in. There's also a cake on the counter, please cut yourself a slice."

Before she'd left, Melanie had put glasses, dessert plates, and silverware on the counter next to the cake stand.

He stood. "Would you like some cake?"

"No, thank you, just some iced tea."

It was strange to hear him moving around in the kitchen that had once been theirs. She closed her eyes, thinking back fifty years to how she used to listen to him in the kitchen while she was getting ready for work. The gurgle of the stovetop percolator, corn flakes spilling into a bowl, and the sound of toast popping up. After he'd left, it was one of the many things she missed about him: the comforting sounds of someone else in the house, someone you loved.

He returned shortly, carrying in two glasses of iced tea. He handed one to Carol and set the other down on a coaster on the coffee table. He headed back to the kitchen and soon returned with a plate of cake.

As they sipped the refreshing iced tea and as Todd ate his cake, they spoke of generalities, what they'd been doing. Like her, he'd been retired for years. In his case, almost twenty. He was enjoying retirement. He played a lot of golf, traveled extensively, and belonged to a few seniors' clubs. He asked after Lottie.

"She has a lot of grandkids, so that makes her happy."

Todd laughed. "Good for her."

"Can I ask you a question?" she started. She figured, now that she was a dying woman, she'd hold nothing back.

"Shoot," he said, scraping the last bit of frosting off his plate.

"How come you never remarried?" she asked. She knew he had a lady friend of long-term standing, but they'd never married.

Todd set his plate on the coffee table. He leaned forward, hands clasped between his knees. "That's a good question. I've come close to remarrying twice."

She had not known that. "But you didn't."

He shook his head. "No, I didn't. I didn't think I could ever love anyone the way I loved you. You were the only girl for me."

Carol swallowed hard but could not dislodge the lump that had taken up residence in her throat. "I'm sorry, Todd."

"Yeah, me too," he said wistfully, without rancor. "That we couldn't find a way to make things work is the only regret of my life."

She had more than one regret, but her broken marriage was definitely one of the things at the top of her list. "I'm sorry it didn't work out too. But I couldn't leave, and you couldn't stay."

"Looking back, I should have stayed," he said.

"Don't say that." Too much time had passed to start second-guessing decisions they'd made years ago. "You wouldn't have been happy staying. It's easy to say that now but at the time, if you had stayed, you probably would have been miserable."

"I suppose," he said. "And you couldn't leave your mother."

Carol drew in a deep breath. "There was no way I could leave Ben."

Confusion clouded Todd's face. "Ben? Why in the world not?"

"It's complicated," she said, her expression pinched.

"How?" he asked. He held out his hands, palms up and said, "I don't understand."

She looked at her iced tea, the glass still half full. Did she dare tell him now the secret that had kept her in Hideaway Bay? The secret she'd been too afraid to tell him fifty years ago?

He waited, patient and expectant.

Finally, she looked over at him. "Ben is my son."

Todd blinked, stared at her, and said, "I'm sorry?" As if he hadn't heard correctly.

Carol lost her nerve.

"Ben is *your* son?" Todd repeated.

"Yes," she whispered, almost choking on the truth.

He leaned back and let out a long, low whistle. "Well, shame on me. I didn't see that one coming."

Carol's eyes darted around the room looking at anything but Todd.

"Carol," he said softly, bringing her attention back to him.

"Yes?" she asked. She was afraid he was about to say goodbye. That he was about to get up and leave.

"Tell me what happened," he encouraged.

So she told him the whole story: how she'd been sent to live with her aunt in Pennsylvania, how the difficult delivery had left her unable to have any more children. How that fact—that she would have no more children—had led her parents to make the decision to adopt the baby and raise him as their own.

"That's why you wouldn't leave Hideaway Bay. It's why you've never left," he said.

"I couldn't."

He put up his hand. "You don't have to sell it to me, Carol. I understand. Now."

He seemed to digest this news, delivered late, and it took him a few moments before he asked, "Why didn't you ever tell me?" His tone was not accusatory; it was more one of concern.

Carol swallowed hard and tried to control the tremor in her voice. "I was afraid. I was afraid if I told you that I had had a baby at the age of sixteen that you'd leave me. That you'd never look at me the same. And I could bear you leaving me; I have borne it. But I'd never be able to bear it if somehow it had diminished your love for me."

"I could never think any less of you," he said quietly.

"We say that now, but what about *then*? Times were different."

"I wish you had trusted me with this information," he said.

"I wanted to, I really did. You have no idea how much of a burden it is to hold on to a secret like that for your whole life."

She took a leap and asked a question she had always wondered about. "If I had told you, would you have done anything differently?"

"The noble part of me wants to say yes, but I was young then and very selfish."

Carol laughed and it lessened the tension in the room. "Todd, a lot of things could be said about you, but being selfish isn't one of them."

"But I left you and went to Chicago to pursue my own dreams," he said. His voice was pained, and this was not what Carol had wanted, not this late in the game. It was too late for remorse or regret.

"Don't beat yourself up, Todd, promise me you won't," she pleaded. When he didn't say anything, she said, "It will change nothing, we'll still end up in the same place."

"Does Ben know that you're his mother?"

Carol shook her head.

"Please tell him," he said. "Tell him, before you go."

Chapter Twenty-Nine

Jackie

Three days passed before Jackie returned to the field. The weather had turned in her favor; the rain had stopped, and the warm sun had dried out the field enough for her to plant the seeds again.

Mimi came out from behind the produce stand to say hello while Jackie pulled the seeder out of the storage shed. Anna looked at her shyly but soon warmed up to her. The teenager kept Anna occupied while Jackie rooted around in the shed, looking for the bags of seeds. Once found, she heaved a bag up off the ground and set it on top of the seeder.

She called out to Anna to come along to the field, and the response that came back was, "Can I stay with Mimi?"

Jackie was about to say no when Mimi piped in. "I don't mind. I can keep an eye on her up here."

"Are you sure?" Jackie asked. She didn't want to take advantage.

"It's not a problem."

"All right, then. I'll be as quick as I can."

"Take your time," Mimi replied.

To Anna, Jackie said, "Behave yourself, please, and listen to Mimi."

"Okay, Mommy."

Jackie pushed the seeder back to the field, set it up as Tom had showed her, and got to work. She walked the contraption along, making sure the seed was deposited and the furrow closed behind her as she went. As the seeds depleted in the hopper, she was confident they were being planted. Occasionally she glanced toward the fruit-and-veg stand but as the stand faced away from the field, there was no glimpse of Anna or Mimi. She hoped Anna was behaving; Mimi was working after all.

The sunshine was sharp and bright, glinting off the aluminum frame of the seeder. She hoped it meant summer weather would be there soon. In the distance she could see the lake through the trees, looking shiny and new under all that sunshine.

She walked the length and breadth of the two acres that morning, the muscles she'd used the other day protesting.

Since she was last there, she'd created different color markers for each row because she'd read somewhere to stagger the planting of the seeds. Today she was planting the rows marked with blue tape. In two weeks, she'd plant the ones marked with yellow tape and then two weeks after that, she'd plant the red-taped rows. She had to admit to a certain level of excitement.

She sank down onto the grass and stretched out her legs, taking a gulp from her water bottle. After a few moments, she pulled out her phone from her pocket and texted Tom to ask about watering, and he replied with a simple *Let Mother Nature do her thing*.

She supposed she should get Anna and return home, but she opted to remain there, sitting out in the sunshine, looking out at the dirt-brown field with tracks of evidence that she'd been there and had got something accomplished.

Jackie finally stood, her muscles aching. Time to get Anna, pack up, and return home. She hauled the planter back to the shed and stored it, pouring any remaining seed back into the bag.

Her daughter was parked on a stool behind the stand, eating out of a small plastic sample cup. More cups lined the stand, holding bite-sized servings of canned peaches.

"Whatcha got there, Anna?" she asked.

"Peaches! And they have their own syrup, but it's not pancake syrup," Anna informed her.

"Can I have a bite?" Jackie asked.

Anna turned halfway on her stool, guarding her cup. "Get your own, Mommy."

"Okay," Jackie said, laughing.

Mimi handed her a sample.

"Thanks, Mimi," Jackie said, taking a mouthful. "I hope she hasn't been too much trouble."

Mimi beamed at the little girl. "Not at all. She's been helping me, haven't you, Anna?"

Anna nodded, her mouth crammed with sweet, syrupy fruit.

The peaches were plump and ripe and sweet. "These are delicious," Jackie said. She glanced over at the Mason jars lining the shelves behind Mimi. "I'll take two." She'd give one to her parents, she thought.

As Mimi rang up Jackie's order and placed the jars in a brown paper bag, an SUV pulled into the parking lot.

Baddie Moore emerged from his vehicle, clearly enthused about the sunny weather in his fluorescent orange board shorts and bright pink polo shirt. He made his way to the stand, nodding in acknowledgement to Jackie.

"Hey, Mimi, please tell me you haven't run out of peaches yet," he said.

"Nope. How many jars, Mr. Moore?"

"Four, please." Turning to Jackie, he said, "I keep telling her to call me Baddie, but it falls on deaf ears."

Jackie laughed. "She's well mannered, that's all. Not a bad thing."

"I suppose not. How's it going?" he asked, with a gesture toward the newly planted field.

"A little bit of a hiccup but we're on track. Planted some more seeds this morning. I'm staggering them so they grow at different times." The confidence in her voice surprised her.

"I don't know the first thing about gardening, but I believe you," Baddie said with a laugh.

Out of the corner of her eye, she spied Anna whispering something to Mimi and pointing to the samples of the peaches on the counter.

"That's enough peaches, Anna, we have to share," she said.

Anna looked at her and scowled. "Aw."

"I think it's a great thing you're doing," Baddie continued. "Carol has done so much for this community."

"Yes, she has," Jackie agreed. And the way Ben and Tom clearly thought so highly of Carol spoke volumes.

"Hold on a minute," Baddie said. "I want to show you something."

He trotted back to his SUV, opened the passenger-side door, and pulled out a book, jogging back to her.

The hardcover book had a plastic cover that was filmy and cracked. The edges of the pages were yellowed and stained.

"Do you always carry a book around with you?" she asked with a grin.

He smiled his easygoing smile and held the book out to her. "I do. That's why I never mind waiting anywhere."

Jackie took it in her hands and studied it. *The First Deadly Sin* by Lawrence Sanders. She lifted her eyebrows at the depiction of a pickaxe on the cover.

"It's my favorite book," he explained. "I've read it about a million times. Every time I do, I discover something new and different about it. When the library had a sale years ago, I bought this and all the other books they had by Lawrence Sanders."

Jackie read the blurb on the back and nodded.

"Before I moved to Hideaway Bay, I'd never picked up a book in my life," Baddie said with a smile. "Then I got laid off and I was home for three months. Leslie was getting sick of my being in the way." He stared off into the distance, perhaps lost in a memory of his late wife. "She suggested I go to the library and get a book." Baddie continued to smile as he told his story. "I went not because I was interested in reading but because I was bored."

Jackie smiled, waiting for him to finish. She handed the book back to him.

"Anyway, Carol asked me what I liked to read, and I said, 'I don't know, I'm not a reader.' She said—and I'll never forget this—that everyone was a reader and that

I simply hadn't found the right book yet. She asked if I was willing to take a recommendation. Not thinking that it would amount to anything, I said sure. Anyway, she gave me two books, and the title of the other one escapes me. But this one"—he propped the book in his hand, cover facing out, and leaned it against his chest—"I couldn't put it down and as they say, I was hooked."

"That's wonderful," Jackie said.

"I read all the detective fiction and thrillers that come into that library. It has been one of my most pleasurable hobbies."

"Hold that pose, Mr. Moore," Mimi called from behind the stand.

Jackie and Baddie exchanged a glance as Mimi dug through her backpack, retrieving a mini instant camera. She ran over and stood in front of Baddie and Jackie. Jackie stepped back, out of the frame.

"This will make a great picture," Mimi said, looking through the viewfinder.

Baddie looked both amused and agreeable. He resumed his pose, casual and relaxed in his board shorts, polo shirt, and battered deck shoes. He held the book in front of him and smiled. Mimi snapped the shutter button, then pulled out the photo.

"That's amazing," Jackie said out loud.

"I know, right?" Mimi said enthusiastically. "My grandmother gave me this for Christmas. I love it!"

"That's a great idea," Jackie said.

"It's like those old Polaroid cameras," Baddie said.

As they hunched over the photo, waiting for it to develop fully, a thought occurred to Jackie.

"I've got an idea."

"Let's hear it," Baddie said with an encouraging smile.

"I think we should take instant snaps of people in the community with a book that Carol recommended to them. A book that either hooked them on reading or had a profound effect on their life."

"Jeez, Jackie, that's a great idea," he said enthusiastically. "It would be a way of showing Carol how much she means to the town. After Leslie died, I was lost for a while. But one day Carol stopped over with a book from the library. A new writer. It helped, the distraction and pleasure of reading if only to take a break for a while from being sad."

"I can take the pictures," Mimi said excitedly, holding up her camera.

"You don't mind?" Jackie said.

Mimi shook her head.

"But that'll get expensive with all the film," Jackie said. After all, she was only a teenaged girl working a part-time job.

"I'll tell you what," Baddie said. "I'll supply the film if Mimi takes the pictures."

Jackie and Mimi looked at each other and smiled.

"Deal?" Baddie asked.

"Deal," Mimi said, sticking out her hand, which Baddie vigorously shook.

"How will we let people know about this project?" Jackie asked, voicing an immediate concern.

"Not to worry," Baddie said. "We'll get the word out without Carol finding out—if you want it to be a surprise, that is."

"I think it would be a lovely surprise," Jackie said softly.

He nodded and said, "I agree." He thought for a moment, rubbing his hand along his chin. "Say, how about we make an announcement at Della's social group and Thelma's card club. We'll swear everyone to secrecy, and those that want to have their photo taken with their favorite book can pop over here to the fruit-and-veg stand so Mimi can take their picture. Is that okay with you, Mimi?"

"Yep."

"Of course, we'll need to do this sooner rather than later," Jackie said softly, thinking of Carol's diagnosis.

"Maybe we should shoot for the next two or three weeks," Baddie suggested.

The three of them went quiet.

"We should ask Ben for permission to take the photos here at the stand," Jackie said, redirecting the subject to the previous topic. After all, the stand was a business, not a photo booth.

Baddie nodded. "You're right."

"I can ask Ben," Mimi said brightly. "He said he'll be here later."

"That's perfect," Jackie said. "If Ben says it's all right, let me know. I'll talk to Della and Thelma about announcing it to their groups."

"Okay, thanks again, Baddie," Jackie said.

"I'll be talking to you," he said, and he ambled off, carrying the hardcover book at his side, whistling.

Ben thought it was a great idea and that the fruit-and-veg stand was the perfect place to take the photos. He mentioned that as Carol wasn't getting out as much as she used to, they could even put up a sign at the stand with something vague like, "Inquire about photos with Mimi."

Kyle wanted to help, and his father's girlfriend, Isabelle Monroe, bought him his own instant camera to use when Mimi wasn't scheduled to work.

Response was good, and at the end of each day, the photos were labeled with the subject's name along with the title of their book, as sometimes the brightness blurred the titles. All the snaps were then put into a box. When a copy of a book couldn't be found, a sign was made, as was the case with Thelma Schumacher. Never much of a reader, she'd surprised them by admitting she had checked out a book from the town's library—once—when she had a mole problem in her backyard and Carol had suggested a book. The title was long out of circulation, but Thelma made a sign that read, "Thanks for the book, the moles are long gone!" and held it up in front of her while posing for her picture, smiling broadly.

Chapter Thirty

Two weeks later, Jackie arrived at the field with her travel cup of coffee just after dawn to plant seeds along the rows marked with yellow tape. She chose a different variety of sunflowers from what she'd planted two weeks ago, to keep it interesting.

Anna had spent the night at her grandparents' house. Jackie woke early and decided she might as well get a head start and was out at the field when the sun came up.

The sky was striped in alternating shades of soft blue and pink. The air was warm for mid-May, and it looked like it might be a decent day.

Off in the distance, she spotted Tom leaving the old farmhouse and getting into his truck. She hadn't seen him since that day when the field flooded. She was pretty sure that between Carol's illness and the vineyard, he was busy.

The fruit-and-veg stand wasn't open yet. It was too early.

As she pushed the seeder from the storage shed with a bag of seeds tucked beneath her arm, something caught her eye. A blanket of fluttering black covered the sunflower field. The whole area was teeming with birds.

"Oh no you don't," she muttered. She abandoned the seeder and ran, yelling, arms waving above her head, as the flock of crows took off en masse in flight, in a squawking cacophony of protests. She halted right in the middle of the field, watching the birds ascend and spread out, putting distance between themselves and her. She stood there for a few minutes, making sure they didn't return.

She blinked. Then frowned. At first she thought she was seeing things, but then she squinted and walked closer and saw the first sprout of green leaves in the middle of the two-acre plot. She stood still, her hand to her chest, not quite believing it. She did a full three-sixty pivot.

There was more than one sprout. In fact, there were several. They dotted the field randomly. Jubilant, Jackie jumped up in the air and shouted, "Yes!" Her shirt became untucked from her shorts with her exuberance.

Behind her there was the sound of someone laughing.

Mortified, she pulled down her shirt and spotted the source of the laughter.

Tom.

That's the kind of luck I have, she thought irritably. Of all the people in Hideaway Bay, it had to be him to witness her jumping up and down in the field at the crack of dawn like an idiot.

He approached her from the highway side of the field, and she saw his truck parked in the gravel lot.

"You're very lively and spirited this morning," he said with a grin. "Are you always like this, this early?"

Appalled at being caught out, she said quietly, "No, not normally."

"First I thought something bad had happened, the way you were running toward the field and waving your arms and yelling, but then I saw those crows take off and—well, you really showed them," he said. He was still grinning.

"I sure did," she said, still feeling a little embarrassed at being caught chasing after a flock of birds.

"You've got some sunflowers!" he said, pointing to the emerging green shoots.

Jackie nodded, unable to keep from smiling. "Yes. That's the good news. The bad news is I'm not sure how to keep those birds away. I'm planting more seed today and I don't want them getting at it."

"The birds can be a pain. What I would suggest is some silver reflective tape on bamboo stakes throughout the field."

She nodded, making a mental note.

"When the flowers are at their full height and produce more seeds, they'll go after them then too."

Jackie decided she'd worry about that later. She still had a long way to go, she thought, until the little green shoots were high in the sky with big heads of flowers.

"I've got silver tape and bamboo back home in the garage," Tom said. "I'll set it up for you later."

"I hate to impose," Jackie said, scrunching up her nose.

"You're not. Besides, it'll only take five minutes."

She had an idea that it would take more than five minutes.

"Leave it to me," he said.

They stared at each other for a moment and finally, Tom said a bit sheepishly, "I better get going."

"Okay, see you around," she said, sticking her hands in her back pockets and shifting from one foot to the other.

Getting back to work herself, she stood at the edge of the field with her hand on the seeder, ready to go, visualizing how those little sprouts would look all grown up and reaching for the sky with their sunny, daisy-like flowers. She couldn't wait.

Her enthusiasm gave her pause. She felt true, unabashed excitement over these sunflowers. Of course there had been times since Jason's death when she'd been thrilled about something, usually to do with Anna—when she spoke her first word or took her first step—but those moments had always been tempered with sadness that Jason was not there to witness it. But now there was this, something independent of her late husband to be excited about.

Not wanting to dawdle, she got to work, planting the next batch of seeds in the rows she'd previously marked off. As it was getting late in the planting season, she wouldn't wait another two weeks, she'd seed the red-taped rows in about ten days.

After she finished sowing the seeds, she returned everything to the storage shed and locked it up.

The sound of tires over gravel made her look up. Ben pulled into the parking lot.

Jackie gave a wave and walked over to say hello.

"How's everything going?" he asked.

She smiled. "Great. We have our first shoots."

"That's always exciting," Ben said.

"How's Carol?" she asked. "I haven't seen her in a while."

He shrugged. "She's been in the inpatient unit for a few days. They're trying to get her pain under control."

Jackie's face fell. "I'm sorry to hear that."

"Carol never complains," he said, shaking his head. "I'll tell her about the new shoots. That'll cheer her up."

"I hope so. Maybe the photos will help too. Mimi says she's gathered quite a few." She hoped they would lift Carol's spirits.

She waved to Ben as she headed to her car. The sunflowers weren't the only things sprouting in the field, and she wanted to do some weeding before the afternoon sun got too hot. But she thought Anna might like to join her, so she drove over to her parents', picked her up, and returned.

Careful not to trample on the newly sprouted shoots, Jackie placed knee pads on the dirt in between the rows. She knew from working on the garden beds at home that to avoid a sore back, it was best to get down at weed level. She began pulling weeds, throwing them into a large mesh bag. She showed Anna how to do it, and Anna did her best, but wasn't quite strong enough to pull the weeds out with the roots intact. Jackie thought it didn't matter that much, as she was removing more weeds than her daughter.

Wouldn't it be amazing if flowers and vegetables grew as fast as weeds, she thought. Her goal was to keep the field neat and not let it get overrun. How nice it was to be working outside and getting her hands dirty.

Every so often, she looked up to keep an eye on Anna. Currently she was sitting on the dirt, staring at something.

"Anna, what are you doing?"

"I'm looking at this butterfly. She's so pretty," Anna squealed.

Jackie stood, groaning as she straightened her knees. She walked over to the spot where her daughter was hunched near the ground.

"Look, Mommy," Anna said, pointing. The butterfly's orange-and-black wings flapped once. Twice.

"That's a monarch. He's pretty," Jackie said.

"I think so too," Anna said.

And the butterfly flew off.

Chapter Thirty-One

A MONTH LATER, THE two-acre plot of land was covered in four-leafed shoots of various heights. It made Jackie happy to look at it, to see all that green covering what had once been a field of dirt. Ben had told her that he'd driven by with Carol, and she'd been buoyed by the sight of all that green. That made Jackie happy.

Anna was full of chat that morning as they walked from the gravel parking lot to the sunflower field. She skipped alongside Jackie, talking about this and that. Jackie loved it when she skipped. There was something about a child skipping and hopping that indicated happiness. And lately, her daughter had been doing a lot of skipping.

In one hand, Jackie carried her travel mug of coffee and in her other, a juice box for Anna. She liked to drink her coffee sitting on the grass at the edge of the field, looking out across all that green.

There was heavy fog that morning, and it appeared to float thickly just above the ground. It was supposed to clear up later, though, and be another scorcher of a day. Jackie smiled to herself. All that sunshine was good for sunflowers.

"Look, Mommy," Anna said, pointing toward the field.

Raising her chin, Jackie spotted about six grown deer in the middle of her sunflower field. The deer lifted their heads in unison and froze, staring in their direction. In a moment, the herd bolted, fawn-colored and graceful, their white tails bobbing up and down as they disappeared into the fog.

Jackie ran to the area of the field where the deer had been. When she landed at the spot, as evidenced by the hoofprints, her mouth fell open. They'd been eating the leaves off the plants.

"Arrgh," she muttered.

They'd done a lot of damage. How had she not anticipated this? There was going to be a big, gaping hole in the middle of the field. She stood there for a few minutes, thinking of what to do. She'd have to figure out something as a deterrent. As beautiful as the animals were, they had to be kept out of the field. They'd destroy it.

She told herself not to panic, not to give in, not to quit. She'd come too far and invested too much time and emotion already.

No, she'd search for a solution, but she hoped it wouldn't cost too much. She made two decisions about her problem. First, she'd take a ride up to the hardware center and see if Frank was around. He might have some ideas about keeping the deer away from Carol's sunflower field. Then she was going to replant seeds where the deer had destroyed the plants.

"Anna, come on," she called out behind her.

Feeling slightly better for having a plan of action, she headed back to her car with Anna still skipping alongside her.

Although it was early, the sun was hot and the morning fog was beginning to dissipate.

As she reached her car, Tom pulled in beside her and waved.

"Hey, Jackie," he said in greeting. He leaned against the side of his truck.

"How are you, Tom?" she said, folding her arms across her chest.

Anna gave Tom a small wave. He immediately waved back.

With a nod toward the field, he asked, "How are things going?"

"I've got a deer problem; they're snacking on the sunflowers."

He winced in sympathy. "The early leaves are really sweet, that's why they go after them. Once the sunflowers get taller, the leaves won't taste as nice and they won't bother with them."

"If there's any left," Jackie said dryly.

"Don't worry. We can throw up some stakes and wrap chicken wire around the perimeter."

"Is that what I need?" she asked. "I'm on my way to the hardware store."

"I can pick it up for you," he offered.

"No, I'll get it," she said. Not wanting to appear as if she didn't appreciate his offer, she added hurriedly, "But maybe you could help me get the stakes in the ground."

"Sure," he said easily. "Can I meet you back here in an hour? I've got an appointment in town."

She nodded, threw up her hand in a wave and said, "See you later."

They met back again at the field.

"How are things at the vineyard?" she asked as they pulled the stakes and the rolls of chicken wire out of the back seat of her car and the trunk.

He nodded. "Things are going well. On schedule."

"That's great to hear."

"Do you like wine, Jackie?" he asked.

"I do," she said, although she didn't drink much of it. The occasional glass here and there, maybe a couple if she went out for dinner.

He appeared to hesitate, then asked, "Would you like to take a tour of the vineyard sometime?"

"I'd love to." She hoped she didn't sound too eager.

"I'll send you a text."

"Great."

As he walked out toward the far end of the field, stakes under one arm and chicken wire beneath the other, his back toward her, she wondered, *Did he just ask me out on a date?* No, she thought. Of course he didn't. He was so proud of his new business venture, he was probably happy to show off his vineyard to anyone with a pulse.

She accepted Tom's invitation to go out and tour the vineyard. Her anxiety increased as the day approached, and she reminded herself that this wasn't a date and she needn't worry. But when she mentioned it to her mother, her mother couldn't contain her enthusiasm.

They were sitting at the kitchen table in her parents' house, enjoying a cup of coffee and some raspberry and almond pastries. Helen looked well, Jackie thought. She'd had her hair done recently. She wore it short, and she was trying to get ahead of the salt-and-pepper look by dying it white. Jackie liked it; she thought it brought out the blue in her mother's eyes.

"I'm going to bring Anna with me," Jackie said. That had been her solution when she was going back and forth about the possibility of it being a date. Bring Anna, and she could act as a buffer or a pseudo chaperone.

Her mother scoffed, her eyebrows knitting together. "Nonsense. What is Anna going to do in a vineyard? She'd have no interest in that."

"She might like the grapes," Jackie said.

Helen frowned. "Your father will pick Anna up and bring her to our house."

When the day arrived, Tom met Jackie at the office of his winery, a fabricated-steel affair. He showed her the watercolor renderings, and she was impressed. She hadn't known there was going to be an onsite shop as well. That would give the area a definite boost. She could see he was proud of what he had accomplished so far.

By the time they stepped back outside, it was dusk. The vineyard looked almost ethereal in the grayish-lavender light of early evening. Her white T-shirt looked almost blue in the gloaming. The warm breeze was as gentle as a caress. Crickets buzzed loudly around them. Clusters of green grapes hung from the leafy vines, row after row of them, supported by posts and wire.

"I didn't see you at the last social club meeting," Tom said.

Jackie looked at him blankly.

"Della's new group," Tom clarified.

"Oh," she said. She had the schedule of meetings at home on a printout, but she hadn't paid it much attention. "Did I miss anything important?"

He chuckled. "Parasailing this Saturday."

She rolled her eyes and laughed. "I'll give that one a miss. I like my feet on the ground."

"I'll let you know how it goes."

"Please do," she said with a smile.

They walked on in silence, but it wasn't uncomfortable by any means.

"Is this your first year having grapes?" she asked.

"Yes. You see how some of the grapes are turning purple in color?"

Jackie nodded.

"The fancy name for it is veraison, which, to put it simply, is the ripening of the grapes. It's when they change color. All part of the process."

"You learn something new every day," she said softly. She liked being in his presence. He was calm, and he didn't get riled up over a lot of things. Or at least not that she could tell.

"I know the area has a lot of vineyards, but when I think of wine, I always think of California," she said as they walked side by side down one of the rows.

"After California, the Lake Erie region is the second largest grape-growing region in the US," Tom told her.

"Hmm, I did not know that," Jackie said. "But it's not all used for wine, right?"

"No. Grape jelly. Grape juice."

"Oh, I see," she said. As they walked, she reached out and let the tips of her fingers graze the leaves on the vines.

They walked quietly for a while.

"What made you decide to become a grape grower and start a vineyard?" she asked awkwardly.

"I love farming and I love wine," he said with a laugh. "And we had enough land. Dad and Mom and Aunt Carol were very supportive of my idea."

"That's nice to have family support."

"Yes, it is. Dad said it would be a good idea for the farm to branch out."

"How long does it take to get the operation up and running?"

"One to three years. This is year two. We'll see how it plays out. I'm very hopeful for next year. Hopefully next year, we can start making wine."

Even in the deepening twilight, she did not miss the brightness in his expression or the excitement in his voice.

Chapter Thirty-Two

As Jackie drove down Erie toward the field early in the morning with Anna in her car seat in the back, she always looked left, to the growing row of sunflowers. They were dense now and their heads were burgeoning, just waiting to open. The sun was coming up in the east on the other side of the highway and shone brightly on the dark green leaves of the flowers. The sky was already a deep blue, and the rising sun was a bright yellow orb.

She smiled to herself, loving this part of the day before the traffic increased on the highway as people made their way to work, before the fruit-and-veg stand opened and customers pulled into the gravel parking lot. She loved having all this outdoor space to herself, this quiet time alone with her daughter and her coffee, if only to enjoy Anna's prattle as she hopped and danced among the sunflowers Jackie had labored over all summer.

When she'd left the field the previous night, the sunflowers were facing west, in the direction of the lake. Now they faced east. She never tired of this, and each day it was a thrill to see it. Tom had explained to her that it was part of a young sunflower's internal clock. But a mature sunflower settled down and faced east permanently. With a wink, he'd added that the bees prefer warm sunflowers.

Out of the corner of her eye, she spotted something in the field.

"No way," she muttered, slowing down.

As she continued down Erie Street toward the entrance to the stand, she looked in her rearview mirror, trying to catch what she thought she'd seen.

Quickly, she pulled in and parked the car, hustling out of it, taking Anna by the hand and trotting back to the plot. Her keys jangled against her travel mug in her other hand. She walked on the outside of the field, the side facing Erie Street, and when she saw it and realized she had not been mistaken, she stopped in her tracks, her expression contorted into a mixture of happiness and disbelief.

Her first bloom of the field. There it was: its large face, brown in the middle, that would become heavy with seed, and its yellow petals like rays of sunlight surrounding it.

It was absolutely beautiful.

Overwhelmed, she dropped Anna's hand, threw her hands to her mouth, and huffed out a breath in excitement.

She'd done it.

"What's the matter, Mommy?"

Jackie bent down beside Anna, wrapped one arm around her, and gestured with her other arm. "Look, Anna, our first sunflower."

"I can't see it."

Jackie stood and lifted her daughter up until she was almost at the top of her shoulder. Anna broke into a wide smile and giggled. "I see it, Mommy! I see it!"

That first bloom meant everything to Jackie. No matter what else happened, she had grown one sunflower successfully for Carol. It didn't matter to her whether the field flooded or the sun burnt the stalks or there was a drought, or a hurricane blew all the stalks down—she had done it. From a seed and with everything that had happened, she had grown a sunflower. All by herself. She'd done it.

Buoyed by that first bloom and encouraged when another flower opened up by the end of the day on the northeast side of the field, Jackie decided she would go to the movie at the beach later that evening being shown by Della's social club. Suddenly she had the urge to be with other people.

Her mother was shocked when Jackie told her she wanted to go out for the evening and asked if Anna could sleep over, but she immediately said yes.

Jackie left the field early and went home to shower and get ready. She'd bought a nail brush at the drugstore and lathered her nails and gave them a good scrub, trying to dislodge that tiny, stubborn strip of brown beneath her fingernails that resulted from digging weeds out of the dirt, despite wearing gloves. She washed her hair and let it dry naturally, thinking she wasn't going to fuss too much, and applied a light coat of mascara and some lip gloss. She traded in her shorts and T-shirt for a maxi dress and carried her jean jacket with her in case the night air turned chilly.

Despite leaving the field early, she arrived at the gathering late. The beach was packed with people and their lawn chairs, and dusk had settled in around them. Della's group had somehow propped up a big, white screen to show the movie. The sun had almost disappeared, leaving a thin peach line above the dark horizon.

She spotted Tom Anderson walking through the crowd, carrying a lawn chair and a canvas bag, looking for a place to park his chair. For whatever reason, she was unable to take her eyes off him.

Finally, he spotted her and did a double-take. Jackie realized he was used to seeing her in T-shirts and shorts with her hair stuffed up beneath a straw hat, not looking tanned in a flowery maxi dress with her hair hanging loose to her shoulders. His reaction flattered her.

"Jackie, I almost didn't recognize you," he said. He looked at her and said quietly, "You look beautiful."

She blushed and was grateful for the cover of darkness to hide it.

With his finger, he outlined the shape of her hair and said, "I like your hair like this."

Now heat rose to her cheeks. "Thanks."

He looked at her lawn chair beneath her arm. "Are you meeting anyone here tonight?"

She shook her head and said, "No, I'm here alone." After a moment's hesitation, she asked, "Would you like to join me?"

"I'd like that," he said. With a grin, he held up his canvas bag and said, "I brought snacks."

"Then by all means, I'll have to insist," Jackie said with a laugh.

Chapter Thirty-Three

Carol

By the end of July, Carol had moved permanently to her den, as the bedroom and bathroom were simply too far away for her to get to. Gail ordered a hospice bed and had it delivered and set up in the den. Tom removed some smaller pieces of furniture to make room.

Although it wasn't ideal, it was perfect. Carol was surrounded by all her books, and she couldn't ask for anything more.

She knew her time was dwindling. She could feel it, could feel herself diminishing. The weakness and the fatigue were increasing, her vitality and life force slowly draining from her.

She could feel herself pulling away from those she loved. Sometimes when they visited, she had a hard time focusing. If she was in her bed, she turned toward the wall, happy to listen to the drone of their conversation.

And her appetite had waned. She was now taking her meals on small saucers. Lottie fretted around her, trying to cook, bake, or order something Carol might eat. Finally, Gail explained to Lottie and Ben that this was normal, all part of the process. Both stood there silently, looking sad.

Through sheer force of will, Carol hung on. She wasn't ready yet. She had two things left to do: to see that field of sunflowers as she had envisioned it and to tell Ben her secret. One she looked forward to, the other she did not. She knew she would have no choice but to tell him soon. It was a matter of summoning some courage.

But just now, she was waiting for him for a different reason.

Physically, she was unable to do much anymore, and these days, she liked to be close to her home. But once a week, Ben and Tom arrived in the middle of the afternoon to get her into the car and drive her out to see the sunflower field. More blooms had started coming on, and it was nice to see the change from week to week.

They arrived in Dawn's sedan as Carol was no longer able to step up into the pickup truck. After they had her seated comfortably in the passenger seat, Tom hopped in the back and Ben drove to the field, entering from the highway. They all waved at Kyle, who manned the stand, as Ben drove past, heading toward the field.

The field itself had a natural curve that sloped toward the water. In the distance just over the tops of the sunflower stalks, Carol could see a thin, shining strip of the lake.

The sun was high in the sky and shone brightly on the few blooms that had appeared. The field was dense with sunflower stalks. In the bright sunshine, their leaves were like green satin. Some of the ray florets that surrounded the heads of the sunflowers were golden-hued, and some were bright yellow. The entire field had not yet bloomed, and she couldn't wait to see it when all the flowers were in bloom. How magnificent that would look.

Please God, just give me a few more weeks, she prayed silently.

Ben parked the car and rolled down the windows. The heat was ferocious and descended around her like a heavy blanket, but it felt good. It felt luxurious. Lately, she was always cold. No matter what she did or how many blankets she piled on, she couldn't get warm. She leaned her head back for a moment and closed her eyes, enjoying the moment. After a bit she opened her eyes to look at the few sunflowers that had bloomed.

Tom got out of the back seat and stood next to Carol's open window.

"It looks magnificent," she said, her voice a whisper.

"For someone who's never farmed before, Jackie's done a great job," Tom said quietly.

"She sure has," Ben agreed.

Well done, Jackie, Carol thought. *Well done.*

Two weeks later, more than half the field was covered in sunflowers, and it had buoyed her. Ben was quiet on the ride home, and she looked over at him more than once.

"Ben, is everything all right?" she asked, feeling the furrow deepen between her eyebrows.

"Huh? What?" he asked. "Yep, everything is fine."

He said nothing more but tapped on the steering wheel.

Carol leaned against the window, bit her lip, and wondered what was bothering him.

When they arrived back at her house, there were a few cars parked on the street out front.

"Someone must be having a party nearby," she said absently. It was summertime—people always got together in the warm weather.

There was no response from Ben, and she looked at him again, but he did not volunteer any information.

Tom met them in the driveway with the wheelchair; he'd opted to stay behind at the house, although Carol did not know why.

"We stayed a little longer than usual," Ben said to Tom.

"Is there a problem with that?" Carol asked, wondering again what was up.

"No, no, nothing wrong," he said.

Together, Ben and Tom helped her into the wheelchair and took her into the house. Recently, Tom had built a ramp to the front door to get the wheelchair in and out.

As they crossed the threshold, Carol heard voices coming from inside the house.

"What is going on?" she asked.

But neither Ben nor Tom said anything.

Tom did not wheel her back to the den; instead, he took her to the living room, which was at the front of the house. There, seated on chairs and the sofa, were Dawn, Lottie, and Jackie. Jackie's little girl, Anna, sat on the floor, playing with Melvin. On the other side of the room were Thelma Schumacher, Baddie Moore, Mimi, and Kyle.

"What is going on?" Carol asked again. Even though she was unsure, she smiled.

"We've brought a little gift for you, Carol," Baddie said, unable to contain his smile.

Tom parked Carol's wheelchair next to the end of the sofa where Lottie sat. Lottie reached out, took hold of Carol's hand, and gave it a gentle squeeze.

Carol peered at her best friend. "Are you in on this?"

Lottie grinned. "I'm afraid so."

"Gifts aren't necessary," Carol said, summoning all her strength to sound firm and forceful but afraid that she had failed.

There was a little buzz of side conversations around the room, and she was mesmerized by the way Melvin lay next to Anna, his tail swishing from side to side. He had rarely been around children in his six years. Meanwhile, Anna rubbed his fur and giggled from time to time.

Ben cleared his throat and the drone of the conversations died down. "As we were saying, Carol, we have a gift for you."

"Just a little one," Thelma said brightly.

Baddie looked at Mimi and said, "Will you do the honors?"

The young girl nodded and stood. From behind her chair, she lifted a large white box—the size that would fit a coat—wrapped in a wide red satin ribbon with a big bow on the front of it.

Mimi carried it over and handed it to Carol.

The box was big and bulky and had a glossy white finish. It threatened to slide off Carol's lap.

"Hold on, Aunt Carol," Tom said from across the room. He grabbed one of the nesting tables from the corner and set it down in front of her, picking up the box and laying it on the table.

"Thanks, Tom," she said.

Carol's brow furrowed, but she smiled as she couldn't imagine what this could possibly be. She removed the bow, handed it to Lottie, and untied the ribbon.

She lifted the lid, set it on the floor beside her, moved the tissue paper aside, and frowned. The box was full of Polaroid photos.

Confused but still smiling, she looked up at everyone present in her living room and asked, "What is this?"

"Look through it and see," Ben prompted. He had his arms folded across his chest and rocked back and forth on his heels, smiling.

Carol dug through, picking out a snapshot. It was a photo of Tom—taken recently—holding a book. *Goodnight, Moon.*

She held the photo up. "Tom?"

He smiled. "It was the first book you gave me as a kid. I loved that book."

"Oh."

She picked up another photo. This one was of Mr. Lime from the Five-and-Dime. He held up an Agatha Christie book, *The Mysterious Affair at Styles*, the first in the Hercule Poirot collection. She remembered recommending that series to him. That had to be decades ago; Mr. Lime had still had his hair at the time. The next photo was of Sue Ann Marchek holding up a copy of Laura Ingalls Wilder's book, *Little House on the Prairie*. Those books had been the rage of the 1970s, followed by the popularity of the television show. Her mother, Barb Walsh, used to come home for the summers and she'd gotten a library card for both her and Sue Ann. There was Connie Machlan, longtime town resident, holding up Ken Follett's *Pillars of the Earth*. And on and on it went.

It dawned on Carol that all these snapshots were books she'd given or recommended to people, books they'd read because of her.

She slumped in her chair and looked around the room at everyone, her lips parted slightly. Her breathing came fast, and her eyes filled up. It was emotional. It was overwhelming. It was wonderful.

"How did you ever come up with this idea?" she finally asked.

Baddie relayed the story of how Mimi had taken a photo of him holding his favorite book, and that had been the impetus for Jackie's idea for the gift. When Carol looked over at Jackie, she lifted her hand in a wave and smiled.

The tears spilled over as Carol's throat swelled. "It's an amazing gift. I love it."

Chapter Thirty-Four

Carol waited for Ben's arrival. Today was the day, she'd decided. She was going to tell him the truth about his birth. There was no sense in putting it off any further.

After the excitement of the day before with the gift from the residents of Hideaway Bay, she spent the evening sitting in her hospital bed, going through the big white box, carefully studying each snapshot. Then she'd slept all night, a deep sleep.

She rubbed the back of her neck, whether to relieve real or anticipatory pain, she did not know.

It was time. She was now sleeping more hours than she was awake. It was as if she couldn't keep her eyes open. Better to tell Ben the truth now before she slipped away altogether, and the opportunity was lost.

As she waited for his arrival, she looked through the box of snapshots again, smiling at each photo. Comforted.

She would have liked a cup of tea, but Melanie wouldn't be there until later. She stared at the shelves and shelves of books, crammed with favorites she'd reread down through the years. Quite by accident, she'd discovered the joyful realization that your perspective changed from the time you were twenty to forty to sixty and that it was a beautiful thing to rediscover a book at another age, from a different angle. She hated to leave them. If it were up to her, she would have preferred to remain at home and slip away surrounded by her books and her things and Melvin. But her end days would be spent in the hospice unit; she didn't want to be a burden to anyone.

A lone tear escaped. That was the problem with living alone and dying; there was too much time to think.

"Carol?" a voice called from the front of the house.

Ben.

"In here," she croaked. Even her voice had gotten weaker. She sighed.

Ben appeared in the doorframe in his usual attire: jeans and a plaid shirt, though in the summertime his shirts were lightweight and short-sleeved. Like most human beings, he was a creature of habit. She couldn't ever remember seeing him in shorts. In one hand, he held a large bouquet of sunflowers. Automatically she smiled.

"From your field," he said, smiling and holding up the bouquet. "I'll put them in water for you." He disappeared into the kitchen and returned with the bunch of flowers in a vase, setting it on the coffee table.

In him, she could see bits of her own father and of Roger Harrison. If she'd had her baby in current times, she would have been able to raise him by herself. It might not have been easy, but she would have been able to support him. The two of them had simply been born at the wrong time. Too soon.

But it was time to do what she had put off doing all his life: telling him the truth about his parentage.

"How're you feeling, Carol?" he asked.

"I'm fine," she lied. No sense in worrying him.

She was glad to see he was no longer limping. It appeared that the knee replacement had been a success. Like Carol's father and grandfather, Ben was happiest out in the field, on the farm. It must be in the blood, although it had certainly skipped her, as she often mused. But that was okay because in the end, it had all worked out perfectly.

"Can I get you a cup of tea or something to drink?" he asked.

"Tea would be heavenly," she said, closing her eyes in relief. Her mouth was parched.

"Coming right up."

"Make one for yourself," Carol called out. "And Thelma Schumacher dropped off a coffee cake, cut yourself a slice."

She'd been surprised by Thelma's spontaneous visit but she'd welcomed her, finding she was actually glad to see her.

"Would you like a slice?"

"Sure," she said to be polite, ignoring her lack of appetite.

Ben whistled as he headed through to the kitchen. The sounds of tea-making commenced: the running of the tap, the click of the stove being turned on, the clinking of cups being brought down from cabinets, and the jingle of cutlery.

Within minutes, Ben returned with two slices of cake. One he set down on the coffee table and the other he handed to Carol, which she took but set on the over-the-bed tray.

On his second trip, he carried one mug of tea and a glass of water. He set the mug on the table next to her. Carol picked it up and sipped from it.

Perfect.

Ben got comfortable on the sofa, leaned forward, and balanced the plate of coffee cake on his knees. "What did you need to talk to me about?"

Despite the tea, Carol's mouth went dry, and she fingered the edge of the blanket covering her lap, her heart beating faster, hoping against hope that she was doing the right thing.

Ben looked at her, his expression expectant as he forked coffee cake into his mouth.

"There's something I need to tell you," she started. Now, she wished she had had this conversation with him years ago. Lack of courage, fear of rejection, she supposed, had prevented her from broaching the subject.

Ben's fork paused midair, a large, crumbly piece of cake balancing precariously on it.

"It's about your adoption," she said, stuttering. She felt as if she'd fumbled the ball right out of the huddle.

"What about it?" He frowned, setting his plate down.

"Mother and Dad adopted you," she started. For someone who'd most likely read thousands of books in her lifetime, words, the right ones, had abandoned her when she needed them most.

"Yes, I know." He took a sip of water.

"The woman who gave you up for adoption"—she lowered her head now; she couldn't look at him—"was me."

There was silence on the other side of the room and Carol continued to look at her lap. Her pants had become way too big. She was practically swimming in them.

"I know that too," Ben said quietly.

Carol's head snapped up and she looked at him, filled with confusion. "What do you mean, you know?"

"I know you're my mother," he said softly. "My real mother."

"But how? How did you know? And why have you never said anything?" she cried. In front of her, the coffee cake was forgotten and the tea was growing cold.

Ben shrugged. "I don't know. As I got older, I figured it out. I put two and two together."

"Why didn't you ask me about it?"

He shrugged again. But importantly, he didn't seem put off by the revelation. "I thought after Mom died, you might say something. And when you didn't, I thought maybe I was wrong. But I always suspected you were my real mother. As sisters go, you were pretty maternal. You treated me more like a son than a brother."

"I couldn't help that."

Ben smiled. "I know, and I appreciate it."

"But you never said anything."

"I figured if you wanted me to know, you would have told me. That it was your secret to reveal." He looked at her and said, "Besides, what if I was wrong? If you weren't my mother and I questioned you about it, how would that look?"

That pain that had been buried deep within and covered up by the passing years began to emerge, and Carol knew there was no painkiller in the world that could relieve it. Finally, she whispered, "I'm so sorry." Tears swam in her eyes.

"It wasn't your fault," he said. "It was just the way it was back in those years. An unmarried woman couldn't have a child and raise it on her own." He said it so easily, as if he were ordering replacement parts for the tractor.

"I'm sorry I wasn't strong enough to tell you the truth," Carol said, her voice breaking.

He leaned forward a little further on the edge of the sofa and smiled. His hands were folded, and his elbows rested on his knees. "I consider myself very lucky. I didn't end up in an orphanage. Mom and Dad loved me. I love farming. And most of all, I grew up with my mother."

The pain and sorrow slowly ebbed out of her, and she could feel herself deflating with relief. "I tried to be there for you."

Ben was quick to answer. "I know you did. You always were. Your sacrifice must have cost you a great deal of hurt."

"It did, but it was the way it had to be. When my mother suggested adopting you, I couldn't believe it. I'd be able to be with you while you were being raised. Times were very different back in 1956."

"Can I ask about my father?"

"He was a boy from town. When he found out I was pregnant, he promised to cause all kinds of trouble if I told anyone he was the father. You see, he was going to college on an athletic scholarship," Carol said.

"He sounds charming."

Carol laughed but it sounded weak. "He was very charming before I got pregnant."

"Was he your boyfriend?"

Carol shook her head. Feeling parched again, she reached for her cup and took a sip of tea, now cold. "No, not really. I got caught up in the attention he gave me. I thought he liked me."

"Is he still in Hideaway Bay? Do you feel comfortable telling me his name?"

"Of course I do. His name was Roger. Roger Harrison. When he left for college, he never came back. I don't know where he is. Or if he's even alive."

When Ben didn't say anything, Carol asked, "Were you thinking of looking for him?"

Ben shook his head. "I don't think so. I had a happy childhood. And I'm not that curious. Besides, I had my mother with me all along."

For the first time in her life, Carol felt as if everything was going to be all right. She felt as if a huge burden had been lifted now that it was out in the open about being Ben's real mother.

"I'd like to tell Tom and Dave," he said.

"I'll leave that up to you." That was his decision to make.

"Dawn knows, I told her my suspicions years ago," he admitted. He stood, slipping his hands into his pockets. "Today, you have a baby outside of marriage and no one blinks an eye."

"Times are different," she said and thought, *Thank God*. "I'm grateful to my parents for adopting you, at least you were with me, if not in the traditional sense."

"I am too," he said.

"How's Dave doing?" she asked, changing the subject. The gravitas of it was beginning to weigh her down.

"He's fine. He likes his new job in IT."

"Any chance he might come home for a visit?" she asked. Ben and Dawn had taken Carol down to visit him last year, and she had loved Philadelphia. She only wished he lived closer, preferably in Hideaway Bay.

"Not for right now. He likes Philly too much."

"Any sign of a girlfriend?" she asked, hopeful. She didn't want either of the boys, as she still thought of them, to end up alone. Tom worked too much and was all about the farm and the vineyard.

"Not yet but we're hopeful. We'd like some grandchildren someday," Ben said with a laugh.

Carol held up her hand and crossed her fingers. "Fingers crossed."

Ben stood. "I should get going. I'll drop off some dinner later. Dawn's making a pot roast."

"You don't have to go to all that trouble," she said.

Ben carried his plate and cup into the kitchen.

"Take that coffee cake home with you," she called out after him. There was too much there, and she'd never eat the whole thing. It would be awful if it had to be thrown out. She'd prefer to think of someone else enjoying it.

"Okay. Can I do anything for you before I leave?"

"I'd like to go see the sunflower field tomorrow." She didn't add what her gut was telling her, that her time was dwindling.

"All right, I'll pick you up in the afternoon," he said.

He stopped in the doorway and looked back at her, smiling. "I'll see you later, Mom."

Carol's eyes filled up and her nose stung. Her voice abandoned her, but she nodded.

Chapter Thirty-Five

End of August

Carol

Carol sat with an afghan over her lap and Melvin perched on the arm of her chair. Before Melanie left, she'd helped her out of bed and into the chair. Ben was coming over to take her to see the sunflower field.

She was trying to keep her eyes open, desperately hanging on. But as hard as she tried, she couldn't. It wasn't that she was tired or sleepy—or maybe she was, but she felt like she was fading.

The hospice nurse, Gail, was due to come out later that week. Carol felt it was time to go into the inpatient unit. The last few nights, Ben, Lottie, Dawn, and Tom had taken turns sleeping on the sofa in the den next to her. That couldn't continue, they'd be worn out in no time. David had decided to come home after all, his flight due in the morning. She was eager to see him.

Ben stood before her, looking serious. She wished she could reassure him. She wanted to tell him that everything would be all right. And it would be. When she looked at him, she was full of nothing but love. Despite the rocky circumstances of his birth, he had turned out wonderful. Sometimes when she looked at him, she was overcome with emotion at how she almost lost him at birth. First, through the process and then almost having to give him up. Despite the less than ideal circumstances, he'd been brought up by her parents and her and he'd blossomed. It made her smile. Some babies were just meant to be.

"Ready? Tom said he'd go with us," Ben said.

She didn't think she could do it. The five-minute drive there and then back would sap her of any remaining energy she had. She was so tired. If only she could go to bed and pull the blanket up over her shoulder. It wasn't that she no longer cared; it was that she was ready for them to go on without her. She could feel herself beginning to pull away.

As if to reassure her, Ben said, "We won't be gone long, and it will be the last thing I'll ask of you."

"Ben, it's too much trouble," she said. "Just take some pictures and you can show me."

"We've got you covered. We'll drive slowly."

Finally, she relented if only to avoid disappointing Ben. Tom arrived. They made small talk with her as Ben readied the wheelchair. He parked it at a ninety-degree angle to her chair as the nurse had taught him.

"I can transfer Aunt Carol, Dad," Tom said.

Carol was relieved about that. She didn't want Ben exerting himself too much.

"I see I'm just in time," Lottie said, poking her head through the doorway. "Are we all ready?"

"Almost," Ben said. "We're about to take her outside."

"Here, let me help," Lottie said, inserting herself between Ben and Tom. She removed the afghan that covered Carol's lap, folded it, and laid it on the couch. She picked up Melvin and put him in the kitchen.

Tom stood in front of Carol. "Okay, Aunt Carol, you know the drill." She put her hands on his shoulders, and he placed a gait belt around her waist and pulled her to a stand. She felt lightheaded and her knees buckled, and she collapsed back into the chair.

Tom leaned down and said, "Aunt Carol, I'm going to lift you."

Before she could protest and wave him away, he scooped her up and set her down gently in the wheelchair.

Once in the chair, she took a deep breath, trying to regulate her breathing. Even though Tom had done most of the work, she was the one who was breathless.

Carefully, as if she were made of spun glass, Tom wheeled her outside to his truck. Ben walked ahead and opened the door. Carol looked up at the passenger seat and her heart sank. She knew she wouldn't have the energy to get into the truck. She was too weak. She expressed this concern to them.

Tom smiled. "We've figured it all out. Leave it to Dad and me."

She nodded. She didn't know how they were going to do it, but she trusted them.

She shivered despite the August heat.

"I'll run back in and get your afghan," Lottie said, and disappeared back into the house.

Tom parked the wheelchair next to his truck and knelt down in front of her.

"Aunt Carol, I'm going to lift you out of the wheelchair and put you in the truck. You won't have to do a thing."

"I don't know about that. I don't want you to hurt your back," she said.

But again, he lifted her as if she weighed next to nothing and set her down gently in the passenger seat. She closed her eyes for a moment, tired. He pulled the seatbelt from its shoulder harness and reached around her to buckle her in.

Ben spread the blanket out over her lap.

"All set?" Tom asked.

Carol nodded.

He tucked the ends of the afghan inside the cab and closed the door.

"Dad, we'll meet you over there."

"Great. Come on, Lottie, you can come with me." Ben trotted to his truck and when everyone was ready, he pulled out ahead of Tom and Carol.

"We'll take a slow drive through town first," Tom said.

"I'd like that," Carol said.

She looked out the window at the town she loved. The grass was a deep green around the war memorial, and the red and white impatiens that had been planted around the gazebo were in full bloom. Main Street was crowded with pedestrians, and Carol smiled as a group of young boys walked down the street, licking ice cream cones. The beach was crowded, and the lake was a bluish-gray color. Overhead, seagulls circled the beach, their cries shrill. Pleasure boats bobbed out on the lake. They passed the library and Tom slowed down a bit. Carol had nothing but fondness for the place, and the mere sight of it made her eyes fill up. It had been the perfect career for her.

Finally, Tom drove up Erie Street, heading toward the highway. Even before they got there, Carol could see them.

A mass of flowers with their golden heads and thick green stalks occupied the corner space where once there had been a flat field. It was dense with sunflowers, all reaching skyward, toward the sun. She drew in a sharp breath. You visualized how something might look, hoped for the best, but you didn't know, really. But this, this had turned out far better than she'd imagined.

"They're so tall and big," she finally said. She couldn't stop staring out the window as they passed by.

Ben and Lottie were still ahead of them. Tom pulled right into the parking lot and drove past the stand, waving to Kyle, pulling up at the edge of the field and rolling down Carol's window.

And there was Jackie with Anna. When Jackie spotted them, she leaned on the handle of her hoe and waved. She looked like a natural, as if she'd been farming all her life. Carol was happy to see that. Her whole demeanor was different from the woman she'd met almost five months ago. Anna bounced and jumped around the field, oblivious to their presence.

Carol was speechless. For a moment, she remained motionless, staring at the field. But she was curious about one flower that stood taller than the rest. It stuck out like a sore thumb, albeit a majestic one.

Ben and Lottie got out of his truck and approached Carol's window.

She pointed. "Look at that one there! It's the tallest one."

Tom smiled. "I'll let Jackie tell you how tall it is. I won't steal her thunder. She worked hard on this all summer."

"She did a great job," Ben said.

Carol's eyes began to fill, and her chin quivered. Jackie had exceeded her remit.

Tom jumped out of the truck, pulled Carol's wheelchair from the bed of the pickup, and opened her door.

"I'm getting out?" she asked, unsure.

"You sure are," Tom said. "We're going to sit for a few minutes so you can enjoy your flowers."

She nodded, her voice too shaky with emotion to speak. She let Tom lift her out and set her down in the wheelchair. Ben pushed it slowly over the uneven grass and she winced a few times going over the bumps. But soon he parked her chair at the end of the field.

Jackie set down her hoe and walked toward them. Anna followed her, laughing and giggling as she sang some song and skipped behind her mother.

Jackie looked great. Her hair was in a loose ponytail and her skin had some color. Even her countenance seemed different. Brighter somehow. Thelma had been right; Jackie was perfect for the job.

"Carol, it's so good to see you!" Jackie said.

"You've done an amazing job here," Carol said.

"I enjoyed every bit of it," Jackie said. "Besides, I had a lot of help." She glanced over at Tom.

"Tell me though, how tall is that tallest one?" Carol asked. She couldn't stop looking at it. The tallest sunflower in the field was magnetic; she could not avert her gaze.

Jackie looked over her shoulder at it, pleased. "I measured it again this morning. Seven feet, eight inches."

Carol put her hand over her heart. "How wonderful." Now the tears came, she couldn't stop them. She was happy.

Ben put his hand on her shoulder and gave it a gentle squeeze.

"Are you all right?" Tom said.

She nodded. "I am overcome with emotion. Thank you, Jackie. Thank you so much."

Jackie nodded, tears escaping her own eyes.

Carol's tears flowed freely, and she let them. Beside her, she heard someone sniffle and she couldn't be sure if it was Lottie or Ben or both. She looked from left to right over the field and back again and pronounced, "It's beautiful. Absolutely beautiful."

Chapter Thirty-Six

By the time Gail, the hospice nurse, arrived a couple of days later, Carol was barely responsive. She was transported by ambulance to the hospice inpatient unit and overnight, she slipped into unconsciousness. Three days later, she died peacefully in a private room with Ben at her side.

Carol Prudence Anderson Rimmer's funeral was held at the small white church up on the cliff overlooking Hideaway Bay, just as the sunflowers were at their peak in her little plot of land off the main highway. As mourners walked around to the back of the church, they had an amazing view of the lake, and looking in a northeasterly direction, they had a bird's-eye view of Carol's sunflower field.

That field of tall, regal sunflowers in shades ranging from bright yellow to dark orange, with their wide heads and disk florets bursting with seeds and their stalks thick and sturdy, was a welcoming beacon to any traveler driving south on the highway, especially those coming from the city to get away for the weekend or partaking in a cottage rental for a week out at the bay. It was also a surprise to vacationers who spent every summer out there in the little town. The sunflower field gave travelers their first impression of Hideaway Bay, and it proved to be a portent of things to come as they discovered the rest of the town hugging the lake behind the blanket of trees.

But to the residents of Hideaway Bay, the field meant so much more. It reminded them that they had lost someone special. Someone who, although she'd led a quiet life, had touched so many lives in the form of a book.

The church was packed for the funeral service, and residents crammed into pews, lined the walls and the back of the church, and spilled out the front doors and down the steps, standing in the amber-hued late-summer sunshine, the air golden and warm.

Ben and Tom and David, now knowing the truth of the past and the great sacrifices Carol had made to stay with them in some capacity, to be a part of their lives, were affected by profound grief. Numbly, they went through the motions. And although later they would feel as if the days after her death were a blur, there were some things they would always remember.

The kindness of the townspeople. So many people stopped to offer their condolences and share a kind word or story about Carol. It comforted them.

The flowers. Not only sunflowers but roses, carnations, hydrangeas, and dahlias to name but a few. The air in the church was fragrant with the mixture of floral scents. A large spray of sunflowers covered the top of the casket. But the most touching thing was the little bags of sunflower seeds Jackie and Anna had made for mourners to take, using yellow netting and tying it with a yellow ribbon. People were encouraged to grow their own sunflowers, in pots on porches or in garden beds, to remember their favorite librarian.

Chapter Thirty-Seven

Jackie

The doorbell rang and Anna ran to the front door. In her arms, she cradled Melvin the cat. After Carol died, Ben had asked Jackie if she knew anyone who'd be interested in taking Melvin. It had turned out that she did have someone in mind.

She had yet to get used to the cat running around at four in the morning but so far, the transition had been a success.

"It's Mimi! Yay!" In her excitement, Anna squeezed the cat to her, and Melvin let out a loud meow in protest.

"Remember what I told you? Be gentle with Melvin. You don't want to hurt him," Jackie said, arriving at the front door, opening it, and letting Mimi in.

"Hi, Mimi," Jackie said with a smile.

She didn't know who was more excited about Mimi babysitting tonight: her, to be getting out of the house; Anna, who loved Mimi; or maybe even Jackie's mother, who was thrilled to see Jackie going out and socializing. It wasn't her first night out. She had signed up for Lily's beach glass class and had gone to a wine tasting event. Baby steps, she thought.

Melvin jumped out of Anna's arms and took off for parts unknown. Anna stood in front of Jackie and Mimi and jumped up and down.

"Mimi, do you want to color?" Anna asked, smiling.

"Sure."

Anna ran off to the kitchen cupboard to get her coloring books and crayons.

Jackie showed Mimi the list of emergency numbers she'd written out and laid on the counter. Mimi nodded. As she went over Anna's bedtime and her routine, Anna laid out crayons and coloring books on the kitchen table.

Before she left, she kissed and hugged Anna goodbye.

"Be good for Mimi," she said.

"I will, Mommy."

It had been a great day. She'd booked their trip to Disneyworld for the following April. It would be the four of them: Anna and Jackie and her parents. The fact that the trip was all paid for with cash thrilled her. No debt hanging over her head.

She sighed a sigh of contentment. She felt as if she was beginning to emerge from the fog of grief that had gripped her these last few years.

―――⁓⁓⁓―――

Jackie took a pair of shears and cut a bunch of sunflowers to bring home. She pulled a length of twine from her pocket to wrap the bundle. She turned them around in her hand, smiling. They'd look great in a crystal vase on her kitchen table. That was one of the perks of growing a large field of sunflowers; Ben and Tom had told her to help herself. During the day, she bundled bouquets of sunflowers to sell up at the stand. And the demand had been steady.

"They're beautiful, aren't they?" she murmured to herself.

She looked westward, past the sunflower field, toward the lake, staring at the sun as it began its descent toward the horizon. The evening sky was scarlet, orange, and gold. The setting sun cast the field in a pinkish-golden hue. She continued to stare, mesmerized, thinking how lucky she was to be a part of all this. That she had helped create this little piece of beauty in a corner of the world. She was lost in her reverie until she heard a car pull up behind her.

She cast a glance over her shoulder and spotted Tom pulling up in his pickup. Through the windshield, he smiled and waved at her. She returned the gesture. He spun the truck around and threw it into reverse, turning his head and laying his arm along the back of the front seat as he backed it up toward her.

He jumped out of the truck and slammed the door, walking around to the back and dropping the tailgate. He looked over his shoulder at Jackie and waved her on.

He pulled a large canvas bag closer to him. He looked at the sunflowers in her hand. "Perfect, you brought flowers."

She smirked at him, trying to stifle a laugh.

From the canvas bag, he pulled a bottle of wine, a bar of chocolate, and a tray of cheese and crackers.

"What's all this?"

He turned halfway and swept his hand across the vista of the sunflower field. "We need to celebrate. You did it. And it looks magnificent."

Jackie felt the heat creep into her cheeks. It was high praise coming from him. She was touched by his gesture to acknowledge her success.

He moved everything to the side so he could lay a tartan blanket over the tailgate. He looked at her and said, "Hop up."

She laid the sunflowers to one side so she wouldn't crush them, then turned her back to the truck, put her hands behind her, and boosted herself up. Tom held up the bottle of wine.

"Unfortunately, not from my vineyard," he said.

"But someday and soon," she said reassuringly. "And that's a glass of wine I'm really looking forward to."

He uncorked the wine and let it rest while he took out two wine glasses and handed them to her. Next the cheese tray was unwrapped, although Jackie corrected herself mentally: charcuterie board, as it held cheese, crackers, olives, and prosciutto. Her stomach growled loudly and, embarrassed, she looked at Tom, who grinned.

"It seems I arrived just in time," he said.

"Sometimes I get so wrapped up in what I'm doing I forget to stop and eat something."

Tom nodded. He hopped up next to her and set the charcuterie board between them. "I understand that." He popped an olive into his mouth. While he chewed it, he grabbed the bottle of wine and poured a liberal amount into each glass.

He clinked his glass against hers. "Cheers."

"Cheers."

They both looked out at the field. There were sunflowers as far as the eye could see. Tall, majestic, and golden, it was a remarkable sight to behold.

"What will you do now?" he asked.

She'd given this a lot of thought in the last few weeks. The sunflower field would begin winding down with the coming of autumn. Ben and Tom had decided to harvest the seeds for birdseed, and then the field would be plowed down.

It had been a great summer. One thing she'd realized about herself was that she loved working outside, loved gardening, and loved flowers. She didn't want to be permanently chained to a desk in her future. "Actually, I'm going back to college to study horticulture."

"So you've been bitten by the growing bug?" he asked, helping himself to a piece of cheese.

"Yes, I've been looking into taking a course in floriculture at the community college next spring," she said. She'd discussed it with her parents and they'd been encouraging.

"Would you do it full time?"

"I don't know yet. For right now, I like the balance of working three days from home at a desk job and spending the rest of the time outside."

"I'm happy to hear that. Because Dad and I were wondering if you'd like to continue growing sunflowers for us."

"What? Really? I'd love to," she said. The prospect excited her, and she immediately began thinking about what she might do differently with next year's crop.

"That's great. That's perfect," he said, pleased. "If you need any help at all, you know where to find me."

"I appreciate that."

Tom gave her a quick nod of acknowledgement and took a sip of his wine.

Sipping from her glass, she looked at the sunflowers and chocolate and cheese. "Wine, flowers, and chocolate. What more could a girl ask for?"

Tom Anderson burst out laughing.

He refilled their glasses. "Friends?"

She smiled, clinking her glass against his. "Definitely."

Acknowledgments

Although I've dabbled for years growing sunflowers from seeds, I have no experience growing them on such a large scale. For that, I turned to Amy and Bob Rogish of Rogish Farms, Chesterland, Ohio. They were extremely helpful and gracious with all my questions. For that, I am very grateful. Any mistakes are solely mine.

If you're ever in the area, I'd encourage you to stop in and visit their farm. And tell them I said 'hi.'

Also By Michele Brouder

Hideaway Bay Series

Coming Home to Hideaway Bay

Meet Me at Sunrise

Moonlight and Promises

When We Were Young

One Last Thing Before I Go

The Chocolatier of Hideaway Bay

Escape to Ireland Series

A Match Made in Ireland

Her Fake Irish Husband

Her Irish Inheritance

A Match for the Matchmaker

Home, Sweet Irish Home

An Irish Christmas

Happy Holidays Series

A Whyte Christmas

This Christmas

A Wish for Christmas

One Kiss for Christmas

A Wedding for Christmas

Printed in Great Britain
by Amazon